BEWARE OF WOLF

Geonn Cannon

Supposed Crimes LLC • Matthews, North Carolina

www.supposedcrimes.com

This book is typeset in Goudy Old Style.

PART I

CHAPTER ONE

CONTEXT WAS important. Without context, Ariadne Willow knew that things looked grim for her. She was currently in a burlap sack large enough to hold her wolf-form, the loop of chain that had been used to subdue her still around her neck. She could hear the men who'd abducted her talking because she was stuffed into the trunk of their car. The carpet underneath her reeked, and the road whispered under the tires as the bad guys drove to an undisclosed location for the next step of their dastardly plans.

Just as she planned.

Fifteen minutes ago she had spotted the beat-up blue Oldsmobile idling in an alley that dead-ended at a wooded area. The driver was behind the wheel, a lit cigarette in the hand that hung out the window. Ari stayed low to cross behind the car without being spotted, trying to pick up the trail of his passenger. It was nearly two in the morning so following the freshest scent was her best bet. She put her snout to the ground and let it lead her to the source two blocks away.

The guy was tall and wiry, crouched low and moving slowly so he wouldn't startle his prey. Ari mimicked him, but she managed to do a much better job of remaining inconspicuous.

As she watched, the guy crossed someone's side lawn and moved up to the chain-link fence. He moved with purpose, avoiding the furtive movements that would have been a giveaway to his nefarious motives. He quietly fiddled with the latch and almost immediately received a barked warning from further in the backyard. The man ignored it and pulled the gate open the rest of the way. He stepped back and to the side, waiting patiently until the border collie came running. The man extended the long pole he'd been carrying and readied the loop.

Ari moved out of the shadows that she'd been using for her cover and sent a thought across the yard to the dog.

Run. Go back to your people.

The dog skidded to a stop, confused. The man was confused as well, torn between getting what he came for and crossing into the people's yard. Ari didn't like 'speaking' with dogs. *Canidae* could do it with normal dogs, and to a minor extent could manage it between themselves, but other *canidae* at least had the benefit of knowing what was happening. For a dog to suddenly have a head full of human commands was perplexing to the poor beasts. Ari tried to keep it simple.

Danger! Run away!

The border collie turned tail and ran back into the yard.

"Oh, you stupid mutt..." the man muttered.

He started to go after it, but was stopped when Ari began barking. He turned and, when he saw her racing toward him, decided to go with the bird in his hand. He faced her full-on and brought the pole around. A short length of chain looped around Ari's neck when she was close enough and the man pulled a trigger to tighten it. Ari's bark was cut off to a wimpy squeak, her forepaws lifted off the ground as the man lifted the pole. He used the pole as a safety measure, keeping her from biting him as he examined her.

"Looks strong. Mean, too." He lashed out with his right hand and slapped the side of her head. "You got a temper, huh?"

Ari blinked to steady her vision. *Oh, you're gonna pay for that...*

The man looked around and pushed the fence shut to hide the fact he'd been there. He jerked the pole and started walking, half-dragging Ari back the way they had come. She put up a valiant fight, making it look good. Even a man this stupid would be suspicious of a dog that was abducted willingly. She snarled and snapped at the chain, throwing all her weight against her back legs. Just because she planned to be stolen didn't mean she was going to make it easy on the jerk. The one thing she didn't do was bark, even when the choke chain allowed it. She didn't actually want anyone coming to her aid.

The man finally got her back to the Oldsmobile. The driver

saw them coming and popped the trunk, getting out so he could help stow her.

"That ain't a border collie," he hissed.

"I still got one. What's it matter? This one is wild. Could be rapid."

"*Rabid*, you idiot. And thanks for tellin' me that before I got near its mouth. Hold him still, will ya?"

Idiot stepped over Ari's back and held her still with both hands. Driver got the bag out of the trunk and held it wide. She got a glimpse of his face - long and thin with a scruff of black beard but no mustache. She would remember that face. The bag was secured over her head and then the rest of her body was shoved inside by Idiot. She was lifted off the ground, tossed into the trunk without finesse, and the lid slammed.

Now the car was thumping over an uneven road. The air smelled salty and cold, and she could hear the lapping of waves. *Industrial District*, she guessed. Judging by the time they'd been on the road, it was somewhere close to the West Seattle Bridge. Driver finally slowed down and Ari heard the rattle of a garage door being manually lifted. The car rolled through and the gate was dropped behind them. The weight of the car shifted as her kidnappers got out.

"What did you get?" someone new asked.

"Some kind of mutt."

I'll show you mutt.

The trunk was opened and Ari twisted inside the bag. The new guy laughed. "Whoa-ho, a lively one. That's a good sign." He put a hand on her shoulder through the bag, pinning her down as he opened it to look inside. "Hm. Nice coloring. Looks strong. You should've seen the stray McCauley brought in the other night. Fuckin' skin and bones. It needed a walker just to stand upright."

"They make walkers for dogs? How's that work?" Idiot, of course.

"Shut up, idiot." The new guy cinched the bag again and hauled Ari out. She was momentarily dangled upside down before he put her on hard concrete. She snarled and thrashed like a fish, the wolf part of her brain panicking at the lack of control. New Guy told Driver to hold her head down, and he grabbed it through the bag. The wolf wanted to try biting him even through the thick burlap, but Ari calmed it and held it back. The bag was opened again and New Guy reached inside. Something was latched to the chain around her neck and she was hauled out. The fish metaphor took on new meaning as she was lifted onto her hind legs and forced to stand.

She was in a garage; three rows of fluorescent lights illuminated a large but empty work space. An open door led into what looked like a dark warehouse. Ari could hear men laughing and cheering. Their shouting was joined by a rattle of chains, and underneath it all was the snarl and barking of her cousins. She could smell blood, and it made her twist and buck against her captor's arms.

"Definitely a fighter!" New Guy was bulky and bald. His face was wide and flat at the chin but tapered to a smooth dome not far above his eyebrows. The reek of cigarettes was strong on him, as were other odors Ari didn't feel interested in identifying. She snarled and bared her teeth at him, twisting her body in an elaborate move designed to look like escape. Instead, she took a quick look at her new environment. A wall of lockers stood as barricade to a series of dark offices, with several tools strewn about between the two.

"It's a female."

Idiot frowned. "Huh? You didn't say nothin' about whether you wanted a boy or a girl."

"No, it's good. Females are called bitches for a reason." He tilted his head to the side and then nodded. "Okay. Go to the office and tell J.J. to get you some cash. Usual rate."

Driver nodded and tapped Idiot's arm to make sure he followed. New Guy let Ari's front legs drop and started walking, pulling the rigid pole he'd attached to her chain. Ari tried to fight, but the ground was too smooth to give her traction. After skidding a few yards she got her feet under her and reluctantly trotted into the warehouse behind him.

They entered into a room full of cages stacked two high, running along the length of the interior wall. Ari lifted her head and looked at them as she was dragged past, meeting their eyes. She heard some of their thoughts as she was pulled along.

Not like us.

Help?

A few of them were too aggressive and riled up to make sense, their spittle glistening on the bars of the cage as they barked at her.

"Come on," New Guy growled. He hauled her through another door into a blindingly bright room that reminded her of a doctor's exam room. The diagrams of canine anatomy and pictures of dogs on the wall revealed it was actually a veterinarian's realm. New Guy bent down and grunted as he hauled her up onto the table in the middle of the room.

"You behave. We're just gonna make sure you ain't got no diseases or anything, all right? Wanna make sure you don't keel over your first time out."

Ari flattened her ears against her skull, widened her eyes, and whimpered.

He kept his steady glare on her.

Ari coughed, trembled, and hunched her shoulders. When she looked up at him again she rolled her eyes back in her head and went limp. She dropped onto her side and let herself fall as limply as if she was dead onto the hard tile floor. *Ouch.* She lay perfectly still and held her breath as New Guy stared in shock.

"What the hell. What the hell." He got onto his knees next to her, both eager to try and help but reluctant to touch her. He finally seemed to decide the ruse was too complicated for a dog to fake and put his hand on her throat to feel for a heartbeat. Ari didn't have to fake a rapid pulse. "Those assholes..." He got to his feet and ran from the room.

Ari immediately flipped onto her stomach and pushed herself up. She brought up one forepaw and pushed it through her collar, holding it there until the claws flattened into fingernails. The hair receded from her hands and arms, her body changing shape with pops and cracks that sent waves of pain through her body. As soon as she had opposable thumbs, she got the choke chain off and tossed it. She arched her back and felt the last few bones pop into place.

Her hip and shoulder ached where she had taken the tumble, but she couldn't focus on that. She limped out of the exam room and back down the row of cages. All the dogs were now staring at her in confusion. The aggressive ones still bared their teeth but they were too confused to actually bark.

Back in the garage Ari ran to the lockers she'd spotted earlier. There was a thick brown jumpsuit hanging on a hook by one of them and she grabbed it. She had just yanked up the zipper when she heard New Guy shouting curses from the direction of the vet's office. She eyed the row of tools nearby and grabbed the shovel. She ran back to the cages and arrived just as New Guy and the Vet came running out of the office. They stopped in their tracks when they saw her.

"Who the hell are you?"

"You oughta be careful who you call a mutt," Ari growled.

She swung the blade of the shovel and both men jumped back even though she was too far away to hit them. She wasn't aiming for them, anyway. The sharp edge of the shovel hit the padlock on the nearest cage and snapped it. The impact shot up both of Ari's arms to her injured shoulder but she ignored the pain as the dog launched out of the tiny space. Given the choice between his rescuer and the people who had tormented it, the dog charged at New Guy.

"Go get him, cousin."

She went back to the garage and used the shovel to break the office window. There was a couch just underneath and Ari used it as a step to enter. She walked to the desk and dialed 9-1-1. When an operator answered she said, "Yeah, anyone you can spare to this location. And bring Animal Control."

She put the receiver down on the blotter and left the office just as Driver and Idiot came back for their car.

Driver looked at the broken window. "Hey. What's going on?"

Obviously New Guy and Vet hadn't raised the alarm yet. Ari could still hear the ruckus coming from the bowels of the warehouse which told her the evening's entertainment hadn't been interrupted. She was still holding the shovel so she gestured past them. "Gotta muck out some of the cages. Don't suppose either of you want to help me out."

"Sorry. I don't do dog shit," Idiot said. "You new here? I ain't seen you around."

Driver tugged on Idiot's arm. "Come on. Flirt on your own time."

"This is my own time. We just got paid." He smiled and walked closer to Ari. "I'm Kevin. What's your name?"

Ari gestured with the shovel again. "I really should get to work."

Driver was leaning against the car with his elbows resting on the roof. "Kev, she just chose shoveling dog crap over talking to you. Take the hint, man. Sorry to bother you, miss. We'll get out of your hair."

Ari didn't want them leaving before the police arrived. "It's not from a lack of interest, you know. It's just that my boss is a real hard-ass. If I leave that stuff sitting around too long, he acts like it becomes radioactive. You guys seem nice. I wish you were sticking around so we could get to know each other better."

She directed that at Driver. She knew Kevin the Idiot would stick around no matter what; Driver was the one she had to convince.

Kevin was looking at Driver, too. "C'mon, Tommy. What are we gonna do, just go home and go to bed?"

Tommy sighed heavily and looked at the door, obviously eager to get away from the scene of the crime. But finally he tapped his hands on the roof and pushed away.

"Sure. Whatever. How long you think it'll take with the shit?"

"Not long." She stepped closer to Kevin and lowered her voice. "Kind of gets boring back here in the garage all by my lonesome. Be nice to have you boys keeping me company." She winked, then looked at Tommy and bit her lip. He finally seemed interested so she smiled. "I'll be right back. Don't you go anywhere."

She walked through the door, looking back once more just to make sure they were both on her hook. Once she was out of sight, she put down the shovel and went back to the exam room. New Guy and Vet were cornered in the vet's small office and the pit bull she'd freed was clawing at the door. He spun at the sound of Ari's arrival and barked at her, but Ari held up a hand to soothe him.

"Easy, fella. Friend. Remember?"

His growl was a low rumble in his chest, but he didn't attack her.

"Good boy. Keep them inside there. If they step out, bite them."

The dog scampered around to face the window and directed its growl at the men behind the glass. New Guy glared at Ari.

"Who the hell are you?"

"Not your ordinary bitch."

By then the sirens were close enough that Ari could hear them even over the commotion in the cages. She followed the narrow and winding corridor into an open area where the spectators had gathered. A chain-link fence supported by steel poles stood in the middle of the space, the sides rattling occasionally as one of the victims slammed against it. Ari skirted the edge of the crowd until she found the front door. There were security guards posted at all three of the visible exits, but only one of them had taken a position where he couldn't see the cage in the middle of the room. He was at least a full head taller than Ari, and his shoulders made him twice as wide as she was. She walked over, approaching from an angle he couldn't see, and spoke only when she was close enough to touch his arm.

"Hey."

His shoulders straightened and he assumed a defensive posture.

"Your job is to keep people out, right? I'm already in, so you can relax." He considered that and then slumped against the wall again. "Something is about to happen. Something very dangerous. You wanna get hurt protecting these people?"

He glanced toward the cage and then quickly away. "Not really."

"Then follow me."

He looked at the crowd one more time, then followed Ari back the way she had come. Kevin and Tommy were waiting in the garage, leaning against the front panel of the Oldsmobile. They straightened up when Ari returned, and Kevin looked confused when he saw her huge escort.

"Whoa. Who is this, your pimp?"

"No. He's gonna help me with my chore."

"What chore?"

"I told you. There's some shit that needs to be picked up." She turned to the bouncer and pointed at the dognappers. "You've probably thought about hurting the people who come in here and watch this shit. You only did it because you needed the money. Right?" She could see the truth in his eyes. "These are two of the guys who provide the fighters. Make sure they can't leave before the show starts. You do that and I'll forget I ever saw you here."

The bouncer moved forward. Kevin and Tommy, torn between fight and flight, got the option taken from them as he closed the distance between them with two steps. He grabbed Tommy and threw him into Kevin, knocking them both down. Ari didn't bother sticking around to see what happened next.

The sound of sirens was unmissable now, and the crowd began a panicked shuffling toward the exit. The dogs howled inside their cages and Ari tossed a quick apology over her shoulder as she ran past them again. Freeing them would only cause more damage and the police would have to use deadly force to make them stop. They were safer in their cages for the time being.

A few people had noticed the door Ari had come through and, assuming it led to a secondary entrance, began bottle-necking there as well. Ari shoved through the crowd of them like fighting a current, slipping her hand into someone's pocket and absconding with their phone. When she got free, she moved toward the fenced area. The dogs inside the cage were oblivious to the pandemonium going on around them. They had been poked, prodded, provoked, and conditioned to fight to the death.

Ari grabbed the fence with her hands and shook it until the dogs turned toward her.

Stop.

Both dogs barked at her but she silenced them by barking herself. The sound was so accurate that they fell silent, their lips curling to show their teeth but most of the fight seeping out of them. Ari dropped into a crouch and flattened her hand against the cage. Both dogs were torn and bloody, and one was holding its left paw up off the concrete. The fight most likely wouldn't have gone on much longer.

You can stop. Just stop. Stop.

The most-injured of the two wavered.

You're safe.

The one with the hurt paw eyed its opponent warily, shuffling off to one side before lying down. The other dog watched and then sat on its haunches. It looked at Ari and whimpered.

"It's okay. You're gonna be okay."

She stood up and watched the people scrambling around for exit. Policemen were using loudspeakers to order the people who had made it out of the building onto the ground. Ari took a deep breath and blew it out through her lips, turning on the phone she'd stolen. She dialed Dale's number and walked to a quieter part of the warehouse interior as it rang in her ear.

"Ari?"

"Yeah. Do you have the police scanner on?"

"Yeah. I assume that's you?"

Ari smiled. "Who else? Wanna come down and give me a ride home?"

"It would be my pleasure. I'll call Detective Lorne and be there are quick as I can."

"Appreciate it. I love you."

"Love you, too."

Ari hung up and went back to the garage. None of the men she'd left there were present. She was hurrying to the door, hoping Kevin and Tommy hadn't managed to slip away, when she heard a muffled thud from the car trunk. She stopped, tilted her head, and knocked.

"Hey!" The car shook as someone in the trunk shifted his weight. "Hey, let us out!"

"Sure thing. An officer will be by shortly to help you out."

From the movement of the car, Ari assumed Tommy and Kevin started wrestling each other. She walked around the car just as a uniformed officer came through the door. He swung his weapon up and got a bead on her, but she stopped dead in her tracks and held out her hands to show she was unarmed.

"Get on your knees."

"Yep, you got it." Ari did as she was told, lacing her fingers together on the back of her head. "My name is Ariadne Willow. I'm a private investigator. When Detective Lorne gets here, let him know where to find me."

"Sure."

One of the dognappers made a noise and the cop turned to see where it had come from.

"Oh. And you might want to let those guys out and take them into custody before they kill each other."

Chapter Two

The past four nights, Dale had gone to bed wearing clothes in which she would feel comfortable leaving the house. She always wanted to be ready as soon as possible when Ari called but this case was different. This time Ari was deliberately putting herself in a dangerous situation, and it was all Dale could do to keep calm about it. A Vice detective had come to them a week earlier with suspicions that there was dog-fighting happening somewhere in the city. He had a good idea who was operating it, a few names of the attendees, but no proof. He couldn't even find out where the fights were taking place.

Ari took the job. It was their first official job with the police, and Dale was nervous about making a good impression. She had gotten Ari a handful of cases for a local law firm that was now seriously considering putting her on retainer, and adding a police consulting job on top of that would put them firmly in the green. All Ari had to do was get herself captured by dog fight organizers. No cause for concern there.

First Ari drove through neighborhoods looking for "Lost Dog" posters. The 'winner' was NewHolly, with posters and flyers for twelve different dogs. Ari cross-checked the dates and discovered that all the dogs had gone missing within the same six week period. She determined that the organizers were abducting people's pets and using them to train their pit bulls and the other official fighting dogs. After that she just had to transform into the wolf and wait to catch them in the act.

"At which point you'll either be a wolf in chains or you'll be naked and unarmed. How is that gaining an advantage, Ari?"

"I'll know where they are. Trust me."

Dale did trust her. She had absolute faith that Ari would come through with a win, no matter how badly the odds were stacked against her. But that didn't make sleep come any easier. The police scanner was a constant companion while Ari was out putting herself in danger, soothing voices in the night that assured her people with guns and pepper spray were out there if Ari needed them.

When Ari's call finally came in, Dale was already wide awake. Police were responding to a 911 call with sketchy information about needing Animal Control. She already had her socks and shoes on when her cell phone rang and Ari asked her to come pick her up. She called Detective Lorne on her way out of the apartment just in case there were any legal issues with Ari being present at an illegal dog fight. He wasn't a client, but he could certainly vouch that they were the good guys if anyone made a fuss.

Lorne told her the address matched a warehouse on Harbor Island and offered her a ride to make sure she could get through the police barricades that were sure to be up. Five minutes later she was in his personal vehicle being driven south.

They first met Kyle Lorne during the Gavin case, and their paths had crossed a few times since then. He respected their results, even if he was becoming suspicious about just how they were achieved. He was a few years older than them, if the gray at his temples was any indication, but still young enough that he was willing to work with a couple of freelancers as long as they got results. He drove in silence for the first few blocks, streetlights flashing across his features as he considered the situation. Finally he glanced at her and said what was on his mind.

"So we've been trying to find these guys for a good long time now, but your partner managed to succeed in, what, under a week?"

"She has a special skill set."

Lorne pursed his lips and nodded. "Yeah. She certainly seems to."

They passed over the bridge and followed the eerie, flash-strobe glow of red and blue police lights until they found the warehouse. Lorne parked and led Dale across the pavement, using his badge to get past the uniformed officers guarding the area. He asked if Ariadne Willow had been found and was pointed toward a squad car closer to the building. Ari was sitting in the back, slumped down so she could rest her head against the back of the seat. Lorne opened the door and she looked up at him, then looked past him to smile at Dale.

"Still good at getting yourself into trouble, I see."

Ari said, "We all have to be good at something."

"Who put you here?"

"Officer Hearst."

Lorne nodded. "I'll find him and clear things up for you. Stay here."

Once he was gone, Dale crouched down in the open door of the car. "Hey, you."

"Hey." Ari took Dale's hand, intertwining their fingers and smiling at Dale's strong grip. "I'm fine. A little roughed up... I got thrown in a sack and manhandled, but otherwise I'm fine."

Dale smiled and kissed Ari's fingers. "Good. No violence?"

"A little. But I got someone bigger and stronger than me to do all the punching."

"Good girl." She leaned forward to kiss Ari's lips. "I'm glad you're okay."

Lorne came back with Hearst, who released Ari from her handcuffs. He looked more irritated than apologetic. "Sorry about this. But you understand our position."

"Sure." She nodded toward the building. "You had to make sure you got everyone who was in there. I'm glad you erred on the side of caution."

Hearst nodded. Lorne patted the officer on the shoulder as he turned to walk away. Ari watched him go then raised her eyebrows at the detective. "You need anything from me?"

"No." Lorne seemed to suddenly notice her outfit. "Nice jumpsuit. Is that typical stakeout apparel for you, Ms. Willow?"

She looked down at herself. "Yeah. All the kids are wearing them these days. Greasy jumpsuits with someone else's name on the chest. They're all the rage."

"Well, anything's better than belly shirts I guess."

Ari saw a few Animal Control officers walking toward the building. "What are they going to do with the dogs?"

"Rehabilitation programs. That was part of your original arrangement with Detective Southall, right?"

"Just making sure everyone is aware. They're good dogs who were forced to be bad. I don't want them to suffer any more than they already have, and I don't want anyone putting them to sleep just because it's easier than treating them like the victims they are."

Lorne checked his watch. "Okay. It's late, and there's no reason for me to lose any more sleep on a case I don't officially have. I suggest you ladies do the same. They're going to want statements from you about everything that happened here, but that can wait until tomorrow morning. They'll be booking these jackasses all night, so you might as well get some sleep."

Ari glanced at Dale. "Actually, if you're on your way home, do you think you could drop us somewhere?"

He stared at her for a moment. "You don't have a car?"

"Not here, no."

"So how'd you get here?"

"I hitched a ride with one of the dognappers. You don't think they just told me where the illegal dog-fighting ring was, do you?"

Lorne's gaze lingered on her, waiting for her to break. When she didn't, he sighed and motioned for them to follow him back to his car.

"We'll have a check for you tomorrow, too. Even if I can't figure out how you pulled this off, you did good work. Caught them in the act, very few if any of them got away... I'm impressed. I'll talk to my captain about taking you on as consultants. I think we have enough cold cases to keep you busy for a while."

"We appreciate it." Ari put her arm around Dale and pulled her close. They both got into the backseat of Lorne's car, and Dale told him to take them back to her apartment. Ari guided Dale's head to her shoulder and stroked her hair as Lorne drove back over the bridge. They rode through the dark in companionable silence, Dale lulled to sleep almost immediately due to the darkness and the hum of the engine. Her sudden relaxation was also at least partially thanks to the fact Ari was safe and sound.

She woke when she heard Ari vaguely giving Lorne directions. She opened her eyes and saw they were passing the University. "It's on Madison," Dale said through a yawn.

"I know, sweetie," Ari whispered.

Dale put her head back down. She heard Ari speak to Lorne without really listening, then woke up enough that Ari wouldn't be forced to carry her upstairs. She said goodbye and thanked Detective Lorne before he drove off, then she took Ari's hand and guided her inside. "I know you couldn't say anything in front of Lorne, but do you need to go for a run?"

Ari shook her head. "I'm fine. I've been the wolf every night this week."

"Yeah, you've been the wolf, but you've been forcing it to work. Walking around in the same neighborhood, back and forth and up and down the same streets. I know I'd go crazy with a schedule like that." She crooked a finger and stroked Ari's cheek. "I know you want to go upstairs with me, but I also know a part of you wants to run. I'm letting you know it's okay if you want to do that. We can reunite tomorrow after a big fancy dinner we get with our police department check." She kissed Ari's bottom lip.

"I do love you."

Dale smiled. "I'm just being pragmatic. I wouldn't be much fun tonight anyway. I'm exhausted. So we'll both take care of biological needs - running and sleep - and tomorrow we can do the fun things when we're both conscious enough to really appreciate them."

"Sounds good." Ari smiled and kissed Dale. "I don't want to wake you, so I'll just go to my place when the wolf is tuckered out. I'll see you tomorrow morning and we can go get our big fat police check together."

Dale smiled. "Be safe."

"I always am. Come on... I'll go upstairs and tuck you in before I leave."

Dale took Ari's hand and led her upstairs. Ari looked down and plucked at her jumpsuit.

"Oh. I guess I stole this."

"I don't think the owners will press charges."

Ari escorted Dale into the apartment and down the hall to her bedroom. She helped her undress and tucked her in, as promised. She kissed the tip of Dale's nose, which made Dale chuckle. "I won't stay out too late."

"Good. I'll see you in the morning."

Ari nodded and smoothed down Dale's hair. She kissed her forehead and then her lips. "Sweet dreams, sweetheart."

She left the apartment and went downstairs, her bare feet slapping on the tile as she went back outside. She stepped into a recessed walkway and, after checking for any security cameras, took off the borrowed-slash-stolen jumpsuit and crouched down onto her hands and knees. She closed her eyes and let the change take her over. She bared her teeth as her skin stretched and tightened, her bones shifting into a new shape.

It was over in a matter of seconds, and she rose to shake out her fur. She flexed her muscles and stretched her neck out, turning her head first one way and then the other. She lifted her snout to scent the air, looked around to see if there was any food lying around that she might have missed, and then trotted out onto the sidewalk. She stopped on the corner, closed her eyes, and focused on the wolf.

Okay, baby. It's all you. You did a great job this week, so you can take over. Animal Control has their hands full with the dog-fighting ring. The city is yours. Just try not to eat anything too disgusting, for my sake.

The wolf seemed hesitant after a week of being kept on a tight rein, but after a moment Ari's vision began to blur. It felt like slipping into a daydream, falling into a veil of distraction, but she'd felt the wolf take over enough times to recognize the sensation of another consciousness taking precedence. She retreated mentally and let the wolf run.

The wolf was kind to her. She left Dale's apartment at a quarter to four and, if she could trust her dead-reckoning of the sun's position, it was almost six before she came back to her senses. She was still in the wolf's form, but it had handed control back to her so she could find a stash and get home. Early commuters were out starting their day, so she kept to alleys and back roads until she got her bearings and figured out where the nearest stash was. She was on Genesee Street, so she headed east for the cover of Lake People Park. Once she was safely out of view from the street, she paused next to a tree and transformed.

Her shoulders popped and her spine crackled, and she dropped to one knee as her skin rippled through the final stages. She flexed her fingers and the middle one popped, sending a bolt of pain up her forearm. She hissed and clung to the tree, bark flaking around her fingers as she rode the initial surge of pain. She'd gotten lucky at the warehouse, the pain of falling off the exam table and adrenaline from the mission distracting her from the pain of transformation. But it was back now in full force, lighting all her bones on fire and twisting her muscles.

When she caught her breath, she pushed her sweaty hair out of her face and got her bearings. The bag she was heading for was newer than most of the stashes so she didn't have its exact position memorized. Dale had only filled it once, and Ari had yet to need it.

She didn't know exactly what was in the bag, but anything would be better than taking the morning commute in the buff. She had entered the park from the north, so she headed south for about thirty yards before cutting to the east again. Her mother had taught her dead-reckoning when she introduced the concept of hiding stashes of clothing and supplies throughout the city. It was one of the few lessons Ari actually appreciated.

She was so distracted by her now-fading pain that she didn't notice the scents in the air until it was too late. She stepped into the small clearing and spotted the interloper when it was too late to hide or abort her approach. An athletically-lean woman with white, almost ashen skin was crouched over the bag. Her back was to Ari, strong muscles at play under the skin. The lines of her spine and shoulder blades were sharp and pronounced, and her pose made her seem animalistic even though she was in human form. Her entire body tensed at the sound of Ari's bare feet brushing across the mulch of dead leaves and twigs.

The woman stood up and spun to face Ari with a wary expression. She was slender and muscular with dark hair that draped her face like a hood. One side fell back to expose her high cheekbone when she tilted her head in consideration. She narrowed dark eyes, nodded once at Ari, and then pointed at the bag.

"This is yours?"

"Yeah." Ari moved cautiously forward. Neither of them seemed overly concerned with their nudity, something Ari had only experienced with other *canidae*. She sniffed the air and was surprised by what she discovered. She raised an eyebrow. "Wolf?"

The other woman nodded. Her nostrils flared as well and the tension seeped out of her. "Yeah. You too?" Ari nodded. "I'm Milo."

"Milo?"

She shrugged. "Millicent Duncan. But I don't like Millicent and I loathe Millie."

"Nice compromise. Ariadne Willow. Ari."

Milo nodded once in greeting before she gestured at the duffel bag. "I was going through the park trying to keep away from all the people, trying to figure out how to get home. I could tell that someone had been through here and I followed it to the bag. I was a little worried it was a serial killer's mementos or something."

"You wouldn't be the first to make that mistake. You're British?"

She smiled, revealing a small gap between her front teeth.

"What gave me away, guv? Me accent a bit limey for ya?"

Ari chuckled and moved closer. Even her hyper-paranoid wolf paranoia was relaxed, so she pointed at the bag. "Go ahead and take what you need. Wolves have to look out for each other, right? My girlfriend packs these for me and hides them all over the city, and she always puts in more than I'll need so she doesn't have to replenish them every time I use one. So wherever I end up after a run, I don't have to go far for clothes."

"Ah, that's nice of her. Whatever I take, I promise to return to you."

"It's fine. Goodwill stuff, mostly. Things that will do in a pinch but you wouldn't want to be seen in under normal circumstances." She unzipped the bag and pulled out one of the shirts. She turned it around so Milo could see the design on the front: a small princess holding a wand that sparkled with glitter. "Heh, case in point."

"I think it's smashing," Milo said.

Ari tossed it to her. "We look to be about the same size. How far are you trying to get?"

Milo lifted her head and looked toward the street. "Don't know where we are now, so I'm not exactly sure. I'm new in town and part of tonight's run was supposed to acclimate myself to the new territory. Seems I've only succeeded in getting myself hopelessly lost. I'm staying on East Crescent Drive."

"Wow."

"That far?"

"No. Well, yeah, kind of. But it's a pretty swank neighborhood." She took a pair of jeans out of the bag and stepped into them. "There's a bus stop nearby. I'll pay your fare."

Milo shook her head as she put on a pair of lime-green shorts. "That's far too generous. I'm already taking your clothes."

Ari raised an eyebrow and looked at Milo's princess shirt and radioactive shorts. "Trust me, you're doing me a favor taking those. Besides, wolves shouldn't have to fend for themselves in new cities. Consider me your *canidae* ambassador."

"I appreciate it, Ari." She examined one of the sneakers Ari held out to her. "These won't fit me."

"Oh." She dug through the bag. "Here, try the sandals."

"Shoes and sandals?"

Ari shrugged. "Dale can't know what time of year I'll need the stashes she hides, so she tries to cover as many bases as possible."

"Nice girlfriend."

"Yeah, I think I'll keep her."

Milo made a noise halfway between a snort and a grunt. Ari looked up, but she didn't expand on it, so she went back to tying her shoes. There was a hidden inner compartment in the bag and Ari pulled out fifteen dollars. "This should get us some coffee while we wait for the bus. Follow me."

They walked through the park together, Ari moving gingerly until the pain of her transformation finally began to fade.

"You all right?"

"Yeah. Why?"

"You're walking a little~"

Ari waved her off. "It's fine. Just a little sore after the change, that's all."

"Oh."

They stepped out into civilization again. Ari pointed to a Starbucks nearby and they joined the line. By the time they received their caffeine, it was fourteen minutes past six and the next bus was due any minute. They took their coffees to wait at the bus stop. Both sides of the bus stop were plastered with Missing posters bearing the face of Melody Scott, the little girl who had now been missing for three days. Ari was a little ashamed by the fact that she no longer looked at the posters when she saw them. The story had broken while she was scouting neighborhoods trying to find Lost Dog posters, so when a little blonde girl's photo began taking over, her initial and shameful response was annoyance.

They settled in amid people in suits and the uniforms of their trade. Ari didn't mind joining them despite her Fraggle Rock T-shirt and second-hand jeans. Milo seemed just as comfortable, slouching in shorts and sandals despite the chill in the air, holding her coffee with one hand as she settled in.

"So what do you do, Ariadne?"

"Please, call me Ari. I'm a private investigator."

Milo raised an eyebrow. "In real life?"

Ari laughed. "Yeah. How about you?"

"Hem." Milo brought the coffee to her lips and took a drink, although Ari got the impression it was more to stall than for thirst. "At the moment I don't do anything, exactly. I inherited a lot of money two years ago, but before that I was a bicycle courier. I also drove a taxi cab for a few years in college. Private eye, though... I never thought of that."

"Don't get any ideas. I don't need the competition."

Milo chuckled as the bus pulled up. They boarded and Ari confirmed it would take Milo all the way to East Crescent before they took their seats.

"The bus is going past my street first, so I'll have to abandon you."

Milo grinned. "That's all right. I'm a big girl, I think I can find my way from here. I would like to repay you for your generosity. If not for your clothes, then I at least owe you for the coffee. No 'pay it forward' malarkey. I want to reward you for your kindness."

Ari tapped the person in front of her on the shoulder and asked if he had a pen. She took Milo's coffee cup and wrote on the side of it. "This is my office number, and my cell phone. You want to buy me and Dale dinner, I'd be more than happy to oblige you."

"That's more like it."

Ari returned the pen. "Oh, and before you ask, Dale isn't... like us. But she knows everything. So you don't have to worry about that."

"Oh. That's a little odd, don't you think?"

"Maybe a little. But we can't choose who we love, right?"

"Hmph."

Ari glanced at her again. "You okay?"

Milo nodded. "Yeah."

Ari decided that Milo's relocation had something to do with a relationship gone south, so she decided not to press it. They may have seen each other without clothes on, but it was still too early in their friendship for them to be completely naked with one another. She settled in against the vinyl of the seat and closed her eyes, dozing for the few minutes it would take to get to her street.

Chapter Three

DALE OPENED the office at ten the next morning and did busywork until Ari showed up at noon. "Hey, sleepyhead. Have a good run last night?"

"Yeah, it was pretty good." She smiled as she leaned over the desk to kiss Dale hello. "I didn't get home until six-thirty, though. Then I just showered and headed downtown to give the police my statement." She held up the check like a trophy and placed it in front of Dale on the desk. "You can deposit that whenever you desire."

Dale whistled. "Yay, cops."

"Amen. Now, I'm still pretty wiped out. I might take a nap in the office if we don't have any appointments."

"Nope, we're all good. I'll try to keep it down out here."

"You could always come in there and join me."

Dale clicked her tongue. "That's not really restful."

Ari shrugged. "Who needs sleep? Don't let me sleep past three."

"Okay."

"Oh, and if a woman named Milo calls, let me know. She's another wolf. I ran into her digging through the Lake People Park stash."

"She was stealing your clothes?"

Ari shook her head. "Borrowing. I really don't mind. She

wanted to take us out for dinner as a thank-you."

"Oh! I won't say no to that. Sleep well."

Ari waved and shut the door to the inner office. Dale turned on some music, the volume loud enough for her to hear it but not so loud it would disturb Ari's rest. She opened the Document related to the dog-fighting case and began typing up the conclusion. Ari claimed they didn't necessarily need hard copies of all the case files, but Dale liked having them on-hand in case of an emergency. She also used it as a means to keep track how often Ari transformed while on the job. They couldn't exactly put in for health benefits related to *canidae* shifting, but it helped her keep track of how often Ari was transforming, and if she pushing herself beyond safety limits.

Things were finally quieting down after the maelstrom caused by the Gavin case. She still thanked whoever was listening to her prayers for how lucky they'd gotten during those crazy days. The case was supposed to be a simple 'observe and report' on a wild-child heiress, but it turned out to be a scam to use Ari as a scapegoat for murder. Ari had gotten out of it by the skin of her teeth, but clearing her name nearly cost them everything.

Dale reached up and touched the left side of her head. For her, the difference between living and dying was whether or not a douchebag took the time to aim. He'd been more interested in being melodramatic, so he had just brought the gun up and pulled the trigger. The kick caused the bullet to graze her skull rather than penetrating it, but sometimes a graze was enough. She still felt the scar every time she washed her hair and remembered how close she had come to dying.

Of course once she healed from the injury and Ari was back in fighting strength after her most strenuous transformation in memory, the agency had taken off in ways neither of them could have imagined. They were namedropped in all of the press releases about Katherine Gavin's arrest, an example of 'the little guy' who went up against 'the man' and won. In the face of great adversity and overwhelming odds, Ari had stuck up for what she believed. There were enough people who respected that to want Ari working for them.

The cases had been hit and miss, some daunting while others were quiet and refreshing. Over the past few weeks Ari had begun referring clients to other agencies when she couldn't fit them into her schedule, and their coffers were full enough that they could afford to pass on clients to take a night off when the mood struck. They might not have been rich, but the bills were paid and they treated each other to nice romantic evenings a few times a week. Who could ask for anything more?

She was printing out the file when there was a quiet knock on the door. She could see the shape of her guest through the fogged glass.

"It's open."

The woman came in and quietly shut the door behind her. She wore a cream blouse and a brown skirt that was just a shade lighter than her skin, eyeing the office with unease before she finally stepped closer to the desk. "Hello. I'm sorry. This is a private investigator's office, right? You do miss~" Her voice cracked and her eyes filled with tears. Dale took the Kleenex off the desk and stood as she handed them over. "Sorry. Thank you." She wiped her eyes. "You look for missing people."

"We do. Please, sit down. Take your time."

"Time," the woman sighed. "I don't think I have time." She let Dale guide her to one of the seats and gingerly lowered herself. She telegraphed every movement as if she was worried she would shatter.

Dale rubbed the woman's shoulder. "Why don't we start easy? I'm Dale Frye."

She smiled gratefully. "Madeline Morris. I want to hire you~"

Madeline was cut off by the inner office door opening. Ari stepped out and glanced at the new arrival, then at Dale. "Everything okay?"

"Yes. Madeline, this is Ariadne Willow."

"Hello. I'm sorry if I came at a bad time, but~"

Ari shook her head and sat on Dale's desk. "Not at all. How can we help?"

Madeline looked down at the Kleenex she had destroyed and brought the tatters up to her face to wipe at her eyes. "I assume you've heard of Melody Louise Scott."

"Everyone in Seattle knows her," Ari said, thinking of the posters at the bus stop again. The little girl, blonde and beaming in the school photo used in all the posters, had been abducted outside of her school. No one had seen her go with anybody, and no sightings had been reported in the seventy-two hours she had been gone. Posters were everywhere, and every news broadcast started with an update on what was being called Missing Melody. At this point Ari assumed the story was getting national attention.

Madeline looked down at her hands. "The police are sparing no expense to find her. They have a special unit dedicated to tracking her down." She sniffled and fresh tears appeared in her eyes. "My daughter Jenna is Melody's age. She's a beautiful little girl. She plays the violin." She laughed and a tear rolled down her cheek. "This morning I packed her lunch, and I kissed her goodbye, and waved to her from the porch when she walked off to the bus stop. An hour later I got a call from the school saying she had never shown up."

Dale took Madeline's hand. "Oh, my God. I'm so sorry."

"The police a-are... I called them to report her missing. They sent a man out." She held up one finger. "One man. And he looked around and told me he was sure she was just playing hooky. She's seven years old, Ms. Willow. Second graders don't play hooky." Her voice broke. "He said to call back if she didn't come home by tonight. So I'm supposed to wait until dark before anyone lifts a finger to find her. While Missing Melody gets a task force.

"The simple truth of the matter is that a little girl, a blonde-haired white girl is missing. And as long as she's in danger, the police aren't going to expend any effort on a missing black girl. I was so angry. I was furious. But I remembered reading about you online. Your agency was hired by Katherine Gavin but you did the right thing. It's because of you that her daughter is remembered as a charitable person. I want to know someone, *anyone* is looking for Jenna. I want to know that she's the top priority for at least one person besides me."

Ari glanced at Dale, but she could have guessed what her response would be. "Of course. We'll take the case."

Madeline pressed her lips together. "Thank you." She touched her eyes again. "I can't pay you very much. I have some money set aside, of course. For Jenna's future." She smiled sadly. "I didn't think I would be using it this soon, but if you can find her..."

"We'll work something out. Come on into the office and we can talk about what I need from you."

Madeline stood up. "Thank you, Ms. Willow."

"We'll do everything we can to get your daughter back safe and sound." She put her hand on Madeline's elbow and glanced at Dale. Dale nodded and gave Ari a thumbs-up, hoping she knew it meant she would clear the schedule. Ari mouthed 'thank you' and closed the office door. Dale went back to her seat and opened a new case file and entered the information.

Jenna Morris. Missing. Age seven. Client, Madeline Morris (mother).

She looked toward the office door and hoped Ari would be able to bring the girl back.

Madeline Morris lived in a cul-de-sac off Lake Dell Avenue in a beautiful A-frame house. The front yard was elevated about two feet above street level, ending at a wooden retaining wall that separated it from the sidewalk. Madeline parked in the street, blocking her own driveway, and stepped out to look up and down the street before she turned back to Ari. "The bus stop is just up there." She pointed, but the curve of the road was so dramatic that there was only visibility for a few dozen feet. She seemed to realize that and dropped her hand. "I never thought about... how long she's out of my sight."

"Don't blame yourself for this, Mrs. Morris. You said that Jenna usually walked with friends. Where were they today?"

"She left later than usual. She was helping me with laundry so she left about five minutes later than usual. Five minutes couldn't make that big of a difference... five fewer minutes waiting in the cold for a bus..."

Ari remembered waiting for the bus that morning with Milo and tried to imagine Jenna, alone and shivering. "How far is it from here to the bus stop?"

"Um. Not far? It takes about four minutes to walk there."

Only four minutes. Ari fought back a shudder at how quickly something could go horribly wrong.

"What was she wearing?"

"A pink cap, a sort of..." She held her hands over her torso and ran them up and down. "It's a puffy coat. Light-purple. She was carrying a bookbag shaped like a koala." Her eyes welled up again.

"Mrs. Morris, I want you to stay here. I'm going to trace her route. Do you have anything of hers?" She stopped herself from specifically asking for anything that had Jenna's scent on it.

Madeline nodded. "Yes. In the car, I have..." She opened the back door and ducked inside. A few seconds later she produced a pair of mittens. "She forgot these when I picked her up from school yesterday."

Ari took them. "Thank you. I'll be right back. Go into the house, lie down, and try to keep yourself calm. You can't help Jenna if you aren't thinking clearly. I'll be back as soon as I can."

"Okay. Good luck."

"Thank you." Ari watched her go back into the house before she brought the mittens up to her nose. She breathed deeply and looked up and down the street in case anyone was watching. Both sides of the winding road were shaded by tall trees. The houses were relatively far apart and, in many instances, blocked from view by trees and bushes. In the dark of morning before the sun rose, it would be all too easy to make a little girl vanish in no time flat.

She knew she would get a better scent at the wolf, but even as a human her olfactory senses were more heightened than the average person's. She kept the mittens in her hands as she started walking toward the bus stop. After a few feet she looked back and saw that Madeline's car was out of sight. A few more steps and she couldn't see the house. On a good day, the tightness would make the neighborhood feel cozy. At the moment it just made the entire street seem closed off and confined on all sides.

Foot paths led off the main road at uneven intervals. She stopped at the mouth of each one and breathed deeply but Jenna hadn't gone down any of them. She reached the bus stop sign in half the time Madeline had predicted, owing to the fact she wasn't keeping pace with a seven year old. She stood next to the pole and inhaled deeply.

Kids had a certain ineffable smell, and a group of them had definitely stood here for a prolonged period. She tried to separate Jenna from the rest and failed. Two houses flanked the bus stop on either side of the road, and Ari went up the front walk to the nearest. She knocked and the door was answered almost immediately by a doughy, middle-aged man in a hooded sweatshirt and bare feet. He smelled of pot and glared at her with undisguised hostility.

"Yeah?"

"Hi. I'm Ariadne Willow. I'm a private investigator. Could I ask you a few questions about that bus stop?"

He looked past her. "The bus stop? You mean the magnet for screaming, bratty kids who scream me awake every morning at seven? What about it?"

"I was wondering if you happened to notice a little girl~"

He rested his elbow against the door frame and squeezed the bridge of his nose. "Lady, I don't notice any particular brats, okay? They're just a swarm. You want to ask me if I noticed a particular seagull who shit on my car, you might have a better chance."

"This morning she was wearing a puffy coat and a pink hat..."

He started to bite her head off again, but then he stopped. "Wait. The black girl?"

"Yeah. Her name is Jenna."

"I don't know what her name was, but I know she wasn't at the bus stop on time this morning. I heard the bus go by when I was getting my coffee, and I looked out and I saw her walking. It must have gone right past her, and she was still just trudging on." He looked at the street again. "She was about there."

Ari looked where he was pointing. Even with the curve in the road, she would have been visible from the bus stop. How long would it take her to run that distance, thirty seconds? What kind of bus driver wouldn't wait for a kid who was that close?

"And she kept walking even though the bus left without her?"

The guy shrugged. "She didn't seem too bothered. She just kept walking."

"Where?"

"Lady, I don't know. I just happened to look out the window and saw her going along. What do you care anyway?"

Ari couldn't resist puncturing the guy's superiority complex. "She's missing. Right now you're the last person to have seen her."

The blood drained from his face. "Oh. Hey, look, I didn't... I didn't know. How could I have known?"

"Thanks for your help." She turned and walked away with him still sputtering on the porch. She breathed the air again and caught a hint of Jenna's scent coming from the west. She had kept walking past the bus stop. But why? If she missed the bus why not just go home and have her mother drive her to school? If Madeline didn't have time, she could have driven her to one of the other stops on the route and let her wait there.

But Jenna had kept walking. Why?

The road curved sharply to the south and then became 32nd Avenue. Without the confines of the hills, the curve of the road, and the trees that acted as windbreaks, the scent dissipated almost immediately. There was a large parking lot to her left and, across the street from that, a city bus stop.

Would Jenna think of that? A part of her wondered if there was any chance Jenna had decided to trade one bus for the other and, if she had, the possibility that she and Milo had been on the bus at the same time as the girl she was now searching for. She crossed the street when the traffic allowed and approached the glass cubicle.

Posters of Melody Scott were hanging on the side facing Ari, and she knew there were more on the other side.

The only person on the bench was an older woman in a flowered dress with shopping bags tucked tight against either hip like levees. When she saw Ari, she began to move her bags.

"Hello. No, you're fine. I'm not waiting for the bus. I was just wondering how far this particular route went. Do you know if it goes past Dearborn Elementary?"

The woman looked up and down the street and then touched her chin. "Hm. I'm fairly sure it does. It certainly goes in that direction."

So even if the city bus didn't take her directly to the front doors, it would at least cut down on how far she would have to walk. "Thank you very much."

"Of course, dear."

Ari jogged back to the Morris house. The front door was open and Madeline was standing just inside watching for her. She perked up when Ari stepped onto the porch. It was obvious she wanted to ask if she'd found anything, if she had picked up any clues about where her daughter had gone, but she was pragmatic enough not to voice her hope.

"I talked to someone who saw Jenna after the bus went by. Would she have expected you to drive her to school if she'd missed the bus?"

Madeline frowned and shook her head. "No. I leave for work right after she leaves most mornings." Her voice trailed off and she hugged herself. "She just kept walking? It's more than a mile and a half to her school..."

Ari guided Madeline back into the house. The living room was small but tidy, and the curtains had been pulled back to let the meager natural light in. Madeline sat on the couch out of habit, lowering herself to the overstuffed cushions without even seeming to notice it was there. Ari sat next to her, elbows on her knees and hands clasped in front of her.

"She could have ridden the city bus most of the way. Does that sound like something she might have done?"

"No! My gosh. She's never been on a city bus in her life."

Ari considered that. "Do you mind if I take a look in her room? She might have left something that will point us to where she is. If there's something going on that you don't know about, she might have left a clue in a diary."

Madeline frowned. "Something going on... like *what?* Drugs? A boy? She's seven years old, Ms. Willow."

"I'm sorry, Mrs. Morris, but wherever your daughter is~"

"No. You're right. Of course you can look in her room. It's right down the hallway. The first door without coats hanging on the front of it."

Ari nodded her thanks and stood up. Jenna's bedroom door was painted white with pink accents. She rested her hand on the knob and braced herself for a flood of girliness, a too-precious environment that would make her heart ache if the case ended less than perfectly. She took a steadying breath and pushed the door open.

The four-poster bed had white muslin curtains protecting the plush mattress. The bed wasn't made, and a pair of stuffed animals - a penguin and a lemur - slumped against each other near the pillow. There was a desk under the twin windows and Ari walked over to it. She found notebooks and pens, some books suitable for a few years above Jenna's grade-level, and a few picture books meant for younger kids that showed animals in their natural habitats. She picked it up and flipped through it before deciding it wasn't a clue.

She had turned to examine the framed pictures on the wall - Madeline and Jenna whale watching, then in the snow, at some school function - when Madeline rushed into the room. She held her phone out at Ari like it was a gun, trembling as her fingers gripped the phone hard enough to leave imprints on her skin. Ari stared and Madeline jabbed the phone at her. After a moment, Ari took it. She only heard a faint hiss on the other end of the line.

"Hello?"

A near-frantic man snapped, "Who the hell is this?"

Ari frowned at Madeline, who had covered her mouth with her hand. Tears were filling her eyes. Ari put her arm across her stomach and rested her other elbow against her hand. "Why don't we start with you, pal? Got a name?"

Another long, hiss-filled silence. Then finally, "I have your daughter. If you want her back, you're going to play by our rules. No cops. You call the cops, she... the girl is dead. If you want her back, start getting the money together. You know how much you need. You know how much she's worth. We'll be in touch tomorrow."

"Hold on. I didn't answer your question."

Another pause. "What?"

"You asked who I was."

"You..."

"My name is Ariadne Willow. I'm a private investigator that Madeline Morris hired to find her daughter." Madison's face trembled and she turned her back to Ari. "I'm not a cop, so she's not breaking your rule. You can consider me a private employee of Madeline Morris. Do you know what that means? It means I don't care about you. I don't need to bring you to justice on principle. My job is making sure my client is happy, and getting her daughter back is her only concern. It's all I'm after. You want money. I want Jenna Morris safe and sound when this is all over. I'm willing to cooperate to make that happen. Are you?"

More silence. Ari waited and then spoke again.

"What's your favorite color?"

"Huh?" Exasperated now, almost panicked.

"Never mind. You said you would be in touch. Mrs. Morris needs time to get the money together. Call me back on this cell phone in twenty-four hours with an update." She gave him the number. "During those twenty-four hours, Jenna is going to be treated like a princess. She's going to have a nice bed, she's going to watch all the TV she can stand." She glanced at the desk. "She likes nature shows, but let her pick. Get her whatever she wants for dinner. As long as we're both happy, this can be a win-win situation. Twenty-four hours. I'll be waiting for your call."

She hung up before he could reply. Madeline spun around and snatched the phone out of her hand.

"What the hell are you doing? How can you talk to them like that? They have my baby!"

"That guy wasn't in charge. He was reading from a script."

Madeline blinked. "How do you know?"

"He got more flustered when I didn't do what he expected. I asked him what his favorite color was and he nearly wet his pants. They want money. They don't care if they get it the easy way or the hard way, they just want it. I'm going to play along with them so that you can rest assured that Jenna is safe."

"You're just going to let them get away with this?"

"Oh, hell no. They took a little girl. I'm going to make them pay. Right now I'm practicing diplomacy. I'm just saying 'nice doggie' until I can pick up a rock."

CHAPTER FOUR

DALE HATED being stuck at the office while Ari was busy on a case. She finished filing the dog-fighting case and manned the phones for an hour before she took the check to the bank and deposited it. When she got back, a woman was leaning against the wall across from the front door of the office. After the Gavin case hit the news it wasn't unusual for them to get two walk-in clients in a single day, but something about the woman's demeanor told Dale she wasn't there to hire them. She wore a slightly rumpled white shirt under a black blazer, the cuffs of her jeans rolled up to reveal a good length of brown leather boots. She glanced up, a hopeful look on her face as she waited for Dale to confirm her identity.

Dale smiled, took off her cap, and nodded at the front door. "Hi, can I help you? I work here. Dale Frye."

The woman's face lit up. "Ah, yes, Ariadne told me all about you. She suggested I could stop by, show my appreciation for what she did this morning. Milo Duncan."

Dale smiled. Ari hadn't said her new friend was British. "Oh, she mentioned you, too. Sorry, she's on a case right now."

"So she really is a private eye?"

"Well, we prefer private investigator. Or detective if you want." She unlocked the door and gestured for Milo to follow you in. "Seems like you two really hit it off."

Milo nodded. "Yeah, she really saved my life last night. Or I guess you get the credit for that, with those stashes. Brilliant idea."

"It was actually Ari's mother who taught her that." Dale put her keys down and filed the bank deposit slip in the proper place. "I just streamlined and maintain it. You know, office manager, receptionist, sidekick, werewolf handler."

Milo laughed. "I should have someone like you for myself. Where'd she find you, Craigslist?"

Dale leaned against the desk. "We actually just kind of stumbled over each other. I was walking home with my dinner and saw what I thought was a stray dog being harassed by some kids. So I ran them off and took the poor thing home where it would be safe." She smiled at the memory. "Ari apparently changed in her sleep, got confused, and crawled into bed with me."

Milo raised an eyebrow. "That's one way to meet your girlfriend. Was she still naked at the time?"

"Oh, yeah."

Milo whistled.

"We actually didn't... get together... then. I needed a job and she obviously needed help here, so she hired me. We kept it strictly professional for almost four years before we finally, um." She shrugged. "Before we gave in to the undeniable."

"Aw, that's sweet." Milo chuckled softly. "Strictly professional, huh?"

Dale blushed. "Okay, maybe not a hundred percent. But we behaved for the most part."

Milo had been eyeing the waiting room while they talked. "This is a brilliant idea, by the way. Wolf detective. Skulking around in the bushes and peeping in windows, no one would suspect the pup. There aren't a lot of jobs out there that combine both sides so fluidly. May I?" She gestured at the closed office door.

"Uh. I guess. It's not really anything special." Dale opened the door and stepped inside. The couch to the right was where Ari occasionally napped after long nights as the wolf, and it was where Dale had given dozens if not hundreds of massages even before they were a couple. The file cabinets were across from the door, and a huge clock hung on the wall above them. Dale had been working for Ari five years and shared a bed with her for one of them, and she still didn't know the story behind the clock.

"Ari said you offered to buy us dinner tonight."

"It's the least I can do after the kindness she showed me."

"We might have to postpone that. She took a case this morning that could end up being time sensitive. A little girl is missing."

Milo nodded. "Oh, right, I've seen the posters. Missing Melody."

"Actually no. A second little girl is missing, and her mother is afraid the police won't take resources away from the Missing Melody case to look for her, so she hired Ari to make sure someone was giving her daughter top priority."

"That's so noble. And it's disappointing I can't repay you both tonight, but I understand. I actually only stopped by to give Ariadne my information in case there was a problem." She took a card from her shirt pocket. Dale took it and gave the information a cursory look before she slipped it into her own pocket. "And let me know if you need any help with the case. A little girl in a city like this, well... just let me know if you need help."

"Will do. And we're definitely going to take advantage of your dinner offer. Girls and wolves all have to eat, right?" She winked.

"Indeed we do," Milo chuckled. "I'll get out of your hair in case she needs you for some private detecting work. It was really nice to meet you, Dale. I look forward to getting to know you better."

Something in her tone hit Dale the wrong way and she smiled. "Me and Ari, you mean."

"Of course." She held out her hand. "I'll see you around, Dale."

Dale shook her hand and led her back to the door. "I'll let you know if Ari is able to get free for dinner tonight. Otherwise we'll just work something out. Oh, and if you happen across any other stashes, I'm sure Ari won't mind you using them. Just let me know so I can refresh them."

"I will. And I think I'll just follow your lead and set up some of my own once I know the city a little better."

Dale shrugged. "I could help you with that. I know some good places that I haven't used yet. I'd be happy to donate them to a wolf in need."

"Fantastic. I might owe you two dinners for that."

Dale laughed. "You're becoming our meal ticket."

Milo stopped at the door. "I look forward to evening things out between us."

Again Dale felt a touch awkward, but she put it off to being unfamiliar with Milo's British wit. She said goodbye and shut the door behind Milo, scratching the back of her head as she walked back to the desk and took a seat. If she became friends with any other sexy *canidae* she was going to have to register the office as a kennel.

"They'll kill her."

"They won't." They were back in the living room, where Madeline was hugging herself on the couch. "Right now they have one goal. They just want money. Jenna is their way to get it, and they have to keep her healthy if they expect us to pay. We learned a lot with that phone call. Whoever took Jenna didn't do it on a whim. Someone took her for a reason. Can you think of anyone who might want to hurt you?"

"*Hurt* me? I work for CenturyLink. I'm an account representative. I suppose if they wanted access to someone's telephone records they could..." She squeezed her eyes closed and shook her head. "No. There have to be a hundred other people who have more access than I do. It would be ridiculous to take Jenna to get me to do something."

Ari said, "What about Jenna's father?"

Madeline shook her head and looked toward the window. "No. He's been out of the picture for years. He left when Jenna was two."

"Is there a chance that he could have come back?"

She pressed her hands flat together and closed her eyes. "Ms. Willow, if my husband came back, he wouldn't have taken Jenna and I wouldn't be alive to hire you."

Ari winced. In that case, there was still a chance he'd taken Jenna as a way to hurt her, but Ari decided to let that trail go for the moment.

"All right. We'll go for a different angle. Let's look at what the guy said."

"You said he was reading from a script."

Ari nodded. "But that can still be helpful. It was a ransom demand, but they didn't give an amount. They just said you'd know how much you need."

"Right. What the hell does that mean?"

"I assume it means you'll pay as much as you can to get your daughter back. If they ask for a hundred grand when you could pay a million, they're short-changed. If they ask for a million and you don't have it, they have to give up a little of their power and drop their asking price. So they left it up to you. They know you'd pay as much as you possibly can to get Jenna back safe. How much would that be, just so we can give them a number if we have to stall?"

Madeline shook her head. "Everything. I would..." She sighed heavily and leaned back, rubbing her cheek with the back of her hand. "With the savings and her college fund and... if I put the house up for sale~"

"Don't count stuff like that. You don't have time to sell anything. Just count the funds you could gather in the next two or three days."

She chewed her lip as she thought. "I could get a hundred and fifty thousand by the weekend. But that would be every dime I have."

"Okay. When they call back we'll tell them a hundred. It's a nice round number and I think it's big enough that they'll be satisfied. Don't worry, we're not actually going to pay anyone anything. We're just using it as bait."

Madeline rubbed her hands together and looked down at her thumbs. When she spoke, her voice was quiet. "Ms. Willow, if we just paid them... wouldn't it be easier? And safer?"

"Probably. But then they could turn around and do this to someone else." She put her hand on Madeline's shoulder. "Right now, Jenna is safe. They're doing what I asked because they think I'm on the level. But these assholes took a little girl away from her mother. I'm going to make sure they're punished for that." She paused. "If you really want to just pay them and end this, then we can do that, too. I think in the long run it would be a bad plan. Maybe not for you, but for the next family."

"I just want her back."

"I know. I understand. You have my word that I'm going to do everything I can to get her home as quickly as possible."

Madeline nodded. "Thank you."

"Sure. Now I need to go back to the office and figure some things out. Can I take your cell phone? That's the number they called, so just in case they didn't write down the number I gave them..."

"Oh, God." She pressed it into Ari's hand as if it was poisonous. "Yes. Take it. I don't want to talk to them again."

"Do you have someone you can stay with?"

Madeline only had to think for a moment. "Erica. We work together. She's the only person at work I've told about this and she said if I needed anything..."

Her voice trailed off and she began to cry. Ari guided her back to the couch and sat her down. She found an Erica Webber on the

Recent Call list of Madeline's phone and called to see if she could come over. She waited with Madeline until her friend arrived. Madeline provided her with a photograph of Jenna she could use if it became necessary to question potential witnesses.

"Mrs. Morris, Jenna is safe right now. I'm going to make sure she stays safe. Whatever it takes and whatever I have to promise these guys, getting her back is my goal."

"Thank you, Ms. Willow."

"You're welcome. I'll let you know if I need anything else."

She got Erica's phone number so they could stay in contact. Madeline offered to drive Ari back to the office but Ari opted to walk. It gave her another chance to try finding where Jenna had gone after missing the bus even though her scent trail was all but gone by the time Ari left the house. It was a little past three, so she waited at the corner until the school bus rolled into view. She waited until the kids unloaded and then climbed on.

"This isn't a public service, lady."

"I just have a few questions. Do you drive this route in the morning?"

He nodded slowly, sagging in his seat as he tried to figure out how long the delay was going to be. He was overweight and dressed in a denim shirt open at the collar, and his lank black hair was dripping sweat onto his forehead. "What's it got to do with anything?"

"I'm looking for a little girl that's gone missing." She showed Jenna's picture. "Someone said she was late for the bus this morning and you went off without her."

"Hey, I have a schedule to keep. If the parents can't be bothered to have their kids waiting when I show up, it's not my problem if they have to drop them off at school themselves. And speaking of the schedule..." He waved her off.

Ari climbed another step. The seat behind the driver was empty and she grabbed the handrail to swing herself into it.

"Hey! Lady, you're not allowed to~"

Ari pointed at the camera mounted above his mirror. "You want to see that footage on the news? Because when this story breaks and people find out you left a little girl behind on the street, and that little girl subsequently vanished into thin air, they're going to play that video nonstop. I'm not talking about KING5, I'm talking about CNN, Fox News, MSNBC. You're gonna be raked over the coals by every talking head with a TV studio. You really want to be the man who got Jenna Morris abducted?"

He sighed, looked past her at the kids left on the bus, and pulled the lever to shut the door behind her.

"Smart choice, pal."

He pulled away from the stop and drove on. He passed the Morris house before he spoke to her. "My name's Louis."

"Ariadne Willow. I was hired by Jenna's mother."

Louis nodded. "She's a nice lady. Sometimes she walks her girl down to the stop. Is she really missing?"

"She is." She saw the guilt starting to settle over him, so she decided to give him a break. "Look, I'm sorry for reading you the Riot Act back there. I think whoever took her has been planning it for a while so nothing you did this morning caused her to be taken."

"She wasn't hurrying or anything. If she'd looked like she was trying to catch the bus, then yeah. Of course I would have waited another few seconds. But she could have been walking to a friend's house, or... I waited, but she didn't hurry up, so I just drove off."

Ari looked out the window as they arrived at the next stop. Kids filed past her to leave, a few of them snickering or trying to look at her without seeming interesting.

One kid stopped next to her. "Hey. What, you been held back twenty times or something?"

"Yep. But don't get discouraged. I'm sure you'll easily beat that record." The kid's friends laughed and shoved him forward. When the egress came to an end, Louis shut the door and continued on. Ari leaned toward Louis again. "Did you notice anyone hanging out around the bus stop? Watching the kids?"

Louis waited until he was at a stop sign then pulled a binder from a slot next to his seat. He handed it to her.

"Suspicious Incident Reports."

"The school makes you keep these?"

"Nope. Do it myself. Make the charts and everything." He ran his tongue over his teeth and flexed his fingers on the wheel. "I never wanted it to be useful. Know what I mean? I wanted to retire and throw 'em all away, and laugh at myself 'cause... 'cause no one would hurt a kid."

Ari nodded and opened the book. "Hope for the best and prepare for the worst." She flipped to the current week and then went back a month. The chart was separated into sections for morning and night, with incidents described in shorthand that Ari quickly cracked. Louis kept track of people he saw near the stop in case a pattern formed. She skimmed but didn't find anything alarming.

"What is this? Three days ago you wrote down C Br Corner LDA. That last part is Lake Dell Avenue, right? That's Jenna Morris' stop."

Louis nodded. "C is car, T is truck... it means there was a brown car on the corner. I remember it now. They were in that parking lot, way at the end away from the building. I thought it was weird, like they had just parked there to watch the street."

Ari pictured the street in her mind. Jenna would have had to walk past that parking lot no matter where she was headed.

"Were they there today?"

"I don't think so. I don't remember seeing anything suspicious."

Ari flipped to that morning's page just to be certain but the page was blank. She closed the binder and handed it back to him.

"No, keep it. If there's something in there worth knowing, I'd rather you have it."

"Thanks."

He exhaled and shook his head. "Thanks for not letting me kick you off the bus. I wanna help. If someone took that little girl, I want him to pay."

"You and me both, Louis."

He dropped her off at the next stop, which cut a mile off her walk back to the office. When she arrived, Dale greeted her with a smile.

"Hey. I got this book from Jenna's bus driver, but it's written in shorthand and he didn't have time to give me any clues. How are you with codes?"

"Just call me Alan Turing."

Ari responded to that with a blank stare.

"He worked on the Enigma machine in World War II. It was a code-breaking..." She shook her head and gestured for the notebook. "Never mind. Gimme."

"You're not impressing anyone with your brains, college girl." She kissed Dale as she handed over the binder. "You know I'm only with you because of your looks."

Dale swatted Ari on the rear. "Bad puppy. Oh, speaking of that, your friend Milo stopped by while you were out."

"Milo came by already? What did she want?"

"She just gave me her information so I could get in touch about that dinner she owes us. I was thinking we should probably postpone until this case is settled."

Ari went into her office and Dale followed. They sat next to each other on the couch, Dale's legs tucked up under her.

"Yeah. Postponing would probably be the best. I need to get some sleep. Then I'm going to go out as the wolf and try to pick up Jenna's scent. She went somewhere after she missed the bus. And according to everyone who saw her, she didn't seem too upset about missing it. Seven-year-olds don't have backup plans." Dale stroked the back of Ari's neck, and Ari closed her eyes. "Mm. That feels good."

"Bad change?"

"Yeah. And I fell off a table last night."

Dale leaned away and stood up. "Take off your clothes and stretch out."

"Are you trying to seduce me?"

"Always."

Ari chuckled and did as she was told. She left her underwear on as Dale got the massage oil from her desk. She stretched out on the couch and Dale sat on the edge of the cushion, turning to face her as she rubbed the oil into her palms. She started at the shoulders and worked her way down Ari's spine, moving her thumbs in tight circles. She smiled as she felt the muscles relaxing as she stroked them, thinking back to the times when this had been a nearly unbearable tease.

"You haven't asked me for this as much since we started sleeping together."

"Mm." Ari adjusted her head on her folded hands. "Maybe I'm more relaxed."

"So your transformations have been easier?"

Ari knew better than to lie. "I wouldn't say that."

Dale smiled. "So you're just nervous about asking your girlfriend for a massage? It didn't bother you when I just was your employee."

"That was different. That was just you helping me out, like when you put together my stashes. Now that we're together I feel like I'm taking advantage of you."

"Aw." Dale leaned down and kissed Ari's cheek. Ari twisted and met her lips. "Whenever you need me, however you need me, I'm here, Ari." She brushed Ari's hair away from her face and sat up to finish the massage.

Her years of treating the massage as a clinical necessity had taught her the topography of Ariadne Willow's body very well. She ran her palms over the smooth planes and dug her fingers into the tight muscles until they relaxed. When she started the massages she had let it act as a sort of mediation in order to keep her mind on the mechanics of what she was doing and not the fact she was touching a beautiful, half-naked woman.

These days, however, their massages sessions ended with sex more often than not. It was so easy to just let her hands slide lower, to cup Ari's breast and nibble her ear and let her hands roam in a more direct manner. She stopped herself this time, gripping the slight curve of Ari's hips with both hands and squeezing.

"You know, that area is bound to have at least a few security cameras. If they were aimed in the right direction at the right time, you may get a better idea of where Jenna went."

"Mm."

"I can call Detective Lorne while you nap."

Ari grunted. "Call the businesses directly first. See if they'll hand them over in the interest of finding a little girl. I only want to involve the police if we have to. Madeline is right; the police have made Missing Melody a priority."

"You're the boss, boss." She bent down and kissed the side of Ari's head. "You good?"

"Much better. Thank you, Dale."

She stroked Ari's hair. "The phone calls I take, the appointments I schedule, the notes I file? That's work. This isn't."

"Good to know." Dale got up and went to the door, but Ari said her name before she could shut the door. Dale turned back and Ari pushed up onto her elbows to look at her. "What you said earlier? Even the first day you started working here, you were never *just* an employee."

Dale smiled. "Good to know. Sleep well, Ari."

She turned off the overhead light and shut the door behind her.

CHAPTER FIVE

THE SUN was coming in low through the window when Ari woke. She had a typical moment of disorientation before she remembered where she was and why she was asleep. Pushing herself up, she retrieved her shirt and put it back on. She checked Madeline's phone, although she had made sure the ringer was on so it would wake her up if the kidnappers tried to get in contact. She could hear music from Dale's desk so she stretched her arms out and went to let her know she was awake.

"Morning, sunshine," Dale chirped.

Ari grunted at her. "No calls on Madeline's phone. Looks like the bad guys are sticking to the twenty-four hour window I gave them."

"Still planning to go out tonight?" Ari nodded. "I'll give you a ride and help you open doors and stuff."

"I appreciate it. What did you find out on the security cameras?"

Dale opened a window on her computer and then pulled a notepad forward. "I found six businesses near that corner, three of which have exterior security cameras. So I called them all and only one of them was facing the right direction. Savoretti Storage. I explained who we are and why we needed the tape and the manager agreed to take a look to see if there was anything to help us. Turns out, voila." She tapped a key and a grainy video appeared.

"What, that's it?"

Dale glared at her. "You just took a three hour nap while I magically turned back time and pulled a slice of the past out of the ether to display on your computer. A little gratitude would be nice."

Ari kissed the top of Dale's head. "You're a magician, Dale, but... the angle is bad, the image isn't clear... I'm not blaming you or saying you pulled off anything less than a miracle. But in terms of helping us with the case, I don't know how far this is going to get us."

"O ye of little faith."

She hit a button and the video came to life. The image was jerky, progressing like a zoetrope, still pictures spliced together to give the illusion of movement and life. Ari was impressed with Dale's ingenuity but disappointed with the results until a small purple blob appeared near the top of the screen. She pointed and leaned closer.

"There she is."

"Yep. Keep watching."

Someone appeared swiftly, seeming to appear out of thin air as he approached Jenna from behind. He lifted his hand in a wave and Jenna stopped. She turned to look at him and, after thirty-seven seconds on the clock, they started walking back toward the spot where the man had appeared. Another twelve seconds and they were out of sight.

"I never should have doubted you. Can you get an image~"

Dale presented a print-out of the man. The image was blurry, his face reduced to a smattering of colored pixels, but it was more than she'd had before.

"You're a princess, Dale."

"Screw that. I'm a queen and you're just the pretty face we present to the public."

Ari smirked and stared at the image. It took her a moment to get her bearings, comparing the odd angle to the street she'd been on that afternoon. "I guess this means I don't have to go out and sniff the ground to see what direction she went. The guy took her east, right?"

"They were walking toward the camera, so... yeah. That's east."

"There's a parking lot there. The school bus driver said he saw a car parked there three days ago. Maybe someone was watching for her. I wish I knew if Jenna was the target or just a conveniently available kid. The guy who called didn't seem to have any specifics about who she was. They could have just been looking for a kid out by herself."

Dale shrugged. "Tomorrow you can ask around again, see if anyone else noticed the car. Or if anyone saw Jenna with this guy."

Ari nodded and put the print-out down on the desk. "In the meantime, if I don't have to spend the night running around wolf-style, I'm going to take you out to dinner. I want to celebrate your genius in getting hold of that security footage."

"I approve. Do you want to invite Milo? I have her number here."

"Oh. I forgot about Milo." She took the slip of paper with the number. "Sure. How about Jak's Grill?"

Dale lifted an eyebrow. "Jak's? Are you trying to impress her?"

Ari rubbed Dale's shoulder. "She'll just be a spectator. I'm going to show her how I treat my lady for a job well done. Besides, we got the check from the police. It'll be nice to splurge a little."

Dale shook her head. "Actually Milo offered to treat, so it'll be her splurging. Not you."

"All the more reason to go somewhere expensive." Ari winked.

Dale chuckled. "You're evil. If we're going to Jak's, I'll need to go home and change."

"No, you actually don't. But if it'll make you feel better."

Dale blew Ari a mock kiss. "You should go change, too."

"Ugh."

"Don't ugh me. I know you, Ari. You're going to obsess over this case until the girl is found. You deserve to treat yourself to one nice night out before it consumes you. Go home, shower, change. I'll swing by and pick you up in about half an hour."

Ari mock-saluted and left the office. She dialed Milo's number as she left the building and started walking toward her apartment. Milo answered on the second ring.

"Ahoy-hoy."

Ari blinked. "Is that how they answer the phone in England?"

"Nah, it's how I answer the phone anywhere. Who's this?"

"Ariadne Willow. Dale told me you stopped by earlier."

Milo cooed. "Oh, right. Sweet little redhead in a corduroy skirt, smells like apples and tea leaves. I can see why you like her. She said you might have to postpone dinner due to a case."

"Actually we decided to go ahead with it if you don't have any plans."

"Nope, no plans. I'd love to go out. What time?"

Ari pulled the phone away from her ear to check the time. "We can swing by to pick you up around eight. East Crescent, right?"

Milo confirmed and gave her the number. "I'll wait outside, flag you down. Should I dress up?"

"Nah, nothing too swanky. Just a nice dinner to welcome you to the country."

"I'm looking forward to it. See you around eight."

When she hung up, Ari made a note on her phone of the address just in case. A part of her felt guilty planning a big night out while Jenna Morris was still being held hostage. Madeline definitely wasn't going to spend her evening having a nice dinner with a potential new friend. But after spending a week tracking down the dogfight ring, Ari needed a mental health night and Dale deserved to have her girlfriend for at least one evening. She doubted the kidnappers would do anything before they made their next phone call. All they could do was wait, and Ari planned to spend the time preparing for their next bout.

Dale parked in front of the small stone house and glanced at Ari. "You're sure this is the right address?"

"Yeah. She mentioned she was living off an inheritance, and given the neighborhood I figured something swank. Even so, this is frickin' impressive."

The house was gray brick with a porch supported by pillars, looming up at the top of a wide rolling lawn. Milo came out moments after Dale asked for confirmation they were at the right place and waved, locked the door behind her, and trotted down the curved driveway. She climbed into the backseat and smiled.

"Hi. Perfect timing. I just finished getting ready." She looked at Ari. "Wa-hey, you certainly clean up nice, don't you?"

"Same to you. Of course anyone looks better than we did this morning."

"Right, right." She touched Dale's shoulder in greeting. "And you look lovely as well, Miss Dale."

Dale grinned. "Thanks. We're going to Jak's... you're not a vegan wolf or anything, right?" She caught Milo's response in the rearview mirror and smiled. "Just making sure. You can never tell with Brits."

Milo chuckled and fastened her seatbelt as Dale got back onto the road. Ari gestured at the house as it receded behind them.

"I knew you'd have a nice place, but that was quite a domicile."

"Yeah. To be honest, I was more interested in the fact it butts up against a big wooded area than anything else. Lots of room to run around without worrying I'll be seen or rounded up by animal control. But I guess I'm just a city girl at heart."

Ari said, "From London?"

"Little town in Yorkshire, actually. But I've always gravitated toward the city."

They settled into a comfortable silence, broken only by Dale asking how Milo liked the city while Ari gave suggestions on which parks were *canidae*-friendly. By the time they passed the University, they were acting as if they'd known each other for years. Milo had moved up to lean forward between their seats to tell a story about two wolf friends she had left back in England.

"I got to the house first, so naturally I got my choice of clothes off the laundry line. Grabbed the trousers and vest, so Paige got the skirt and blouse. And poor Benji..." She swept her hand across her mouth to stifle her chuckle. "Well, let's just say it's a good thing he has the legs for a sundress."

Ari laughed. "Oh, man. You're evil."

"Hey, I'm not going to walk into my friend's pub wearing a bleedin' frock. Got a reputation to uphold."

Dale said, "And the genius of the stash proves itself again."

"I don't know. Even with the stashes, I've had to walk around town wearing some pretty unique outfits."

Milo snapped her fingers. "Worst one. Go."

"Oh, God, I couldn't even..." Ari looked out the window. "A sort-of lime green waitress uniform. It was like I was auditioning for some lame seventies porno."

"My worst was a tarp. Just a big blue tarp I had wrapped around me like a toga."

Dale faked irritation. "Now I feel all left out. I've never wandered around town in a bizarre outfit."

"What about that blue-and-orange dress you got last year?" Ari said.

Dale slapped her arm, and Ari rubbed her thigh to show she was only kidding. Dale smiled and turned onto a side street, craning her neck to look into the restaurant's parking lot.

"Looks like we got lucky. Slow night." She glanced at Milo in the rearview. "We once waited an hour for a table here."

"Wow. Hope it was at least worth the wait."

"Oh, yeah. Normally I'm impatient as hell, but I can wait when the result is something extraordinary." She involuntarily glanced at Dale, remembering how long they'd been 'just friends' before taking the next step, and they shared a smile.

They proved to be luckier as a trio, getting seated and placing their drink orders in less than twenty minutes. Dale and Ari sat across from Milo, and Dale placed her hands on the table and leaned forward.

"Uh-oh. Interrogation pose," Ari said. "Brace yourself, Milo."

Milo tensed dramatically.

Dale said, "I'll go easy on her. Ari said you got an inheritance, but why did you choose Seattle? I mean, besides the fact it's the best city in the world?"

Milo laughed and hunched her shoulders as she looked around the restaurant. "I just always wanted to see America. When I got the means, I thought I should see my own part of the world first. So I bounced around London, spent some time in Scotland and Ireland, then decided to jump over here. I thought maybe Seattle, you know... green and cold... I thought it would be a nice way to acclimate myself before I tried New York or something really jarring."

Ari laughed. "There's also a larger *canidae* population here than anywhere else in the country."

"Yeah, that was definitely a plus. I didn't know for sure, but there was bound to be, right? All these woods and mountains around, gotta be a wolf or two. And sure enough, I'm here less than a month and..." She gestured at Ari.

Dale smiled at Ari. "Yeah. She has a way of just popping into people's lives when they least expect it."

"Usually for the better, I hope," Ari said as their drinks arrived. Ari and Dale ordered for themselves and, with Milo's blessing, chose something for her that was sure to win her over.

Milo waited for the waitress to leave before she spoke again. "How about you two? How on Earth do you decide to be a private investigator?"

"It just sort of happened. I was in the right place at the right time and met a woman who ran an agency. I started out as her assistant and when I had enough hours of apprenticeship to get my own license, I did. Then Dale came along and turned my flailing into an actual business." She shrugged. "The rest is history."

"Wow. I never thought about it being something people did,

like, in real life. The gentleman detective? It's so Sherlock Holmes."

Ari shrugged. "If you're going for literary references I prefer Dupin."

Milo whistled. "Oh, a literature junkie. I love it. So... Dale told me how you two met when I stopped by this morning." Ari glanced at Dale, who shrugged. "When did it go from work partners to more?"

"About a year ago. There was a big case we were working on. I was a person of interest in a murder, so I had to go on the run for a while." Milo threw her head back and laughed, and Ari couldn't help but smile. "Yes, yes, we lead exciting lives. Anyway, Dale stuck by me through it all. And I realized that even if I lost everything else, I was okay as long as I had her by my side. Once I admitted that much, it seemed silly not to be with her."

Milo grinned. "Aw. That's sweet. I myself am terminally single. Had a girl for a while there for a while, but that... didn't... really work out." She worked the edge of her glass around the water ring it had formed on the table.

Dale could tell it was a sore subject, so she latched onto the part that seemed safest. "Girlfriend, huh? Are all *canidae* gay?"

Ari laughed, but it was Milo who answered. "Nah, just the coolest ones." She lifted her glass and Ari clinked hers against it.

They exchanged personal histories over the meal. Milo told them about driving a cab in Wales, Ari and Dale told about some of their more interesting cases.

"Must be convenient to use your wolf to watch without being seen."

"Sometimes," Ari admitted. "Sometimes it can be a hindrance."

Dale brightened. "Are you going to tell her about the time you were rounded up~"

"Nope."

Milo raised an eyebrow. "Oh, now you have to tell me."

Ari lifted her chin and rubbed her neck. She glared at Dale. "I'll make you pay for this." She smoothed her hands over her thighs and straightened in her seat. "I was supposed to be watching this guy for a workman's comp claim. He said he hurt his knees and could barely walk, so I wanted to get evidence he was lying. So I had the wolf watching his house for a while so I could learn his routine without him seeing me. It just so happened that the night I chose to begin my investigation, Animal Control got a tip about stray dogs running around in the neighborhood. I gave them a good chase, but they eventually got me."

Dale smiled. "She had to spend nearly thirty-six hours in a kennel until I finally tracked her down."

Milo shuddered. "Sounds awful."

"It's not as dire as it sounds, really. It was one of the good kennels."

"Sorry, I still don't see how that's a funny story. That's one of my worst nightmares."

Dale snickered. "She didn't tell it right."

Ari glared across the table at her. Dale raised an eyebrow, challenging her. Finally Ari sighed.

"There was a poodle in the next cage. You spend an entire day next door to someone, you get acquainted. So we bonded a little."

Dale said, "And when the poodle got picked up by her owner, she broke out again and came to find Ari."

Milo's grin widened. "Ah. You got yourself a girlfriend."

"Two weeks she followed me around. Outside the office, outside the apartment, every time I turned around, that damn poodle was *there*."

Dale rested her chin on her fist, fingers curled against her lips. "I thought it was cute. Puppy love."

Ari narrowed her eyes and Dale twitched her eyebrows up and down.

"How'd you finally get rid of her?"

"You want to tell her?" Ari asked Dale, who was obviously barely containing her glee.

Dale laughed. "Doggie dating service. She went to a dog park up by Green Lake. The poodle followed her, of course, and Ari waited until she got distracted by a new target and headed home as fast as her feet could carry her. So far she hasn't come back."

"That story is really not as good as you think it is," Ari assured her.

"Oh, sure it is," Milo said. "Your children would have been fierce and fluffy."

Dale snorted through a mouthful of water, covering her hand as she half-coughed and half-laughed. Ari reached over and patted her back until the fit ended.

"Sorry."

"No, it's fine." She took another sip of her water and swallowed it carefully, then glanced around to make sure no one had noticed her choking.

Milo said, "Well, turnabout is fair play. Went home with a girl from a bar. Human girl for a change, because she was just far too hot for me to give a shit about her species. So we were getting the typical one-nighter under way, right, things progressing nicely, when suddenly she starts sneezing uncontrollably. Red face, hives, can't breathe. She looks around and says, well... wheezes is more like it, asks me if I have a dog. Deathly allergic."

Ari winced. "Ouch. Talk about a mood killer."

"Yeah. I couldn't even take her to a hospital because I'd just make her sicker. Kind of shitty to just give her cab fare and hope for the best."

Dale said, "So what did you end up doing?"

"Put her on a bus."

Ari laughed. "Poor lady."

Milo shrugged. "Sex with me may be great, but it's not worth dying for."

Dale snickered and checked her watch. "Well, ladies, it's been fun, but I think we've lingered long enough. There are people waiting for the table."

"Too right." Milo picked up the check and took out her credit card. When the waitress whisked it away, Milo folded her hands on the table in front of her. "I truly enjoyed this evening. Thank you, ladies."

"It was our pleasure," Dale said. "And thank you both for hanging around with a boring, normal human like me."

Milo clucked her tongue against her teeth. "Nonsense. Pretty as you are, who needs a wolf?" She reached out and pinched a strand of Dale's hair between two fingers. "Or I suppose with the red hair you'd probably be a fox."

Ari smiled as Dale blushed. The waitress returned Milo's card with the receipt and they abandoned the table.

They drove south again, stopped by the raising of the Montlake Bridge. As they waited for the boat to pass and the bridge to lower again, Milo spoke up from the backseat.

"So, Dale. Not to be pushy, but when would be a good time for you to show me some of these stash locations? I'd like to get a few of them set up as soon as possible just so they'll be ready if I need them."

Ari said, "I don't think I'll need you too much tomorrow. If you wanted to take the day off to take her around town..."

Dale shrugged. "Sure. We can go in the afternoon, after the

lunch rush settles down."

"Excellent. I want you both to know I really appreciate all you're doing for me. You're really going above and beyond the call. I feel a bit guilty, to be honest."

Ari jutted out her chin and spoke with a raspy accent. "One day, and it may never come, I will ask you to do a favor for me."

Dale wrinkled her nose. "Worst Brando ever."

Ari grinned.

"What do you have to do tomorrow, Ari? Unless you can't discuss the case."

"I probably shouldn't. But I won't need Dale for it. You'll be doing her a favor. I think she goes stir crazy in that office sometimes."

"Mm-mm," Dale said, shaking her head. "It's nice and quiet. I can meditate."

Ari smiled.

The bridge eventually lowered and they continued on. Dale pulled up in front of Milo's house and twisted to look into the backseat. "So tomorrow around one? Should I pick you up, or do you want to come straight to the office?"

"I'll come to you. It's only fair that I pay for the petrol if we're going to be driving all over the city. So I'll see you tomorrow. Thanks for giving me my first great night out in America, ladies."

Dale made sure she safely reached the front door and was inside before she drove off. She reached blindly in the dark and found Ari's hand.

"Want me to drop you at your place?"

"I want to stay at your place tonight."

Dale brought Ari's hand to her lips and kissed the knuckles. "That's a right answer."

Ari smiled and leaned back against the headrest. Her sleep schedule had been screwed up for a week. Naps stolen on the couch in her office, sleeping for three or four hours at home while everyone else was going to work... she was grateful the dogfight case was closed down. The kidnapping case would, she prayed, only fill up the normal working hours of the day. She wanted a real bed, and she wanted to share it with the woman next to her. Everything else could sort itself out for a few hours.

CHAPTER SIX

THE ACT of pulling into her usual spot in the apartment building's garage signaled to Dale's brain that the day was finally at an end. It had started much, much too early with Ari's call from the warehouse and seemed to drag on endlessly. Now her brain seemed to receive the message it was okay to shut down and a yawn escaped before she could restrain it. She stretched when she got out of the car, sagging against Ari's side as they walked to the elevator. Ari put an arm around her waist as Dale rested her head against her shoulder.

"Long day," Dale sighed.

"Yeah." Ari kissed the top of Dale's head and pressed the button for her floor. Dale closed her eyes during the ride and let Ari half-carry her the rest of the way inside. She fished the keys from her pocket, let them in, and turned to Ari in the darkness. Ari kicked the door closed behind her and cupped Dale's face as they stepped toward each other for a kiss. Dale stepped out of her shoes as she lifted her arms to drape them across Ari's shoulders, her wrists crossing behind Ari's head as she stepped backward toward the wall.

Their lips separated with a gasp from both of them, and Dale swept the hair back out of Ari's face. "I've missed you." The words rode out on a gasp, barely spoken before Ari's lips were on hers again. Ari moaned her response, sliding her hands down Dale's sides and then tugging her shirt out of her slacks when they moved back up. She slipped her hands underneath and brushed her fingers over the bare skin underneath, smiling into the kiss as Dale's body hitched and jerked at the touch.

"Missed you, too." Ari pulled back and spun Dale around so she was facing the wall. Dale chuckled and closed her eyes as Ari kissed her cheek, the line of her jaw, and cupped her breasts from behind. She arched her back and bit her bottom lip, knees bent so she could push her hips backward against Ari's.

Ari brushed the hair away from Dale's ear. "Remember before we were together?" she whispered. "Those times when we would kiss or touch and decide it wasn't worth the risk to the partnership to try making it something more?" She nipped Dale's earlobe.

"Uh-huh..."

"Yeah," Ari sighed. "That was stupid."

Dale laughed and reached back to stroke Ari's hip through her pants as Ari began unbuttoning her blouse. She tugged it down and lowered her head to kiss Dale's now-exposed shoulder. Dale's bra was black, and Ari had been teased to glimpses of it through her cream-colored blouse all night. She took the strap between her teeth and pulled it down, then ran her tongue over the lightly freckled pink skin to suck on the base of Dale's neck.

"Ariadne..."

She shivered and brushed her fingers over Dale's stomach, teasing her navel before moving down to her belt. She unfastened it with ease and pushed the material down over Dale's hips without bothering to unbutton. She straightened and pressed against Dale, who craned her neck back to catch Ari's lips as Ari hooked both thumbs in her black underwear and dragged them down her legs.

The bra fell next, and Dale rested her cheek against the wall as Ari ran the flat of both palms over her. She cupped her breasts, pinched her nipples between her fingers, and then rested her hands on Dale's hips.

"Bedroom?"

"Um-hum," Dale murmured.

Ari retreated in order to free her, took her hand, and led her down the short hall to the bedroom. Dale stepped away from Ari just long enough to turn on the bedside lamp. It was dim enough that it only seemed to give shape to the shadows rather than banish them entirely, but it was perfectly romantic. Dale turned, her curves cast into sharp relief. She brought her hands up, stopping just short of covering her breasts and hooking her fingers on her neck instead. Her lips were slightly parted, her breath held as she watched Ari looking at her.

Ari swallowed hard and took a step, but Dale shook her head. "Uh-uh. Stay there."

"What?"

"Undress." It was barely whispered, and Dale turned her head to the side and smiled as she said it. Her eyes sparkled, wide and mischievous, and Ari couldn't help smiling in response. She unbuttoned her blouse and slipped it off, tossing it onto the foot of the bed as she toed off her shoes and kicked them out of the way. Dale brushed her hands down, cupping her own breasts as Ari dropped her pants and kicked them out of her way.

"Wanna help me with this?" Ari asked as she hooked a thumb under her bra strap.

"Yeah..." Dale stepped forward and kissed Ari, reaching behind her to undo the clasp. The bra fell away, and Dale walked her fingers back under Ari's arms. Ari's breasts fit perfectly in Dale's hands and she massaged them as her tongue slid over Ari's teeth, pressing the hard buds of the nipples as Ari guided her back toward the bed.

Dale sat, leaned back and pulled Ari with her, sighing as Ari's weight settled on top of her. Ari pecked Dale's lips and then slid down, kissing both breasts and her stomach. She slid her hands over Dale's legs before lifting them onto her shoulders to settle between them. Dale reached up for the pillows and pulled one down, wrapping both arms around it as Ari kissed her thighs and then moved higher.

Dale pressed her shoulders into the mattress, eyes rolling back as she lifted her lower body to meet Ari's mouth. She flattened her hands on the bed and pushed herself up, falling forward as she tightened her thighs around Ari's head. Ari dug her fingers into Dale's ass and Dale closed her eyes as her body closed around Ari like a fist. She rocked her hips upward, gasping when Ari's tongue slid over a particularly sensitive spot.

"Don't tease me, puppy," Dale whispered, eyes closed and face burning as Ari's tongue moved from inside of her to circle her clit. Dale exhaled sharply and stroked Ari's hair. "My beautiful puppy..."

She came with a sigh, trembling as she pulled Ari's head up and whispered, "Puppy," just before their lips met. It had started as a joke, an off-hand mention that most lovers called each other 'baby' so puppy would be the *canidae* equivalent. Dale had initially only said it when she was teasing, but when Ari admitted that she found it hot the name stuck. Dale's cheeks were warm as she fell back. Ari slid further onto the bed to settle between Dale's legs. She shifted position until she was astride Dale's thigh.

Dale met Ari's gaze and began to rock. Dale put her hands on Ari's hips to guide her, running her eyes down Ari's body and then back up to meet her eyes. Ari smiled, and Dale mouthed, "I love you." Ari stroked Dale's cheek and touched her lip with her thumb. Dale took it into her mouth and Ari rolled her head back. She said Dale's name, tensed, and clenched her legs around Dale's. She gasped and hunched her shoulders, rolling her head forward before she opened her eyes and looked down at Dale.

"I love you," Ari said.

Dale pulled Ari to her, rearranging herself until she was laying the right way. Ari stretched out next to her, face pressed against the curve of Dale's neck and fingers splayed on her stomach. Her nostrils flared at the scent of her lover and Ari's gentle kiss on Dale's pulse point turned into sucking, and then licking. She lapped up the sweat, and Dale's breathing became ragged again. She tensed and pressed her face into Ari's hair, whimpering when she came a silent second time.

"Whoa."

Ari chuckled. "Sorry it didn't last longer..."

"Any longer and it would have qualified as torture." She dragged her fingernails lightly over Ari's upper arm. "I really have missed you."

"The downside of sleeping with a private investigator." She gave her job title a British lilt, matching Milo's voice. She lifted her head and kissed Dale's chin. "No more week-long stakeouts in the future. Promise."

Dale smiled. "You don't have to promise that. Just screw me senseless before you leave for the night."

Ari laughed. "I think I can handle that."

She stroked Dale's stomach and kissed her properly. Dale moaned into the kiss and rolled onto her side. They pressed closer, thighs slipping against each other. Ari pulled back and Dale tightened her lips around Ari's tongue, holding it for a moment before she released it. Ari curled her tongue up, then swept it across Dale's bottom lip.

"How tired are you?"

"Depends on what you have in mind." Ari slid one hand down Dale's side to her ass and squeezed. Her thigh pressed higher and made contact with Dale's sex again. Dale hunched her shoulders, eyes wide, and her lips curled into a sleepy smile. "Oh-h. In that case I think I could be persuaded to stay up a little while longer."

Ari smiled. "I'll try to keep your attention..."

Eventually they slept, using the last of their energy to dress for bed before slumping against each other under the blankets. Ari put on a pair of short pajamas and a baggy tank top while Dale settled for just an oversized T. In the middle of the night Ari woke suddenly, spooning Dale from behind. Some sound had woken her and she lay still as she waited for it to repeat. Dale adjusted position in her sleep, murmuring against the pillow, and Ari soothed her by whispering into her ear and stroking her hair until she settled again.

Ari gently freed herself from Dale, tucking the pillow against her back so she wouldn't miss her presence. She prowled to the window on the balls of her feet. She pushed aside the curtain and peered out.

She was about to give up and go back to bed when she heard the sound again. A wolf's howl, echoing through the streets. It wasn't on their street, but it also didn't sound like it was terribly far away. She listened as the echoes faded, wondering if it was Milo or some other *canidae*.

When the night was silent again, Ari let the curtain fall back into place. She walked back to the bed and crawled under the covers.

Dale lifted her head off the pillow. "Ari?"

"Sh." She stroked Dale's hip under the blanket and kissed the back of her neck. Dale was asleep again before she was actually awake, falling effortlessly back into whatever dream she'd been having. Ari looked toward the window and then buried her face in Dale's hair, breathing deeply and letting Dale's scent surround her as she drifted off as well.

The wolf was sleek, with white fur and black markings. It ran without purpose or direction, stopping only to wait for cars to pass on the occasional streets it came across. After a few hours of running the wolf turned back and headed toward home.

Milo transformed while still in motion, her feet stretching and her legs snapping back into the correct position as she skidded down a muddy slope. Her fur receded and her suddenly exposed skin pebbled at the touch of cold night air. She was panting, allowing instinct to change her course so she didn't slalom into trees. Her pent-up energy was boiling over even after the run. She loved this neighborhood. It was so thick with trees that in several places it was impossible to see the sky. It was a *canidae*'s paradise.

A small pond stretched between two trees and she finally stopped when she reached its banks. She knelt and washed off her arms, cupping her hands to splash her face. She ran wet fingers through her tangled hair and looked around to regain her bearings. This part of the woods was starting to be familiar to her, and the wolf recognized most of the rest of the park by scent if not by sight. She stood up and went to the clothes she'd hung from a nearby tree branch, thinking about Ariadne Willow's stash method.

Stashes, buried under rocks and drainage ditches, tucked just out of sight... it was a great idea. She couldn't count the number of times she'd transformed far from home and wished for something as simple as a pair of shoes. She put on the slip, the lightweight material resting against her skin as softly as dew. She had dirt under her finger- and toenails, but that would wait until she was safe at home.

She walked the remaining fifty yards to her property. A wooden gate hung on the fence and she unlatched it, let herself in, and climbed the steep rise to her back porch. The kitchen light was on, which meant that she had a visitor. Milo sighed and braced herself for a confrontation as she slid open the door and stepped inside. The smell of nature and wildlife was cut off, replaced by the plastic and processed stench of modern life.

He was in the dining room, seated at the table facing the front of the house. Milo stared at the back of his head, the tight curls of white hair shorter than they'd been last time she saw him. He didn't turn at the sound of the door opening and closing, so she walked past him into the kitchen. She was starving after her run, so she opened the fridge and used the door to block her sight of her guest. Finally she couldn't bear the silence any longer. She took a pint of milk out of the fridge and finally faced him.

Benjamin Moss, as sanctimonious as always, managed to look completely composed despite the late hour. His beard was trimmed, his skin light enough to be described as a slight tan. He wore a high-collared shirt with no tie, his gaze directed at the newspaper laid out flat in front of him. She felt slightly embarrassed standing in front of him in her slip, but she wasn't going to show her discomfort by covering up.

"I thought you were going to check my progress over the phone."

"That was the plan, yes." He finally looked up at her. "It's been a month, Millie. We thought you would have made more progress by now."

Milo grimaced and took a swig of her milk. She wiped the back of her hand across her mouth. "I didn't want to tip my hand. It had to look natural. Willow's a damned private detective, Ben. If I gave her a reason to be suspicious, how long d'ya think it would take her to figure out what's happening?"

"How long do you intend to delay?"

"I'm not delaying. I'm being subtle. I made big strides today. I've befriended them, took 'em out to dinner. And tomorrow I'm going to spend the afternoon with Dale Frye. You gave me this assignment because you knew you could trust me. So either trust me or get someone else to do the job. Don't break into my house~"

"*Your* house?"

Milo pressed her lips together. "Don't barge into the house you gave to me in the middle of the night making demands. You want people to behave the way you want, you have to finesse them. Let me do my job, Ben."

He carefully folded his paper and rested his hands on top of it. "There is a ticking clock on this, Millie, so I feel I must remind you that time is of the essence. There's time, but it is swiftly running out. We would prefer if she came to us of her own free will, but it's not required."

"Thanks for reminding me." Milo finished her milk and put the carton in the trash. She took a box of leftovers from the fridge and saluted him with it as she walked out of the kitchen. "Lock the door of *my* house when you go. And if you want me to do my job, stop harassing me and just let me do it. I'll recruit Dale Frye in due time, and I'll make it her decision so she's more likely to go through with what we need."

"See that she does, Millie."

She growled as she started up the stairs. "My name is Milo, you son of a bitch." She didn't look back to see if he left; she didn't care if he stayed downstairs all night as long as he stayed out of her hair.

CHAPTER SEVEN

IN THE morning, the radio was full of news about Missing Melody. The police discovered a green overcoat on the Elliot Bay Trail matching the one Melody Scott was wearing the last time anyone saw her. Now the debate was whether her abductors had dropped it there, if it was placed there to misdirect the police, or if it had been taken by a homeless person who didn't realize its significance and discarded when it proved too small.

Ari silenced the meaningless speculation and went to shower. By the time she was finished and dressed, Dale was awake and had started breakfast. Ari kissed her hello and went to finish cooking while Dale took her turn in the bathroom. The morning talk shows were all talking endlessly about Melody Scott, and Ari had to mute them after a while. Melody had been missing four days now and Jenna was only twenty-four hours gone, but Ari couldn't help but be infuriated by the imbalance. Part of her hoped it would have been different if Madeline had gone straight to the police, but the practical part of her wouldn't let the hope thrive.

Dale came out of the shower with her hair still wet and face bare of makeup. Ari smiled and pushed a cup of tea across the counter to her.

"Thank you, puppy," Dale said, her voice still soft with sleep.

Ari smiled. "You ready for your big day out with Milo?"

"Mm." Dale shrugged. "I'd rather be helping you with the case, but I know there's really not a lot for me to do. Too many cooks." She sipped her tea. "Oh. The blocked number that the kidnapper called from. On Madeline's phone? I tried to trace it, but I hit a dead end. I'm going to dig a little harder while I'm waiting for Milo."

"Did I ask you to do that?"

"You were gonna."

Ari shook her head. "Man, I am a good detective."

Dale snickered and accepted her plate. Ari sat across the counter from her and picked up the remote control. Nonstop coverage of Melody on all the major networks, so she switched the cable and settled on a syndicated rerun of a sitcom about an airport.

"Are you okay?"

She looked at Dale. "Okay? Yeah. I'm... fine. Why?"

Dale shrugged and poked at her eggs. "I was just thinking about this case. You were a missing girl, too."

"I was a little older than Jenna when I ran away."

"Yeah, but you were still a pretty young white teenage girl. The local news would have been scouring the city for you if..."

Ari smiled. "If my mother had bothered to report me missing?" She shook her head. "By that time she was grateful to see the backside of me. I wanted to disappear, so I'm glad she didn't search. This?" She gestured at the TV. "Jenna didn't choose to vanish. She deserves to have an entire city looking for her. But so does Melody. And so do the dozens of other kids I'm sure have gone missing in the past week. I saw a lot of them when I was on the street, and no one looks for them. Even among the people where I was staying, if a kid disappeared we just assumed it was someone else's problem. Kids shouldn't disappear so easily. It shouldn't be so goddamn easy to just take a kid and get away with it."

She looked down at her plate and realized she felt better. She hadn't noticed she was holding back anything until she started speaking, and now it felt like she could breathe.

Dale smiled. "Feel better?"

Ari slid her hand across the counter and covered Dale's. "Yeah. Thank you."

"Sure." They went back to their breakfast and watched the twenty-year old sitcom in silence. When it was time to leave, Ari stepped around the counter and kissed Dale. "Want a ride to work? I'm going to leave in about twenty minutes."

"No, I want to walk. I'll probably leave straight from there to

Madeline's so I might not see you."

"Okay. Ari..." She caught Ari's hand before she could step away. "I would have looked for you. I never would have stopped."

Ari brought Dale's hand to her lips and kissed the knuckles. No one had ever gone looking for her. Everywhere she called home, she eventually left of her own free will and no one ever tried to bring her back. She couldn't express what Dale's promise meant to her, so she just said, "Thank you, Dale. I love you."

"Love you, too. Be careful."

Ari kissed two fingers and held them out to Dale as she left the apartment. The walk to the office from Dale's building was almost a mile, but Ari planned to use it to organize her thoughts. She turned up the collar of her coat and headed west as she thought about what she knew as facts.

Jenna Morris was a seven-year-old second grader. She walked to the school bus stop every morning. On the day she went missing, she was running late because she helped her mother with laundry. The bus driver saw her but didn't wait. Jenna didn't seem overly concerned and, rather than going home, continued south. Ari paused on the corner and put herself in the little girl's position. Would walking a mile and a half be feasible to a seven year old?

Of course, Jenna wouldn't have thought about it in those terms. She was seven, and she'd most likely only traveled the distance in a car or on the bus. In her mind the school was only a few minutes away so it was just a simple little walk.

She only got half a block, however, before someone approached her. He spoke to her briefly and then they walked back to his car together. The picture from the security camera was horrible, too far away and blurry. Their description might as well have been of a ghost.

Then the kidnappers waited until afternoon to make the ransom call. Why? If the teacher hadn't called to reveal Jenna's absence, Madeline wouldn't have known there was a problem until then. The kidnappers could have just been giving her time to panic so that when the demands finally come in she was more willing to cooperate. Whoever had called wasn't the mastermind of the operation, so they were dealing with two or more people.

When she got to the office she gathered her things, including the printout of the person that led Jenna away. It had been cropped so that Jenna wasn't in the picture, which she hoped would be less traumatic for Madeline. She drove back to the Morris house where a car she didn't recognized was blocking the driveway. She parked across the street and walked up to the porch. A woman appeared in the doorway before Ari could knock. She was taller than Ari, with blonde hair parted in the middle and a stern expression that brooked no argument.

"Can I help you? She's not taking any visitors."

"I'm Ariadne Willow. I assume you're Erica. We spoke on the phone briefly yesterday."

The woman's expression softened. "Oh. Yes, Erica Webber." She opened the door. "She said you might be coming by. She's trying to rest right now. She didn't get a lot of sleep last night."

"How bad was it?"

"As bad as you can imagine," she said softly. "Do you have anything?"

Ari shook her head. "Not a lot, to be honest. I do have a photo I want her to look at if you think she's up for it."

Erica nodded and motioned for Ari to follow her. The master bedroom was at the back of the house, and the door was open slightly. The morning light filtered through the curtains to make the room look blue, and Erica gently pushed the door open. "Maddie? The private investigator is here. Are you up for seeing her?"

"Yes. Yes, please."

Erica stepped out of the way to let Ari into the room. Madeline looked like she'd aged a year since Ari last saw her, wan and weary. She was lying on top of the blankets still wearing the clothes from the day before, and her hair was a mess from repeated finger-raking.

"Do you have anything?"

"Not as much as I would like. My assistant did find security footage of someone who seemed to be leading Jenna away. Can you look at the picture and see if you know who it is? It's a terrible picture but maybe something about his posture or what he's wearing will ring a bell." She took the photo out of her bag and held it out. Madeline pinched it between two fingers and frowned at the image.

"This is a... person?"

"The security camera wasn't exactly top of the line, and it was pretty far away. I wish I had more to report, but~"

Madeline wasn't listening. She had leaned closer to the picture and was staring intently at it. "Erica. Is... i-is that...?" She turned the picture around, holding it so her index finger was resting on the person's jacket. She tapped the man's chest with her finger and Ari thought she saw some sort of design.

Erica leaned in close and narrowed her eyes. "I don't... wait. The Boy Scout?"

"Yes." To Ari, Madeline said, "There's a man who works with us named Brandon Kent, and he wears this old jacket that has patches sewn onto the lapel. They look like merit badges, so we call him the Boy Scout. I think this could be him. But that makes absolutely no sense whatsoever."

"Does Jenna know him?"

Madeline tucked her hair behind her ear only to have it fall back against her cheek. "No. Not... not really."

"Maddie," Erica prompted. "You have to tell her everything if you want her to help Jenna."

"We dated. For about three months last year. He met Jenna, but she didn't know we were... we kept it quiet. I didn't want her to get attached. And it ended amicably."

Ari glanced at Erica for confirmation and she nodded with a shrug.

"Would he have any reason to hurt Jenna or you?"

"Now? A year after we broke up? No. We've been friendly toward each other. It wasn't a bad breakup. Brandon's a good man, we just weren't compatible. He wouldn't do this to me."

Ari gave her a moment to accept the possibility. "I'm going to need Brandon's address."

Madeline nodded. "It's on my phone." She looked around. "Where's my phone?"

"I still have it," Ari reminded her. She took it out and scrolled through until she found Kent, then made note of the address. His contact information included a photograph of a reasonably attractive Asian man a few years younger than Madeline. He was smiling into the camera and looked harmless enough. Ari checked the time. "We have a few hours until the kidnappers call. I'll see what I can find out and be back here before that happens. About the money..."

"I spent the night on the computer moving money around in my accounts. I think I could get seventy or eighty thousand of it together today if I had to. Are you sure I shouldn't just give them everything? I can get a hundred and fifty if I have a little more time."

Ari shook her head. "There's a reason they didn't ask for a specific amount. Ten thousand dollars doesn't mean anything if you're rich, and if you're poor then a million dollars is just a number. They don't know what you're worth, so they left it up to you. They know you won't shortchange your daughter so whatever you give them will be a fortune in your eyes."

"But you're making me shortchange them."

"No. I know that you would give a million dollars to get her back. But there's no sense in mortgaging your future just to be honest with these pricks. And the amount doesn't matter. You're not going to pay them one red cent, but we may need to use it as a prop. We don't even need the full amount. We don't have to fill a briefcase with stacks and stacks of hundred dollar bills; a hundred thousand dollars doesn't look nearly as impressive in real life as it does in the movies."

Erica said, "I'll show you out." When they reached the front door, Erica stopped Ari with a hand on the arm. "I need to know if you'll really be able to bring Jenna back. She's so devastated right now that I think if she has any hope in what turns out to be a hopeless situation~"

"It's not hopeless. Keep her thinking positively and let me worry about panicking. I'll be back as soon as I can."

"Okay. Good luck."

Ari thanked her and headed to her car. Brandon's address wasn't far, just on the other side of the interstate near a park she was vaguely familiar with. The difference between Brandon's neighborhood and Madeline's was startling, and Ari couldn't help but think the worst about the man she was looking for. She took out Madeline's phone and found a number listed as "Work" and dialed it.

"CenturyLink, how may I direct your call, please?"

"Hi, I was wondering if Brandon Kent was available."

"I'm sorry, ma'am, Mr. Kent isn't here today. I could direct you to another account representative if~"

"No, that's fine. Thank you anyway." She hung up and drummed her fingers on the steering wheel. Madeline, Erica, and now Brandon all skipping out of work. CenturyLink was facing a severe staff shortage.

His house was the fifth in a row of seven identical houses, its lawn a little shabbier than his neighbors. She parked and walked across the dead grass, scanning both sides of the street for the brown car the bus driver had reported seeing. She knocked and stepped back, hands in the back pockets of her jeans as she waited for an answer. After a few minutes she knocked again, then looked through the side window.

"Mr. Kent? My name is Ariadne Willow... I'd like to speak with you, if I could." She turned and looked down the street. If he was working with a partner, they could have taken Jenna to a more secure location. They wouldn't want to try keeping a kid somewhere she might draw attention. Ari knocked one more time before she stepped off the porch and went around to the back yard.

A barbeque grill stood next to the back door, and at the far end of the property stood a small shack with white paint flaking off the wood. It looked like it hadn't been disturbed since the previous century but she approached it anyway, cupping her face and looking through the dirty and weather-warped glass. Even in the dim light she could see only thick piles of tools, sporting equipment, and what looked like a bicycle missing tires hanging upside down from the ceiling.

She saw no evidence of kids, and little chance anyone was being held hostage there. Still, she remembered the case in Ohio, the three teenagers held in the middle of a suburban street, and took another pass around the perimeter of the house. She cupped her hands over every window, but the interior seemed empty and quiet.

She took out Madeline's phone again and scanned for Brandon's number. It rang three times before going to voicemail and she sighed. She took out her own phone and dialed Detective Lorne's number. He answered on the second ring.

"Miss Willow. Is it too forward to ask what you're wearing today? I'm only curious because you have such a wonderfully eclectic fashion sense."

"I wouldn't win any awards today, Kyle. Sorry. I was hoping you could do me a favor."

"You want a favor? Well, gee, this is such an unprecedented shift in our relationship, I'm not quite sure I know how to process it."

She rolled her eyes. "Yeah, sure, I'll owe you. I want to know if any of the boys and girls in blue have been called out to this house in the past day or so." She gave him the address. "Suspicious activity or weird sounds coming from inside."

He sighed and then, a moment later, she heard him typing. "Going back six months... no calls to that house. Or that street, even. Hell, I want to move there."

"You're probably better off where you are."

"Now that isn't an informed opinion. If you ever wanted to see for yourself, get all the facts before you make a decision."

She chuckled. "Pass. Thanks for the assist, Detective Google." She hung up before he could protest the name and walked to the back door. It was locked, so she peeked through the windows again. She could see a messy dining room, mail scattered across the top of the table with one space cleared for eating, and about two-thirds of a relatively tidy living room.

Disappointed that the trip hadn't borne more fruit, Ari walked back around to the front of the house. There was still plenty of time before the scheduled call, so she had nothing to lose by waiting around for a while to see if he showed up. She walked back to her car and settled behind the wheel to watch and wait.

Dale got lunch delivered from the Other Coast Deli and ate at her desk. She still had the blocked call information from Madeline Morris' phone, and she went through the usual routes of trying to find out where it had originated. Before she started working for Ari, she had never even heard of Deep Web searches. Now she accessed their search engines on a regular basis to track down information that would ordinarily have been out of reach. Today she had an actual phone number she could use to track down the phone used to call Madeline. She had just finished her sandwich when she discovered it was a defunct number. It had been disconnected six months ago.

"Hm. Weird..." Then again, Madeline *did* work for a telecommunications company. If the kidnapper was a coworker, maybe they had access to defunct accounts.

She was in the midst of sending another request when there was a knock on the door. She looked up as Milo stuck her head inside. Today she was wearing a sweater over black leggings, brown boots, and a green scarf. Her hair was down and a few curls clung to her cheeks, which had been reddened slightly by the cold.

"Hi. I think I'm a bit early."

Dale shook her head. "No, actually you're right on time. I just finished lunch and it's going to take a while for this request to be processed." She put the computer to sleep and began gathering her things. "Have you eaten?"

Milo nodded. "Yes, I stopped at a delightful little bistro not far from here. I'm afraid Seattle may be terrible for my waistline."

"If you're anything like Ari, you'll work it off in no time. Being a *canidae* is very good for the metabolism."

Milo seemed to consider Dale for a moment before she shook her head. "You know, it's kind of amazing. I didn't notice it until I met you, but most people who know about us don't bother to use the proper term. They like werewolf, even when it's not accurate. Werefoxes and all... But you actually go to the trouble to use the right word. It's respectful. I like it."

Dale shrugged. She locked the office door and led Milo outside. "Ari doesn't particularly like werewolf unless she's being facetious, so I guess I just responded to that and got in the habit."

"So you deal with us a lot? *Canidae?*"

"Not a lot, but not infrequently. She's run across one or two. There's a *canidae* bar she likes to go to called the, uh, Bull & Terrier."

Milo nodded. "I'll have to ask for the address, see if she doesn't mind me horning in on her territory a little bit more than I already am."

"The more the merrier, I'm sure. Is this your car?"

She couldn't think of another reason for a brand new Mini Cooper Roadster convertible to be parked in front of the office, and it shouldn't have been a surprise after seeing where she lived. But it was still an amazingly nice car.

Milo said, "I picked it up as soon as I got over here. It was between this and an Aston Martin, but a bit too Bond for my taste. I'll let you give it a spin later on, if you want."

"Sounds like fun."

"I went through my bags last night, ones I brought over from home, and culled the herd a little. So instead of just scouting we can actually create a few stashes I can use tonight if necessary."

"Nice planning." Dale got into the passenger side and waited until they were on the road before she started giving directions. "I'm going to start up in your neck of the woods. Ari will sometimes wander up north, but she tends to stick around Downtown and in the eastern part of the city. So there are some good stash locations up there I've never taken advantage of."

"Okay. And speaking of taking advantage, if Ari ever needs to use one of my stashes, she's more than welcome to."

Dale nodded. "I know she'll appreciate that. We have nine right now, so we should be set. But in case of an emergency where she ends up by the University, it'll be a load off her mind I'm sure."

Milo smiled. "How far north has the wolf taken her?"

"One time she got to Port Townsend. But she had a little help on that one. A Good Samaritan thought Ari was a runaway, and it was cold out, so she took Ari home for safekeeping. Good intentions."

"I've been there myself. Has she ever been forced to eat kibble~"

"~given to her by well-meaning animal lovers? Oh, yeah. She'd tell you that the raw steaks are worse. She loves steaks, but to have them thrown onto the ground uncooked... she thinks that's just being wasteful." She noticed their pull-off. "Okay, turn here. Find a place to park. Hope you're wearing shoes you don't mind walking in."

"I expected we'd have to hoof it a bit, so I got my trainers."

She parked in front of a church, where Dale was confident it would remain unmolested. She took a duffel bag out of the backseat and Dale looked around to make sure no one would witness them tromping off into the woods.

"We're going to be walking pretty close to the golf course, so watch out for bogies. Literally and figuratively, I guess."

"Should've brought a helmet. Lay on, Macduff."

Dale saluted and led Milo into the shadows under the trees.

CHAPTER EIGHT

ARI WAS back at Madeline's house with time to spare before the call. Brandon had never shown up, which she found more and more peculiar as the minutes ticked by. He wasn't at work, and he wasn't at home, so where was he? Had he taken Jenna to some out of the way place, a stronghold where he didn't have to worry about his neighbors seeing him with a struggling child? The more she thought about it the more likely it seemed that he was involved. Now if only she could find him. She reported her suspicions to Madeline, who took the information without emotion.

"Do you still have anything of Brandon's in the house?"

"Why?"

So I can isolate his smell from everyone else's if it becomes necessary probably wasn't an acceptable answer. "It's kind of a quirk I have. Right now Brandon Kent is just a name and a photo. If I can touch something of his, like a sweater or a jacket, it would help make him into a real person in my mind."

Madeline was on the couch, chewing on her thumbnail. She had the beginnings of a true thousand-yard stare, but she finally nodded. "Yes. He left a-a T-shirt behind. Sometimes I wear it to bed, but will that work?"

"It could."

She pushed herself up, moving quickly now that she had a task she could easily complete it. "I'll go see if I can find it."

Once she was alone with Erica, Ari said, "You know Brandon. Do you think he's capable of doing something like this?"

Erica crossed her arms over her chest, clutching her elbows with both hands. "I want to say yes. I want there to be a bad guy, you know? But Brandon? He was sweet to her. He wears vests and ties to work. Even after they broke up, there was never... h-he was never vindictive. I remember thinking how grown-up they were being about the whole situation. I can't believe he would do something so horrible."

"What about Madeline's ex-husband? Jenna's father."

"I never knew him. I didn't meet Maddie until after he left."

They stopped talking as Madeline came back into the room with her hands wrapped in a T-shirt. She looked at Erica, then Ari, and her shoulders sagged. "I'm not that fragile. You don't have to tiptoe around me and talk behind my back." She handed Ari the T-shirt. "What do you want to know about Jenna's father?"

"Anything you're willing to tell me. If he's still alive, there's a chance he was involved in this. I don't want to dismiss anything out of hand."

Madeline walked to the couch. "He left when Jenna was two. We met in high school and he had a crush on me. After college I came back and he was still around, and he still carried a torch, and by that time I was just flattered to have the attention of a nice, normal guy. I dated him to save myself from bars and blind dates and the internet." She rubbed her face. "He acted like getting me was winning a trophy. Like he'd worked hard and finally got the reward. That turned into jealousy, and that turned into trying to control everything about my life. I finally got sick of it. I wasn't going to have Jenna growing up in a house like that. So I filed for divorce and moved out here to get a fresh start."

"Jenna wasn't born here?"

"Well, I moved here from Spokane. It's not exactly cross-country. Gerry still lives there. I can't imagine him making the trip here and back just to take Jenna."

Ari conceded the fact for the moment, but she filed it away in case it came in handy later. Erica offered to make lunch for them all, utilizing bread and lunchmeat that Ari knew would otherwise have been used to make Jenna's lunch that morning. Ari was almost finished with her sandwich when Madeline's phone rang.

Madeline rose off the couch as if she had been jolted, eyes on the table where the phone was lying. Ari held up both hands to signal her to remain calm and then answered the call on the second ring. She turned it on speaker and leaned forward.

"Hi. To whom am I speaking?"

"Cut that out." The nervous guy was back. Ari looked at Madeline, whose eyes were closed. Erica pointed at the photo and nodded as the kidnapper spoke up again. "You don't ask the questions, I ask the questions and you answer them. Got me?"

"Sure, Brandon."

A sharp intake of breath that was exhaled as a whimper. "I said shut up."

"No, actually, you didn't. You said no questions and that wasn't a question. It's nice to finally speak to you. I waited around outside your house all morning and you never showed up. Where have you been, Brandon?" She tsked herself. "Sorry. That was a question. I forgot myself."

"My name's not Brandon."

"Denial only works in the first few seconds, guy. If you have questions you want to ask, you better get to them. I think Jenna's gone long enough without seeing her mother. Now, Madeline has to move some funds around. She has to liquidate some assets. When all is said and done, she can pay you a hundred thousand dollars for Jenna's safe return. She can have that money for you..." She looked at Madeline who mouthed her response. "...she can have it ready by tomorrow. But you have to do something for us."

"What?"

"You have to prove to us that Jenna is alive and that she's safe. I want to hear her voice in the next five minutes. You got that, Brandon?"

"Stop calling me that. My name isn't Brandon. And she's... she's not here. She's somewhere else. I can't get her to the phone in five minutes."

Ari said, "Then you hang up, call whoever is with her, and they can call from that phone. This is non-negotiable, Brandon. We're not paying for someone you can't deliver. This is just a business transaction for me, so don't try to make it complicated. I'm going to hang up now, and when I've talked to Jenna you can call me back so we can discuss how we're going to do the exchange. Goodbye, Brandon."

She hung up and folded her hands in front of herself.

Madeline exhaled sharply and shook her head, tears rolling

down her cheeks. "I can't stand the way you speak to him. Can you please just be a little nicer?"

"No. I can't. I don't want him thinking you'll just roll over and do what he wants. He's got to work for this. Now..." She looked at Erica. "You're positive that was Brandon?"

"It was him."

Madeline said, "I-I'm not sure. He sounded strange."

"That's because he's panicking," Ari said. "Last time it sounded like he was reading from a script, but this time he was close to tears. Whatever his part in this is, he's not doing it willingly. Madeline, his neighborhood and his house... they're definitely a step down from where you live. You said you're coworkers..."

"Yeah. Brandon... he has a gambling problem. It's one of the reasons we broke up. He's not a bad man, he just gets in over his head and it costs him." She shrugged. "I tried to get him into a program, but when that failed I told him we had to end it. I didn't want him throwing away Jenna's future on a bad hand of cards." She wiped at her cheek and Erica joined her on the couch.

The phone rang, startling them all. Ari picked it up and turned on the speaker again. "Hi, who's this?"

"Jenna Pearl Morris."

Madeline gasped and clutched Erica's hand. Ari held the phone out, and she clutched it like a lifeline. "Jenna? Sweetie?"

"Mommy!"

The word was filled with such joy that Ari nearly stepped out of the room. She felt like she was intruding just by overhearing it.

"Hi, sweetie. Are you okay?" Madeline had her free hand flat against the side of the phone as if she could feel Jenna through the device.

"I'm fine. The man doesn't have any ice cream, though."

"What man, honey?"

"Unca."

Ari mouthed a suggestion and Madeline repeated it. "Do you recognize him, sweetie?"

"No. He's always wearing a silly mask. I miss you, Mommy. When can you come pick me up and take me home?"

Madeline closed her eyes. "Soon, honey. Really soon, I swear. Is... is 'unca' treating you well? You tell me if you're scared or want to leave."

"No, it's okay. I just miss you." She lowered her voice. "He lets us watch so much TV. I'm sorry."

Ari straightened. Us?

Madeline laughed. "No, honey, no. For right now, you can watch all the TV you want. It's okay, you have my permission."

"Really?"

"Swear. Don't worry about missing school or anything. Just let mommy worry about all of that, okay."

Jenna was quiet. "Mommy, why are you crying?"

Ari stood up and turned her back, wishing she could reach through the phone and pull the girl through. Back to home, back to where she was safe and could have all the ice cream she wanted.

"I just miss you, sweetheart. I love you. You know that, right? You know that I love you so much."

"I love you too, mommy."

"I'll see you as soon as I can. Not a second later. And I'll talk to you as much as I can. Okay? Be a good girl, honey."

"I will. Bye, mommy."

"Bye, baby."

The phone went dead. Erica took it and Madeline covered her eyes with both hands. Her body shook as she sobbed. After a few minutes of silence, the phone rang again. Erica looked at it like it was a foreign object and then held it out to anyone who wanted to take it from her. Ari took a deep breath to steady herself, wiped her cheeks just in case any tears had slipped free, then turned back around. She took the phone.

"What's Jenna's favorite ice cream?"

Madeline whispered, "Cookies and cream."

Ari answered the phone. "Hi, Brandon."

"Please~"

"Tomorrow you're going to get one hundred thousand dollars for the girl. I'll leave the details of the exchange to you. I'm going to be making the exchange myself. When I'm sure Jenna is safe and unharmed, you'll get the money and I'll bring Jenna home to her mother. You'll have the exchange information to me by tomorrow morning at ten. We'll carry out the exchange and the girl will be home by noon. Understand?"

There was a long pause, and Ari pictured Brandon waiting for a thumbs-up or down from whoever was writing his scripts.

"Okay."

"And get her some cookies and cream ice cream, for God's sake."

She hung up the phone and dropped it into the chair. She

rolled her shoulders and shook her arms, feeling like she'd just gone ten rounds. She hugged herself, hands cupped over her elbows as she thought back over the conversation. One thing kept jumping out at her. "She said 'us.' They're letting 'us' watch TV."

Madeline looked confused, then closed her eyes as understanding hit her. "Oh. That might not mean anything. She has an invisible friend that she talks about sometimes. I wouldn't be surprised if she's there now."

"Oh. Well, we're not paying ransom for the invisible friend, too."

Madeline almost smiled at that. "So tomorrow by noon? This will be over tomorrow?"

Ari nodded. "I'll do everything in my power to make that happen, Mrs. Morris. You have my word."

Milo's feet were nearly turned completely sideways as she skidded down the slope. Montlake Bridge, which had slowed their drive home the night before, loomed above them. She turned and offered Dale her hand to help her balance as she joined Milo on the walking trail. When Dale was back on solid ground, she exhaled and brushed off her hands, looking around at the area. Milo had prepared three bags full of clothes, shoes, and emergency funds. One had been tucked under a drainage pipe by the fence of a golf course, the second was hidden underneath the wooden pylons marking the edge of a playground, and now the last one was to be placed in a spot of Milo's choosing. She'd asked to choose the last one as a test, and she would let Dale decide if she needed more practice in choosing locations.

Dale looked up at the underside of the bridge, and then turned to look down the footpath. Out of the way, sure, but a little difficult to reach. All in all, she gave it a grade of seventy-five, still well above passing.

"Okay. This one may just be in case of a dire emergency..."

Milo laughed. "I don't know. My wolf is pretty wily when it needs to be. I can see myself getting down here." She had one of the duffel bags from her car slung over her shoulder, and it bumped against her hip as she looked for a good spot to conceal it. Dale followed her, taking the time to admire the water rolling by a few feet to her left.

She climbed up a little ways from the walking path and crouched down, digging with a trowel she'd brought from the car and sticking the bag down into it. The spot was obscured by bushes and shadow, in a spot where it would be unseen by even the most eagle-eyed boat crew.

Once it was in place Milo climbed down and wiped the dirt from her hands. "And that's all she wrote. Three stashes... not too bad, gotta say. Makes me feel more comfortable with going out for a run now that I know I won't end up jogging home naked."

"Yeah. Ari has a problem with that, too. Although I think her complaint is with the arrests for public nudity. She has no problem with private nudity."

Milo lifted her chin. "Ahh, good to know. So I should always knock before I barge into your office."

"That's probably a good rule to have, yes. Okay, so..." She looked back up the slope. "Back up we go." She began to climb, moving slowly and hunched over in case she had to push herself along with her hands. She had only managed half a dozen steps before her sneakers slipped on the loose dirt and she tumbled backward.

She yelped and twisted at the waist, wanting to see where she was falling so she didn't just plummet into Montlake Cut. Milo was right behind her and, seeing Dale was in distress, reached out and put both arms around her waist. They fell backward together, but Milo caught herself with her foot and remained upright. She twisted on the ball of her foot, turning Dale's downward momentum into a spin and keeping them both from falling.

Dale put her hands on Milo's shoulders, their hips pressed together. When Dale had her breath back, she flipped her head to get her hair out of her eyes and chuckled nervously.

"Heh. Slipped."

"I saw that." Milo's voice was soft. "You okay?"

Dale nodded. "Uh-huh. Yeah." She tensed slightly, hoping Milo would take the hint and let her go, but the strong arms remained around her waist. "Uh... I-I think this footpath ends up there. We should probably just... I mean, it's a little out of the way, but it's better than falling into the water right?"

"Yeah." Milo smiled and, for a moment, seemed as if she wasn't going to let Dale go. Just before Dale was forced to ask her, Milo stepped back and straightened her blouse. "Yeah. Nothing wrong with walking a little out of our way."

"Nope." She cleared her throat. "It's a good spot. I, uh, I have a couple of other places. I can mark them down on a map so you can fill them up later. If you want."

"That would be lovely. Thank ya, Dale."

"Sure. Uh, lead the way." Milo turned and started walking, and Dale let out the breath she'd been holding. She tucked her hair behind her ears and followed. By the time they got back to the car, she had decided she wasn't going to mention anything to Ari about the clinch they'd just had. There was nothing devious about what had happened, no hidden motives on either of their parts. Dale had slipped and Milo caught her, and she'd had a natural reaction to being held by a beautiful woman. It didn't mean anything. Still, it would probably lead to a lot of unnecessary consternation if she brought it up.

Milo glanced over at her after she pulled back into traffic, aiming the car south to take Dale back to the office.

"Hope Ariadne really didn't need you today. I feel like I've taken over your entire agency in the day we've known each other."

"Well, we're new to each other. We're still feeling each other out. That takes time. Once we're familiar with each other it'll calm down. We'll just hang out to watch baseball games or have dinner every now and then."

Milo smiled. "I look forward to that."

Dale relaxed against the seat, then leaned forward and turned on the radio. She scanned the channels until she found something she didn't object to - Hall & Oates, vastly underrated in her opinion - and didn't realize which song it was until Milo started singing the chorus.

"'Rich Girl', huh? Got this one memorized?"

"Yeah, well. I'd bet you have all the words to Springsteen's 'Red Headed Woman' memorized, huh?" She reached over and twirled one strand of Dale's hair around her finger.

Dale grinned and leaned away from her, letting the strands unravel around Milo's finger. "I plead the fifth," she said. "Sorry, you're British... that means I'm not saying a damn word."

Milo laughed and settled for singing the rest of the song in full voice as they drove back across the bridge.

CHAPTER NINE

ARI RECEIVED a text message from the kidnappers on Madeline's phone before she left the Morris house. All it said was "Peppi's Playground 9:30a. ALONE. Stand on the world." When she showed it to Madeline, she pointed toward the front door. "It's at the end of the street, on the right. There's a, a... there's a painting on the pavement." She held her hand out palm-down and patted the air. "A map of the world is drawn on the pavement. I'll have the money for you in the morning."

Erica said, "I can go with you when you leave and show you where it is."

"I'd appreciate that." To Madeline, she said, "This will all be over very soon. Your daughter will be home, and you can start putting this whole thing behind you."

"Thank you." Madeline's voice was soft. "I'd have gone crazy if you weren't here."

Ari smiled. "Just doing my job. I'll be here by eight-thirty. Try to sleep, Mrs. Morris. You're going to want your energy when Jenna comes home."

Madeline smiled and nodded. Erica escorted Ari out of the house and pointed. "The playground is just up here on the right."

They started down the sidewalk, hands in their pockets. Ari looked back to make sure Madeline wasn't following.

"What do you really think of Brandon Kent?"

Erica glanced at her, started a denial, then exhaled sharply. "I couldn't badmouth him in from of Madeline, even under the circumstances. He *is* a nice guy, and this is completely out of character for him."

"But...?"

"But he never really got over their breakup. Part of the reason he stayed on good terms with her was because he still hoped he had another chance. He was sweet. He didn't obsess or force himself into her life. It's more like he was just biding his time until she realizes she made a mistake and takes him back. Now, though, I think he can consider his chances pretty much eradicated."

"She said they broke up because of his gambling. Was it bad enough to lead to this?"

"Gambling." Erica made a rude noise and rolled his eyes. "Normal people gamble. Brandon seems to jump through hoops to give his money to people. Brandon is an ATM for card players. Madeline never really knew the extent of it. He played cards at a club downtown, he played online poker. He wanted to get into that tournament they used to show on TV all the time but he was terrible. But no matter how bad it got, I can't imagine him deciding to use Jenna or victimize Madeline like this. It doesn't make sense."

"If his girlfriend didn't know, how did you?"

"We were friends from work. He didn't want Madeline to know, so when he needed a little cash to get him through to payday he'd come to me."

"Do you know the name of any clubs he might have frequented?"

"I don't. I might be able to find out for you."

"Try. I'm going to get Jenna back tomorrow, and I'm going to make sure she's safe before I make another move, but I won't stop until I get the people who took her."

Erica looked at her as they walked and then nodded. "Maddie made the right choice when she hired you."

They crossed the playground and walked around the corner of a quiet school building to a paved area with patterns for hopscotch and four-square painted on the ground. The opposite side of the playground was lined with basketball goals. In the center of the space were two maps, one showing the fifty American states and the other showing the countries of the world.

"Looks like that's where I'll be waiting tomorrow." She looked at the school. "Hopefully I won't get in too much trouble for loitering outside a school."

"You told Maddie that you weren't going to let Brandon get away with the money."

Ari nodded. "I assume he's going to try to use the kids as a smoke screen. I'll be too busy getting Jenna to watch the money and he'll slip out. But I'll have a secret weapon."

"He said no police."

"No police," Ari assured her. "And if everything goes well, he'll never even notice my backup is there. I just have to see if she's willing to play along."

They walked back to the house and Ari retrieved her car. She had just missed the post-work, pre-dinner rush when she parked in front of the office. The curtain in their office window was glowing gently with light from within, and Ari knocked on it as she passed. By the time she got inside, Dale was standing up behind her desk. The overhead lights were off, but the desk lamp cast enough light to see by.

"Evening, boss."

"Hey, gorgeous. Solve my case yet?"

Dale turned her computer monitor so Ari could see it. "The call from your kidnapper came from a defunct number. I did a little digging and it turns out the account was suspended by one of Madeline Morris' coworkers."

Ari almost didn't say anything. "Brandon Kent?"

"Yeah." Dale looked a little disappointed. "How'd you know?"

"Madeline identified him from the security camera footage. So it was still your work that made the break. You get a gold star." She pecked Dale's cheek.

Dale smiled. "Well, so long as you know I'm indispensable."

"Never doubted it for a second. Madeline and Brandon dated for a while but they broke up because he has a gambling problem. I checked out his house, but he wasn't there and didn't show up for work today."

"So he needs the money to pay off a debt?"

Ari considered that, but shook her head. "I don't know. Maybe. I still think there's more going on here. The guy sounds scared to death on the phone, but I'm also fairly sure he's reading from a script whenever he calls."

"Well, Ari, he's a gambler who is extorting a former girlfriend by kidnapping her daughter. He's going to be nervous, and if he's nervous he's going to prepare for the phone call. He might have written out what he wanted to say on note cards so that he wouldn't slip up when it was actually happening."

"That's true. But when he called today I asked to talk to Jenna. He said she wasn't nearby. He had to get in touch with someone else to make the call."

"Accomplice?"

Ari chewed her lip. "Maybe. Possibly. And both Madeline and her friend Erica say this is out of character for him. Neither of them can imagine him coming up with this plan, so I have to think someone else did the brainstorming." She pushed her hands into her hair and sighed. "Anyway, I'm starving." She stuffed her hands into her pockets. "You wanna go out on a date with me?"

Dale smiled. "I think that would be lovely, thank you."

"Good."

Ari waited while Dale logged off her computer and got her coat. When Dale put on her scarf, Ari took a moment to adjust her collar and smooth her hair down over it.

"Thanks."

"Sure." She brushed her hand down Dale's back and escorted her out. "Indian or Thai?"

Dale considered. "I could go for some curry."

Ari linked her arm around Dale's and guided her down the street. "So how was your afternoon with Milo?"

"It was fine. We found a couple of good stash places up by the University. She said if you ever get up that way you're more than welcome to make use of them. Must be kind of nice having a *canidae* friend."

"Yeah. I think I could get used to it. In fact, I might have a way to make good use of her. The payoff is happening tomorrow at nine-thirty at the playground. He said no cops and to come alone, but even if Brandon does have accomplices they aren't going to be looking for a wolf. If Milo is there she doubles our chances of getting Brandon and making sure Jenna gets home safely."

"Good idea."

"I'll call her tonight to see if she's interested in lending a hand."

Dale hesitated and then nodded. "Okay."

"Problem?"

"No." Dale twisted her head to get a windblown strand of hair out of her eyes. "I like Milo. She's a lot of fun. You deserve to have someone you can hang out with."

"You're the only social circle I need."

Dale slipped her arm around Ari's waist and pulled her close. "You can go play with your friend tonight. And if you want to take the wolf out for a run, that'll be fine. You're dealing with an asshole that kidnapped a little girl. I'd be worried if you didn't need to let off a little steam, four-legged style." She pressed closer to Ari and kissed her cheek. "Just remember to call if you need a ride. And if you want to sleep at my place, make sure your feet are warm and clean before you get into bed with me."

"I think those are reasonable conditions. I'll stop by Milo's place later on. For now, I'm all yours." She opened the door to the restaurant for Dale and then followed her inside. No matter how bad the case was, and no matter how strong her urge to "go for a run" became, she would always take the time to let Dale know what her priorities were.

Ari pulled into the driveway of Milo's house after dropping Dale off. Half the lights on the first floor were aglow, and she sat behind the wheel for a moment debating whether or not she should go through with what she had planned. She didn't even really know Milo, so was it right to include her in something so potentially dire? It boiled down to the fact that she didn't have much of a choice. She had to be in human form in case of unforeseen difficulties, and a *canidae* would be perfect camouflage if someone was looking out for observers.

She got out of the car and went to the porch. She almost retreated again when she heard music coming from within. She imagined a party, but the driveway was empty. She knocked and the music ceased. A minute later the door opened and Milo smiled warily out at her. She appeared to be dressed for bed in a V-neck shirt and sweatpants that ended just above the collapsed tops of her green argyle socks. Her hair was pulled back in a loose ponytail and she leaned against the door, resting one foot on top of the other.

"Ariadne. Uh, hi. I didn't expect you."

"I wasn't sure I was coming. May I come in?"

Milo pushed her hand into her hair. "Uh. Yeah. Come on inside." She stepped out of the door and let Ari in. The stairs were directly ahead, leading up to a darkened landing. To the left was a living room directly out of a finer-things catalogue, and the folding door to the right was open just enough for her to see a dark dining room. Milo stood behind her while she took it in, then finally broke the silence. "Did you, ah... talk to Dale?"

"Oh. Yeah, she said she had a great time. I'm glad she was able to help you with the stashes."

"Yeah." Milo paused. "That's it?"

Ari finally looked at her, confused. "Was there something else?"

"No." Milo shrugged and gestured at the living room. "I just thought that you came by for, ah... I don't know why. Is everything all right?"

"Mostly. I know I said I couldn't talk to you about the kidnapping case I was working on, but it actually turns out you might be able to help me. The exchange is supposed to happen tomorrow on a playground. I have to be there as-is because I'm the one who has been dealing with the kidnapper. But I thought if I had backup it might lead to a... happier conclusion for everyone."

Milo smiled. "Oh, I get it. You want my wolf to keep an eye on things. Brilliant. I love it." She leaned forward with her elbows on her knees. "Is that allowed? I mean, do I need to be deputized or anything?"

"No, I think we're good. I'll pay you part of what I get from the client."

"How old is the missing girl?"

"Seven."

Milo shook her head. "Nah, I'll do it for free. It's my civic duty to take down bastards like that."

"Great. The drop is going to happen tomorrow morning. I'll swing by here around eight to pick you up. You'll probably have to be the wolf for a couple hours."

"That's fine. I do it all the time. Love being the wolf."

Ari stood and noticed a piano against the wall next to the living room entrance. "Was that you playing when I knocked?"

"Yeah. It's soothing. I've loved the piano since I was a girl."

Ari nodded, impressed by anyone who could master an instrument. "Well, I'll let you get back to it. Sorry to drop by so late and for the short notice."

"No problem. I'm happy to help." She followed Ari to the door and then stopped her. "Hold up. Maybe you could help me out at the same time. You've already brought me into your business and you let me borrow your girlfriend for the day so I almost hate to ask, but... do you have a pack?"

"A pack?"

"Yeah, other *canidae* you run with. I mentioned the mates in

Yorkshire I ran with. Gets lonely going for runs by myself, so I was thinking if there was a group..."

Ari shook her head. "Not really. I did run with a pack once or twice, but it never really works out for me."

"So you go out alone? All the time?"

"Yeah. Sorry."

Milo shook her head. "Wow. I'm the one who's sorry, if you're all by your lonesome out there. Maybe we could help each other out. I want someone to run with, and you're here... let's go for a run."

Ari chuckled. "Thanks, but I should probably just go."

"Why not? Could be a lot of fun. And it's a little weird we've never seen each other's wolves. I'll show you mine if you show me yours."

Ari hesitated and looked at the front door. The last pack she'd run with was an undercover sting to help out an ex-girlfriend who happened to be a cop. The pack had been run by a fox - literally, a fox - named Sadie Dillon, who led a gang of thieves in a robbery spree. That ended about as bad as it could have. And her past experiences with *canidae* were less than stellar. It would be nice to have one friend who understood what it was like. And what was she going to do, say no and then go run by herself? She'd never minded being alone before but in this case it seemed ridiculous to refuse.

"What the hell. Why not." She smiled, eager now that she had made the decision. "Where do you want to run?"

"The woods?" She nodded toward the back of the house. "I have a place where we can leave our clothes and get cleaned up afterward. I call it the Thwaite. C'mon."

She turned to go down a hall that ran alongside the stairs and Ari followed. Milo flipped a switch as she opened the backyard and the porch was illuminated by a pair of powerful flood lights. She put a hand against the wall and bent down, perching on one foot and then the other to peel off her socks. She wiggled her toes as she led Ari out into the night air. They crossed the manicured lawn. The woods came right up to the fence, and within a few minutes they were surrounded by thickly-crowded trees and the smell of nature. Milo led Ari to a small pond and peeled off her T-shirt.

"We should have done this yesterday morning. It's one thing to get acquainted on two legs, but our wolves need to meet."

Ari nodded, glad she had changed her mind about doing this. "They do." She turned slightly so she and Milo weren't facing each other and began to undress.

"Shy?"

Ari glanced over her shoulder as Milo pushed down her underwear. "Well, we've only just met. Some etiquette needs to be observed."

Milo chuckled.

Ari draped her clothes over a branch and turned to see Milo was already in the midst of transforming. She was crouched down, one leg against her chest with her arms extended to steeple her fingers against the ground. Her skin seemed to be rippling, her mouth wide as her jaw extended an unnatural distance from her neck.

Ari rolled her shoulders and transformed as well, changing into the wolf on what quickly became hind legs. She dropped forward and pawed at the mud, working her muscles to ruffle her own fur. She turned and approached Milo, who was now a stately white-and-gray wolf. Milo faced her and they sniffed each other briefly, the ritual as natural to them as shaking hands would have been a moment ago.

When the pleasantries were finished, Milo reared back on her hind legs and growled low in her throat. Ari swiped at her with a paw, but Milo easily ducked it and lunged from beneath. She nipped at the side of Ari's snout, making just enough contact to sting without breaking the skin. Ari yelped and threw her weight to the side, knocking herself down and bowling over Milo in the process.

Ari corrected herself first and turned to run. Milo had the benefit of knowing the woods, so she didn't stray too far to give her a chance to catch up. When Milo did reappear, she nipped Ari's shoulder as she past, barking in a way that was almost like a laugh as she ducked around a tree and out of sight. Ari growled and yipped and put on an extra burst of speed to get her revenge.

Within twenty minutes the police had received seven different calls complaining about hearing the "howling of wild dogs" in the park.

CHAPTER TEN

HUMAN AGAIN, Milo dropped flat on her back with her arms stretched out to either side, and exhaled sharply. Her skin shined in the moonlight, sweat glistening off her chest and stomach as she settled against the mud. Ari was right behind her, transforming on all fours and then rolling onto her side. They were next to the pond, their clothes within reach but neither of them willing to waste the energy needed to stand up and get them.

Ari's hands and feet were coated with mud, and she was struggling to catch her breath after what felt like a marathon run. The trees overhead were too thick for her to see the moon, but she still had a general idea of where they were in relation to Milo's house. She looked over to see Milo watching her, a thin webbing of dark hair falling across her face. She smiled, and Ari found something about that hilarious and began laughing. Milo joined her. They had spent at least two hours racing each other in circles, setting ambushes and tackling each other through the underbrush. Even when they were scored by branches or thorns, they didn't bother stopping to check the damage. Ari had thought at one point Milo had raced headlong into a rosebush only to discover a carefully concealed passage that was only visible if it was seen head-on.

Milo finally got her laughter under control and sighed. "God, I'm jiggered." She looked over at Ari and scanned her body. "Not shy now, are ya."

"Screw modesty." Ari chuckled and wiped her hand under her nose, still adjusting to being back in her human body.

"Heh." Milo chuckled quietly and then said, "Did I leave any marks on ya?"

"Oh." Ari raised both arms to look, then lifted her head to examine her body. "No, I don't think so. Did I?"

"Nah." Milo exhaled sharply and pushed her hair back. "Hell fire! That was exactly what I needed."

Ari snorted. "Yeah. Who won?"

"I think you did. You tossed me arse over tit more'n once. Nice job, for a city wolf."

"You held your own." Ari flexed her toes and grimaced. She rolled her shoulders and stretched her back to try working through the pain building at the base of her spine.

Milo noticed. "Y'awright?"

"Yeah. Just a little sore. It happens sometimes after I change." She pushed her elbows into the mud and arched her back, working to find a more comfortable position. She curled her toes and let the mud form around her body shape. She sighed as she settled in and closed her eyes until the pain subsided enough for her to clean herself in the water. She knew she needed to get at least a few hours of sleep before the scheduled meet, but for now the mud was far too comfortable. And a night as the wolf was sometimes as refreshing as a night's rest.

After a few minutes Milo sat up. Mud and sweat marred her back as she pulled her knees up and wrapped her arms around them. She looked down at Ari and then dropped her hand. She dragged her fingers over Ari's thigh and hip, sending shivers up and down her body. Ari smiled nervously and swatted her hand away.

"Cut that out."

"You're gorgeous, you know?" Milo rested her cheek on her knee. "Both you and your wolf." She flattened her hand and ran it along the bottom curve of Ari's belly, between her navel and pubic hair.

Ari looped her fingers around Milo's wrist. She gently but without hesitation moved it. She sat up, ignoring the shock of pain that shot through her bones.

"I'm with Dale, Milo."

"Sure. But your wolf..." She leaned in and pressed her lips to Ari's, starting a kiss that Ari ended by pressing her arm across Milo's chest and shoving. Milo rocked back on her haunches. "What? What's wrong?"

"I'm Dale's. Completely."

Emotions flew across Milo's face too quickly for Ari to name them all. Milo turned to look at the water and then pushed herself up. "Sorry."

"It's fine. Forget it happened."

Milo crouched and began to quickly wash the mud from her hands and arms. After a moment Ari joined her at the banks. The water lapped against their bare toes as they scrubbed themselves clean just slightly more than arms-length apart.

"Still hurt?"

Ari glanced over. Milo's tone was flat, but Ari could tell she was trying to move past the awkwardness. "It's faded a little. It's fine. I'm used to it."

"How come it hurts you like that?"

Ari sighed. "It's a long story. I wasn't exactly born like most *canidae*."

"What, you were bit?" Some of her emotion came back.

"Nothing like that. My mother was *canidae*, so I should have inherited it from her. I didn't. So she found a doctor who did a procedure that..." She waved her hand in the air. "It was highly dangerous, there was probably a fifty-fifty chance that I would die, but instead I grew up to become a woman who is very bitter about her mother."

Milo whistled. "You'd never know it. You're a natural from what I saw of ya. Most of us, we choose one side or the other. They're wolves who can act human, or a human who can become a wolf. You walk the line very well."

"Thanks."

"Could you..." She rubbed her eyebrow with one bent finger. "I'd rather Dale not know that I tried to, ah... take advantage of you. I think the three of us have a pretty good start here and I'd hate to think I ruined it. I got between a mate and his girl once before, and it nearly destroyed us all. It's still hard to be in the same room with them both at the same time. Please. I'd hate to think I've ruined all the hard work we've put into the last two days."

Ari wasn't keen on the idea of lying to Dale, even if it was a lie of omission, but it would be a shame to let such a promising friendship falter because of one indiscretion.

"It's a new friendship, you had to test the boundaries. Now that you know where the line is, you won't cross it again."

"Right. So we're good?"

"Yeah, we're fine." She held out her hand and Milo shook it.

They finished washing up and retrieved their clothes. Ari stuffed her socks into her shoes and carried them back to the house, scrubbing her feet clean on the grass as she walked. When Milo started up the back yard she paused and stared at the back window.

"Something wrong?"

"Did I turn on the dining room light when we left?"

Ari tried to remember. The room they'd left from was off the dining room, and Ari remembered it being dark behind her. But now the window was brightly lit.

"I don't think you did. I have my phone in the car if you want to call someone."

"No. I know who it is." Milo shook her head in disappointment and then looked at her. "Ah, no offense, Ari, but I think I have an unexpected visitor. Would you mind going around the side of the house to your car?"

Ari looked at the house. "Everything okay, Milo?"

"Yeah. It's just far too late for introductions and explanations and... I think it would just be best if we put it off for now."

"Sure. If you're sure everything's okay."

Milo shrugged. "Nothing more dangerous than family. You know how it is. Want to make sure wee Millie is behaving herself in America. Even if I just introduce you as a friend, they'll think you're more and then the interrogation will begin, and~"

"Got ya. We're still on for tomorrow morning?"

"Eight sharp. I'll be ready."

Ari nodded. She took the time to put on her shoes without socks, then let Milo walk her to the side yard.

"And thanks for understanding about the kiss. Sometimes I get a bit hot under the collar when I'm the wolf, and that makes me act daft."

"Happens to the best of us. Good luck with whatever's waiting for you in there."

Milo grunted and groaned. "I'm gonna need it. Give Dale a kiss for us, yeah?"

"Will do. Good night."

"Night."

Ari waited for Milo to go into the house before she took the long way back to the front of the house. A black sedan had appeared at the curb since Ari's arrival, and she took a moment to walk down and give it the once-over. She bent down and sniffed near the door handle, the one place the driver was certain to touch it. She wrinkled her nose. There was a miasma of coffee and cigarette smoke, thick perfume. Whoever was in the house was female, but without becoming the wolf Ari wasn't able to tell anything else.

She decided it was just as Milo said, some well-to-do dowager aunt come to make sure Milo wasn't frivolously throwing away her inheritance in the colonies. She went to her car and checked the time on her phone before she pulled out of the driveway. A few minutes past one in the morning. She waited until she was at a stoplight before she considered which destination she was heading toward. Home, where she could get plenty of rest to prepare for the morning? Or to Dale's, where she could get a little less rest but have the comfort of being in her partner's arms.

In the end, it wasn't much of a choice.

Dale drifted awake to the vague awareness that someone was in her bedroom, but the primal side of her mind recognized Ari's shape or gait and prevented her from panicking. When she woke properly a few minutes before five, Ari was in bed with her and fast asleep. Dale turned around and put her arms around Ari's wait to pull her close. She kissed Ari's neck and fell asleep with her lips still partially pursed.

The alarm woke them both at six. They showered together and Dale took it upon herself to scrub the mud from the soles of Ari's feet to make sure they were fully clean. Ari had a few clothes in Dale's dresser, which she decided made it technically one of her stashes. If it was, it was definitely her favorite. She chose nondescript clothes - a green T-shirt and jeans with a lightweight leather jacket. She found a satchel out of Dale's closet and took it with her into the living room.

"Can I use this to carry the money?"

"Of course you can." She chewed her sausage carefully. "Are you sure you don't want to bring in the cops at this point? At least tell Detective Lorne what's going on."

Ari shook her head. "Madeline is right. They won't waste resources while Missing Melody is still out there. Besides, if I tell Lorne now, he'll fill the square mile around the playground with guys who just stepped out of a cop show. I don't want Brandon to get spooked when we're this close to getting Jenna back. That's the focus. We'll work on getting the people who took her once she's safe." She watched Dale for a minute. "Do you agree with me? Because if I'm off-base... if you think I'm risking her safety~"

"No, no. I think you're doing the right thing. I just wanted to make sure you had thought it through completely."

Ari smiled. "Thanks." She leaned against the counter. "Milo kissed me last night."

Dale blinked. "Hm?"

"When I went over to her house to ask her about helping me this morning, she talked me into going for a run with her. So we ran through the woods behind her house for a few hours and when we got back to this little pond where she washes up, she kissed me. I stopped her and told her that I was completely yours and she apologized. She didn't want me to tell you because she didn't want to affect our friendship, but I decided I can't keep it from you if I'm going to be spending the morning with her."

"Oh." She blinked and raised her eyebrow. "Were you guys, uh... post-wolf?"

"Yeah, we were naked."

Dale hunched her shoulders. "Well... you stopped it. And I guess we've only known Milo for a day so she's not..." She scratched her cheek. "You're a beautiful woman, Ari. And you have so much in common with Milo, I'm not surprised she thought you might be interested. You set her straight?"

"Yeah. Hundred percent."

"Then I'm okay." She stood up and leaned forward. "Kiss me like she kissed you."

Ari pecked Dale's lips quickly.

"Now kiss me like we kiss."

Ari leaned in and didn't pull back for a solid minute. When she did, Dale kept her eyes closed and smiled. "Oh, yeah. That's fine."

Ari cupped the side of Dale's head and kissed her again. "Okay. I'm going to go make sure Madeline's ready."

Dale gripped Ari's wrist. "Be... careful, Ariadne. You hear me? I know a little girl's life is at stake and I know you'll stop at nothing to get her home and get justice. But I don't want you to get hurt. So whatever risks you take, try to make them calculated risks, okay? Come back to me today. That's all I ask."

"Today. Every day. Yes, ma'am."

She kissed Dale again and slung the strap of the satchel over her head so that it hung across her chest. She put on her sunglasses, blew a third kiss to Dale, and left the apartment. She felt relief flooding her core, replacing the anxiety that had been burning in her chest since she promised Milo to keep mum about the kiss. She had felt it building and knew it would only get worse until she confessed. Now she and Dale were completely fine, and she was going to be able to focus on keeping her promise to get Jenna Morris back in time for lunch.

The rental car was no longer parked outside of Milo's house, so apparently the mysterious relative wasn't a houseguest. Milo answered the door in a robe. She smiled and brushed her hair back from her face and motioned Ari inside. "I thought I'd say good morning before I changed. Plus, kind of hard to answer the door with paws."

"Don't I know it. Listen, before you shift, I should tell you that I told Dale about what happened last night."

Milo paused. "Oh. I guess I understand that. How'd she take it?"

Ari shrugged. "We trust each other. She took it at face value. I just wanted you to know the air was completely clear so that things won't be awkward between the three of us."

"Completely clear... so she told you about what happened with us?"

"You and her?" Milo nodded. "No. What happened with you?"

Milo winced. "Oh. Nothing. She might not have even... no. I was just probably misinterpreting the situation. New country, new society, all that. Um." She cleared her throat. "Right. The, ah, wolf." She slipped out of her robe and, as she transformed, Ari tried to push thoughts of what she'd said out of her mind. Her and Dale? It couldn't be anything worth mentioning or Dale would have brought it up. The fact she didn't proved how minor whatever Milo was referring to must have been. But if there was something...

She put the thought out of her mind and led Milo's wolf out of the house. She didn't have time for relationship crises or second thoughts. She and Dale had been circling each other for too long to let an off-hand comment cause any doubt. Ari knew exactly how Dale felt about her, and Dale knew the same thing. She opened the back door for Milo so she could jump in, then circled around the back of the car.

Milo was the unknown in the situation. Bringing up some unknown "incident," now of all times, stank of manipulation. She was up to something, but it would have to wait.

"Let's go catch us a kidnapper."

Milo barked her approval and Ari regained her focus.

Jenna was coming home today.

CHAPTER ELEVEN

ERICA WAS waiting on the front porch of Madeline's house when Ari arrived. She was dressed down, as if she'd just thrown on the first outfit she could find when she rolled out of bed. She came down the driveway and offered Ari a strained smile. Milo trotted a few steps behind Ari in wolf form, and Erica stared at her for a moment before she spoke. She whispered as if a full voice could be heard inside the house.

"Maddie's been sleeping for almost five hours. I didn't want to disturb her until we absolutely had to."

"Good. Let her sleep. Was she able to get the money?"

"Eighty thousand of it. I still don't feel comfortable using it as a prop. What if something goes wrong? What if he gets away?"

"Then I'll hunt him down until we get it back." Erica looked down at Milo again and Ari patted her on the head. "This is Millie. She's going to help me."

Milo made an annoyed sound in her throat and Ari pinched her ear. Milo 'harumphed' and shook her entire body before surrendering to the name.

"Maybe she should stay out here. I don't want her to wake Maddie up."

"She's fine. She's very well-behaved, for the most part."

Milo looked up at Ari, who didn't meet her gaze.

"Okay. Well..." She motioned for Ari to follow her and they went into the house. Madeline was already awake and standing in the living room, looking lost and alone. "Maddie, I thought you were asleep."

"I was. I heard Ms. Willow... and..." She frowned at Milo.

"This is Millie. She's going to help me get your girl back."

Madeline crouched down in front Milo. "Is she friendly?"

Milo responded by ducking her head and pressing up against Madeline's thigh. Madeline chuckled and ran her fingers through the hair at Milo's neck, then hugged her.

"Guess that answers your question." Ari smiled. "Are we all ready to go here?"

"Yes." Madeline stood and went into the living room. Ari and Erica followed her. A large duffel bag was on the couch, the elephant in the room despite the fact it seemed empty. Madeline withdrew a few stacks of hundreds from it and shrugged apologetically. "I thought eighty thousand would take up more space."

Ari patted her satchel. "It'll fit fine in here."

Madeline nodded and they put the money into it. Once it was loaded, Ari said, "I know that I'm still a stranger to you, and it takes a lot of faith to let me walk out the door with this. I want you to know that today, Jenna comes first. The money is second, and then grabbing the bastards who took her is third."

"Thank you. But get the bastards should be second. If I lose the money, it's a small price to pay to get bastards like that off the street."

Ari nodded and snapped the bag shut. "How are you feeling?"

Madeline pushed her hands through her hair. "I feel like I'm paying for my daughter. Even worse I feel like I'm trying to get a bargain." She looked at Ari, obviously considering once again whether they should just pay and get it over with. She sliced her hand through the air between them before Ari could think of an answer. "I know. I know, and you're right. I don't want to reward kidnappers."

"Right." Ari looked at her watch. "In about a half hour I'll go get into position. Millie here will be a safe distance away keeping an eye on things. When I have Jenna, Millie will follow him back to wherever he goes next. She'll get your money back."

Erica blinked at her. "That's... impossible. I don't care how well-trained she is."

Ari looked at Madeline. "What is Jenna's favorite toy?"

"A little stuffed lemur, I guess."

"Is it in the house?"

"In her bedroom."

Ari patted Milo on the side. "Go get it for me."

Milo stood and trotted down the hallway. A few minutes later she came back with the toy clamped carefully in her jaws. She lifted her head and deposited it on Ari's lap, then settled down on her haunches and stared at Erica.

"How uncanny." Erica's eyes were wide, and she looked at Ari with newfound respect. "You're actually going to get her back."

Madeline was as surprised as Ari. "You had doubts?"

"I'm sorry, Maddie. But this girl is... she's..." She looked apologetically at Ari. "You're so young. And your agency is called Bitches Investigations. I guess I can see why now, but it was kind of hard to take you seriously. I apologize."

Ari shook her head and waved it off. "It's fine. I kind of bank on people underestimating me. I like being the underdog."

Ari spent a few more minutes reassuring Madeline that she had the situation well in hand. Before she left, Madeline stopped her and tucked the lemur into the pocket of Ari's jacket so its head was sticking out. She petted the top of its head and then smiled with tears in her eyes.

"Here. Take this so Jenna will know it's okay to come with you."

Ari nodded. "Smart. Thank you. Hopefully I'll have some good news for you very soon. Stay here and try to stay calm even if it takes a while." Ari realized she was taking a fortune out of the woman's house and walking off with no set time of return. "Mrs. Morris, thank you for trusting me with this case. It's an honor."

"You've proven yourself worthy, Ms. Willow. I'm glad I chose you." She held out her hand. "Good luck."

Ari thanked her and then led Milo out of the house. She was very aware of the eighty thousand dollars resting against her hip as she walked, grateful to have Milo at her side even on an idyllic suburban street like this. Jenna's disappearance had proven even the most peaceful places could be the scene of a horrific event.

She took the long way around the school and lingered on the sidewalk until the playground was empty of kids. She looked for signs of Brandon watching the location but the street was quiet. She pointed to a shrubbery where Milo could observe without being seen and the wolf trotted off. Ari walked across the pavement and stood on the world map, planting her sneakers in the Atlantic Ocean with her back to the school.

At nine-thirty exactly, Madeline's phone rang in Ari's pocket. She took it out, saw it was a blocked number, and scanned the playground as she answered. Still no one in sight, but she figured he could be in one of the cars parked along the street.

"Morning, sunshine," Ari said. "Running late?"

"I'm right where I need to be. Are you?"

Ari tapped Florida with her right foot. "Yep. Let's get this over with, Brandon."

"Not so fast. Be on Lake Washington Boulevard in Frink Park in ten minutes."

The phone clicked off. Ari frowned at the phone in disbelief, looked to the south, and checked her watch. Ten minutes didn't give her a lot of time to debate, not that there was much of a question she had to comply. She shoved the phone into her pocket and broke into a running start and hoped that Milo would be smart enough to follow. She had to do rapid mental cartography because she didn't dare stop to think about the best route to take. At the intersection she turned left, cutting the corner sharply to shave a few seconds off her time. She had to sidestep pedestrians, not wasting time with apologies as she entered the park.

Lake Washington Boulevard curved up and around, moving deeper into the park. Ari followed the bend in the road and glanced behind her to see Milo keeping pace a block behind her. A bicyclist nearly mowed her down by Ari avoided her at the last second. The girl shouted a curse, but Ari ignored it as she raced forward.

The phone rang again as she approached the next curve. Ari yanked it free as she trotted to a stop. She answered without looking, panting to catch her breath so she could tell Brandon what she thought of his little game. He spoke before she could get anything out.

"Thirtieth and King. Ten minutes."

Ari cursed breathlessly as he hung up. She wiped her wrist across her forehead and started running again. Just before she left the park she heard Milo running through the brush to her right, keeping up with her. "Thirtieth and King," Ari said. Milo barked a response and the sounds of pursuit faded as she took a shortcut. Ari envied her. She was in good shape, but the wolf would have been a much better runner.

The satchel banged against her hip, the lemur bouncing against her side as she tore down the street. She drew odd glances from everyone she passed but she didn't care. She got to the corner of Thirtieth Street and stopped, hands on her hips as she looked in both directions. The streetlamp in front of her was plastered with pictures of Missing Melody, four days gone now, but they didn't help her determine which way was right. She looked both ways in frustration, and then grabbed the arm of someone passing her. "King Street," she gasped.

He tensed and glared at her. "What? Let go..."

"Which way is King Street?"

The man pointed north and yanked his arm away, and Ari took off again without bothering to thank him. She was approaching the intersection when the phone rang again. She slowed to take the phone out, answering it while she was still running.

"I'm almost there, you prick."

"You're falling behind. Judkins Park, twenty minutes."

"Oh, you fucker." She growled and forced herself to move faster. Despite the cold, sweat was soaking through her T-shirt as she reached the corner and turned left. She had to get her bearings on the fly, scanning to see if Milo had beaten her to the corner. Even if Milo was keeping up, Ari doubted she would spot her. Even a newcomer to the city would know shortcuts through backyards and alleyways. But she couldn't help but worry. If they got separated, the whole plan would fall apart. Brandon would get away with the cash and odds were they would never see him again.

She ran down King Street to its end and turned south. She had a vague idea where Judkins Park was since Dale had once kept a stash for her there. She turned at the far intersection, panting as she slowed and tried to decide which part of the six-block park she was supposed to be when the phone rang again. She exhaled sharply, her body protesting at running another block. Her pulse was pounding in her temples and her face was slick with sweat. It was more than forty minutes since the meet-up time. She couldn't imagine what Madeline and Erica were going through. She pulled the phone out when she reached the corner and growled into the speaker.

"Listen, you son of a bitch~"

"The baseball field. Home plate."

Ari looked directly ahead and saw the field. She approached at a slow jog, scanning the wide expanse between it and the softball field at the other side of the park. She walked to the batter's box and put the phone to her ear again.

"Okay, I'm here."

A hundred yards away, on the other side of the fence, she spotted movement. She recognized Brandon from the photo Madeline showed her, and the little girl he was guiding out ahead of him could only be Jenna. He was holding his flip phone like one of the old *Star Trek* communicators, raising it to his mouth to speak.

"Alone?"

"You probably had your asshole partner keeping an eye on me. Did he tell you I had a platoon of cop cars following me all over the damn city? I'm alone." She lifted the satchel, then reached inside and held up one stack of money so he could see it. The distance between them helped conceal the fact it wasn't the full amount. "I have the money. Let me talk to Jenna."

"Wave to the lady, Jenna," Brandon said. The little girl lifted her arm and waved in a carefree, innocent way that told Ari she had no idea what was happening. "See? She's fine. Here's what's going to happen. Jenna is going to stand on the home base of the softball field. You're going to put the bag down on your home plate. Then you'll walk around the edge of the park while I walk along the other edge. I'll get the money when you get Jenna. Sound good to you?"

"Sure." Ari prayed Milo was nearby.

She lifted the strap over her head and dropped the bag heavily onto home plate. Brandon stepped through the gate on the fence and bent down, pointing to where Jenna should stand. She followed his instruction and stood on the pad, hands behind her back, watching as Brandon started to walk along the fence line. Ari walked to the opposite side of the park, phone still against her ear.

"You try anything," Brandon said, "and you can be sure I can still make things very bad for her. You might have figured out who I am, but you don't know anything about this."

"How much was your debt, Brandon?"

"What?"

"You didn't ask for a specific number, but I imagine it was pretty high. Most of the hundred grand, if not all of it. Maybe this is just going to be a down payment on your sorry ass. I just hope it was a suitably high number since you went to this extreme. So at least tell me if the money in that bag is going to make you free and clear."

Brandon said, "Why don't you just shut up. You're almost out of this. So just shut up."

"No, you want to keep me on the line to make sure I'm not calling for backup. Wasn't that in the script? Keep me on the phone, keep me talking until you have the money? So let's talk, Brandon. You're not acting like yourself. Sure, you're acting like a desperate man, but there's more to it than that. Desperate people don't threaten kids on a whim. Who wrote the scripts for you? Those calls for ransom, making me run my ass ragged the past hour... was that your idea? Because I don't buy it."

"I don't care what you buy."

Ari was at third base, and Brandon was even with first base of the other diamond. Ari lowered the phone and called across the field to Jenna.

"Hey, sweetie. You okay?"

"Yeah..." Wary, as well she should be. She looked toward Brandon, then back at Ari. "Who are you?"

"I'm a lady your mother hired to bring you home. Here..." She pulled the lemur from her coat pocket. "She knew you'd be missing this guy, so she wanted me to bring him to you."

Jenna brightened. "Lolo!"

Ferocious barking suddenly came from the other side of the field and Ari looked to see Milo tearing toward home plate. She skidded past Brandon, nearly knocking him over as she raced for the bag of money. Brandon shouted and began to run as Milo ducked her head and threaded it through the strap. The leather pulled taut against her neck as Milo ran pell-mell toward the opposite side of the park. Brandon gave chase, but it was clear he had no chance.

Ari ran the rest of the distance to Jenna and scooped her up. "Honey, we're going to have to run. Hold tight."

"I'm scared," Jenna said.

"I know, sweetie. Just hold onto Lolo." She tucked Jenna's head against her shoulder and ran for the gate. She hit the chain-link just as a loud cracking noise filled the air. At first she thought it was the sound of her hand hitting metal, but then it happened again and she realized it was a gunshot. She hunched her shoulders forward to cover Jenna's body with her own, and Jenna began to cry as Ari hauled her toward the safety of a nearby building. She ducked down and put Jenna against the wall, knowing the big gray bricks would protect her from any stray bullets. She crouched next to her and ventured a look back the way she had come.

Brandon was sprawled on his back a few yards from where Ari had last seen him. Tires squealed, but the echo was so bad that she couldn't pinpoint the direction.

"You're sweaty."

Ari couldn't help but laugh. "Yeah, sweetie. I was running to come get you so I could take you home. Your mother really misses you."

"I miss her, too."

Ari pulled out her phone. "Do you know how to send a text message?"

"A little."

"Here... send one to your mommy's friend Erica. Tell her you're safe and you're coming home soon."

"I'm only supposed to use phones in case of emergencies."

"This counts. Trust me."

Jenna took the phone and Ari looked back out. Brandon still hadn't moved, and now sirens were picking up. She'd heard no other shots after the first two so she decided it was safe enough to try leaving cover.

"I sent it." Jenna handed back the phone.

"Okay. Come on." She put the phone in her pocket and guided Jenna out of the nook. Jenna was clutching her toy with one hand, so Ari took the other and hurried her to the south and away from the sirens that now seemed to be right on top of them. She didn't want to waste time explaining to the police who she was and what she was doing there.

Jenna looked back and then looked up at Ari. "Did I do something bad?"

"No. Brandon was doing something bad."

"Oh."

"Hey, did you ever get your ice cream?"

Jenna smiled. "Yes!"

"Good." She looked to see if any of the police had noticed her or if, more importantly, Milo was anywhere to be seen. She ushered Jenna onto the footpath, knowing that there was a bus stop somewhere nearby that could take them back to where her jog had started. She put her hand on Jenna's back. "Do you mind riding the bus back to your mommy's house with me? We could walk, but I want to get you back there as soon as I can."

Jenna hesitated. She'd obviously been taught to be wary of strangers, but after what she'd been through she wasn't sure what to say or do. She pressed her face against the head of her toy and then nodded once.

"Okay. Come on. There's bound to be a bus stop somewhere nearby." She took Jenna's hand and walked with her away from the park. "Can I ask you something about the place you've been staying the past few days?"

"I guess."

"Was Brandon there the whole time, or was there sometimes another person?"

"There was another person. I didn't like him. He was a mean man."

"Did he hurt you?"

Jenna shook her head. "He was just mean to us. I mean... me."

Ari remembered the invisible friend and touched the back of Jenna's head. "It's okay. You don't have to worry about him anymore."

They found a bus stop and only had to wait a few minutes before the bus arrived. Ari led Jenna to a seat near the middle of the bus and let her take the window seat. The route was circuitous, and it would take nearly forty-five minutes before it got to where they needed to be. Ari settled back against the seat and relaxed, finally able to catch her breath. She put her hand on top of Jenna's head and then held out her hand for Madeline's cell phone.

"Let me see." She found the games section and, with Jenna's help, chose one that they could play together. Jenna focused on the angry birds and not the harrowing situation she'd just gone through. When it wasn't her turn, Ari would look out the bus window in the hopes of spotting a black and white wolf racing through the streets with a leather satchel of money hanging from her neck.

"You're not very good at this game."

Ari laughed. "Well, maybe you're just *too* good, huh?"

She rested her hand on the back of Jenna's head as she refocused on the game. There was still a lot of work to do. She had to find out why Brandon had really been involved with the kidnapping, and she needed to know who the 'other man' was. If she learned that she would most likely know who had taken those two shots in the park. But for the moment, she could relax. The most important part of the case was closed.

Chapter Twelve

THE BUS delivered them to a stop down the street from Jenna's home. Jenna started walking faster once home was in sight, and Ari spent the walk trying to come up with an explanation for how her 'dog' had run away with the eighty-thousand dollars of ransom money. Just before they made the final turn, Milo emerged from the trees to their left and trotted to catch up with Ari. The bag was still sloppily slung over her neck, bumping the ground as she walked.

"Nice of you to show up."

Milo looked up and gave Ari an unmistakable 'are you kidding me' glare. Ari smirked and reached down to scratch the top of her head.

Jenna had tensed when Milo appeared, but she relaxed when Ari petted her. "Is that your doggie?"

"She's, ah, my helper today. Her name is Millie. You want her to walk you home? She's real friendly."

Jenna nodded and Milo moved up to walk beside her. Ari took the bag off Milo's neck and slung it back over her shoulder as they made the final approach to the house.

Madeline and Erica were both on the porch. Madeline turned, looking over her shoulder in a way that told Ari she had looked every time a car or truck or bicycle had come around the curve. When she spotted Jenna she inhaled sharply and held the air in her chest, grabbing Erica's arm to keep upright. Jenna squealed and ran up the driveway, and Madeline met her halfway. She dropped to her knees and wrapped her arms around her daughter, clutching her tightly as tears flowed from her eyes.

"Baby... I was so worried. Are you okay?"

"I'm fine, mommy. I missed you."

Erica stepped around the happy reunion and looked at Ari with equal parts awe and respect. "I have no idea how you did it, but thank you."

"It was my pleasure." She opened the flap of the bag and checked to make sure all the money was present. It wasn't that she distrusted Milo, but she was still an unknown quantity. It was all still accounted for, so Ari shut the bag and lightly touched Madeline's arm.

"Let's take her inside, okay?"

"Yes. Of course." She stood up and took Jenna's hand, guiding her up onto the front porch. Erica and Ari followed, with Milo bringing up the rear. Once they were inside, Madeline took Jenna to wash up and change into some of her own clothes. It seemed that Brandon and his mysterious companion had bought clean clothes for her to wear while she was in their custody, and Ari didn't blame Madeline for wanting to get Jenna out of them.

While they were gone Ari transferred the money from her satchel to the duffel bag Madeline had left on the couch. Erica watched her and shook her head.

"How did you ever manage to do this?"

"I got lucky. And I had a good partner."

Milo ruffed quietly.

Erica said, "Do you have a business card?"

Ari frowned and took out her wallet. She handed a card across the table. "Do you need a private investigator?"

"No, and I don't foresee needing one in the future. But if I do, I know for damn sure which one I'm going to call."

Ari smiled and dipped her chin in thanks.

Madeline returned alone. "Jenna's exhausted. I tucked her in so she could take a nap." Ari noticed that she was standing between Jenna's bedroom and the front door, standing guard even if she didn't consciously realize what she was doing. She looked at the money in the bag as if she didn't understand what it was doing there. Then she dropped her hands and her lips parted in surprise. "My God. Is that my money?"

"It is. All eighty thousand of it."

"That's unbelievable. What happened?"

That took her a few minutes to explain. When she got to the part about seeing Brandon's body, Madeline sagged and pressed one shoulder to the wall. She hung her head and took a few deep, steadying breaths before she looked up again. The tears in her eyes were fresh, but Ari could tell she wasn't grieving too hard for him.

"He really was a good man. When I knew him. You have to believe that, Ms. Willow."

"I know. You wouldn't have been with him otherwise. But people change. I'm just glad this ended as neatly as it did."

Madeline left the hallway and went to the bag of money. She broke one of the packets and counted out a few hundred.

"Your assistant told me your fees. This... this is double that."

"That's generous, but I can't~"

"You earned it. And you saved me from losing so much more." She held the money out with a steady hand. "Please, Ms. Willow. The kidnapper forced me to give what I could afford. Now I'm giving what I feel like I owe. You brought her back to me."

Ari took the money. "Thank you. I'm glad I was able to help. Oh..." She took out the cell phone and handed it to her. "I probably won't need this anymore."

"Oh. Thank you." She looked at the phone and then met Ari's eye. "Thank you, Ariadne."

"You're very welcome. I'll go ahead and get out of here. You'll need some rest so you can keep up with Jenna when she wakes up."

Madeline blinked in surprise. "Oh. Yes, of course. Thank you." She furrowed her brow. "I know I said that, but I don't care. I can't say it enough."

Erica said, "I'll see you to your car."

They walked out together, Milo staying close by Ari's side. "Will you stay with her today?"

"Of course," Erica said. "She'll need someone to pick up the slack, and I'm happy to do it." She touched Ari's arm to stop her and lowered her voice. "The other kidnapper, whoever shot Brandon... they're still out there. Should Maddie be worried?"

Ari didn't see any sense in lying to her. "Yes. I don't think Brandon came up with this by himself. If there is someone still out there who wants Jenna, they'll try again. The good thing is now that Jenna's home, there's no reason not to call the police. Can I have my card back for a second?" She handed it over and Ari wrote another number on the back. "This is the direct line to Detective Kyle Lorne. Have Madeline call him and tell him everything that happened this week."

"I'll have her call. I know she said it about a dozen times, but thank you. I've known Maddie a long time and I've never seen her as lost as she was this week. Having you take charge the way you did really helped get her through it. Getting Jenna back was just part of it."

Ari handed her card back. "I'm just glad I was able to help. If you need a follow-up, or if Detective Lorne wants to talk with me, you can reach me at that number."

Erica nodded. "Knowing Erica she'll probably invite you back here for a barbeque or something. She doesn't forget when people come through for her."

"I'll consider myself warned." Ari grinned. "It was nice meeting you."

Erica shook her hand and wished Ari well. Ari opened the car door for Milo to jump in, got behind the wheel, and left the Morris house behind her. She heard Milo shifting in the backseat behind her, so she maneuvered herself out of her jacket and tossed it over her shoulder. At the next stoplight she looked back and saw Milo was in human form, wearing the jacket zipped up to mid-chest.

"Were you okay?"

"Fine. Nearly got hit by a thousand bloody cars, though. Kept forgetting to look the right way." She coughed and flipped her hair out of her face. "Hope I didn't overstep or blow things up, taking the bag like that."

"No, that was the perfect call. Were you clear before the shooting started?"

Milo nodded. "I was about a block away, runnin' like hell. I didn't stop until I was a good mile away. Then I had to try'n figure out how to get back to the Morris place. Had a hell of a time, but I managed. Good thing I spent the night cramming with a street map of Seattle. Good God, that checkpoint run! I thought we were done for sure. How 'bout you?"

"The shooter seemed more interested in killing Brandon than getting me. I was lucky."

"You really think whoever it is will come after Jenna again?"

Ari shrugged. "Better have Madeline prepared for that instead of giving her false hope and dropping her guard. I think the real danger is going to be that she gets overprotective of the girl, but that'll pass. Madeline's got a good head on her shoulders. She'll know when the time comes to let her go."

She pulled onto Milo's block and turned into the driveway. The morning's conversation came back to her, the idle comment about something happening between Milo and Dale. She parked and took the money Madeline had given her out of her pocket. She peeled off one of the hundreds and held it out. "Here. I know you said you didn't want it, but you risked car accidents and flying bullets, and you helped a bad situation end happily for the people we like. It's a hundred, so it's nothing to sneeze at, but it's a fraction of what I'm keeping for myself and Dale so I feel a little guilty about it. And considering your address, it feels sort of like tipping someone a penny. Go on. Use it to buy stuff for your stashes."

Milo took the money and hoisted it once in thanks. "You're all right, Ari."

Ari nodded. "One more thing, Milo." She paused with the door open. "Dale and I are together. I don't know what last night was, and I have no idea what you think happened between the two of you yesterday, but that's something you can take to the bank. I trust her. So if you plan to get between us, you can give it up. I like you. You're a good person, and today you proved that you're a hell of an asset to have around. Today would have gone a lot worse without you there, and I like to think Dale and I have made your transition to Seattle a little easier. I think the three of us could be really good friends. But if you keep up this shit trying to incite jealousy in one or the other, you're going to lose us both."

Milo looked out the window during the speech. When Ari was finished Milo looked down at her bare legs under the hem of the jacket, nodded once, and softly said, "Yeah. A'right."

"Friends?"

The corners of Milo's mouth ticked up slightly. Her voice was soft, defeated, and she nodded her head twice. "Yeah. My love to Dale, yeah?"

"Sure. Give us a call, we'll go out to dinner again sometime."

"Aye. Thanks for today, Ari. And I'm sorry about the... games."

Ari shook her head. "It's already forgotten." She held out her hand. "See you around. We'll go running again."

"I'd like that. Sithee, Ariadne."

"Bye for now, Millicent."

Milo managed a smile at that and plucked the hem of her coat. "I'll get this back to ya."

Ari nodded. "Thanks for your help. You may have saved Jenna's life, so..."

"Ah, you did all the hard work. I just swept in at the end. And from now on, the whole... you and Dale thing? I won't, ah... You don't have to worry about it."

"Glad to hear it."

"All right... bye."

When Milo was safely inside, Ari pulled away and drove back toward the office. She felt weak and weary, allowing herself to be exhausted now that Jenna was safe. She turned found a radio station playing Bruno Mars and took the long way home, driving near Downtown before she swung back up toward the office.

As she was driving, she thought about the whole bizarre thing with Milo playing her and Dale off each other. It was a fool's errand destined to fail, but she still felt awkward that it had been tried. There was a store nearby that had piqued her curiosity before, but she'd never gone in. With the bonus from the case burning a hole in her pocket, and with Milo's juvenile games nipped in the bud, she thought the time had come to finally take the step.

She took a detour that passed by the store and parked in the back lot. She took part of the money Madeline had given her, looked at the store, and made her decision as she climbed out of the car.

Milo hung Ari's jacket on the hook inside the front door and slid her hands down the sleeves. It was still strongly filled with Ari's scent, but there was a hint of Dale's as well. She assumed it was Ari's jacket and it simply spent a lot of time at Dale's apartment. Maybe she borrowed it from time to time for quick runs to the corner store or to get something out of the car. She brushed the collar and found a stray red hair that she twirled between her thumb and forefinger as she walked naked into the living room.

The plan had seemed simple in England. But at that point Ariadne Willow and Dale Frye were just names on a piece of paper. There was a bit of personal information on them both but nothing that revealed just how compatible they were. She sat in the armchair that faced the window and thought about their dinner together. She'd known from the first moment that she wouldn't be able to break them apart. They truly loved each other. More than that, they belonged with each other.

She eyed her cell phone for a good two minutes before she

finally picked it up. She dialed an international number and closed her eyes as it buzzed in her ear.

"Hello."

"I'm out."

There was a long silence on the other end of the line. "You assured us~"

"I know what I said. But I can't do it. More than that, I won't do it."

"Millie, if you abort now, you'll be destroying our ability to do this quietly. It was your idea to play it subtle. But if you stop now, we'll be forced to use more dire methods. You're the one who convinced us that Ms. Frye might come willingly. If you've changed your mind we can certainly go back to~"

Milo interrupted. "No." She hated herself, but she knew what lengths the bitch would go to. She looked out the window, defeated. "Don't do that."

"So you'll continue as we agreed."

Milo chewed the inside of her cheek. "Yeah."

"Fantastic. Keep us apprised, Millicent."

The call disconnected and Milo hurled the phone at the sofa, where it hit the cushion with a sound like a baseball sinking into a catcher's mitt.

Dale was at the computer when Ari got to the office. She was carrying a small white bag in one hand, the satchel in the other. She dropped the bag into one of the waiting room chairs as Dale stood up to meet her halfway. They embraced, kissed, and held each other for a long minute until Dale turned her head and kissed Ari's ear.

"Everything okay?"

"Everything great. Jenna's fine. She's home with her mother." Dale audibly exhaled with relief, her arms tightening around Ari's waist. "Just letting it all catch up with me."

"Thank God. You did good work today, Ariadne." She pulled back and kissed Ari's lips again. "I love you."

"I love you, too." Ari stared into Dale's eyes for a moment and then pulled back. "That's why I bought this with some of the extra Madeline Morris paid me." She took it out and tossed the bag so she could hold it with both hands. It was a brown leather collar with a silver clasp. Simple enough, but out of context it was hard for Dale to reason why Ari had it.

"What's that for?"

"It's a promise. It's not a wedding proposal or an engagement ring, but it says that I'm yours. Whenever you're ready to put it on me, I'll wear it."

"Oh. Wow." Dale ran the fingers of one hand over the leather. "Can I put it on you now?"

"Of course."

"Okay." Dale took it and Ari lifted her hair out of the way. Dale slipped the collar around Ari's neck and bit her bottom lip as she slipped the tongue into the metal loop. She looked into Ari's eyes. "Is that too tight?"

Ari worked her head from side to side and smiled. "Nope. Feels great."

Dale let her hands slide down to Ari's shoulders and smiled. "Good. Now, you mentioned being paid...?"

"Yeah. The case is officially closed."

"Officially, but not technically."

Ari briefly explained what had happened during the ransom drop, ending with Brandon Kent's death. "Someone is still out there and they were running the show with Jenna's abduction. I'm not going to feel like she's safe until I know everything that happened. But now that there's been a death, and since Jenna is no longer in danger, I think we can call the police and let them do some of the legwork."

"Definitely. But first, paperwork."

"Can't I just get shot at again?"

Dale hooked her forefinger under Ari's collar and dragged her to the desk so she could fill out a report.

PART II

Chapter Thirteen

THE UNDERGROWTH *shuddered violently as the animals pass through it, the sound of their heavy breathing frightening away the smaller creatures that flee in fright. The forest seems endless, an ever-continuing expanse of scents and uneven ground and trees so tall their tops are out of sight. At a clearing with a lake the wolf skids to a stop and turns, sides billowing with breath as she waits for her companion to join her.*

The sleek fox bursts out of the scrub and slams into her side. Their limbs tangle and they bite playfully at each other, finally ending up in the water where their fur becomes soaked. The fox rises and bolts back to dry land and the wolf follows. Dripping, the wolf crowds the fox as they both begin to transform. Their faces shift and change until they are human, lank brown hair hanging in the wolf's face.

Ari playfully licks Dale's cheek as the fur recedes to reveal soft pink flesh. Dale grabs handfuls of Ari's hair and pulls her head back, lips against Ari's throat as they rearrange their legs and settle against one another. Ari sits up and Dale lifts her hips to meet her, smiling up at her as the fox and the wolf become human once more.

Ari tightened her arms around Dale's waist as the dream broke, blinking the fog out of her eyes and pressing tighter against her partner. Dale's breathing remained steady in sleep so Ari settled against her and closed her eyes in a futile attempt to get back to sleep. She knew it was only a matter of time before the day began. The morning was already bright through the window and she could hear Dale's neighbors getting ready for work.

After trying and failing to fall back to sleep, Ari decided to wake Dale. She kissed her neck, stroked her hip, and gently nibbled her earlobe until Dale began to respond. She rolled onto her back and sleepily draped her arms around Ari's neck, angling her face up for a kiss. She pecked the corners of Ari's mouth and then dropped her head back onto the pillow.

"It's early." Her voice was rough with sleep. She turned her head to cough quietly into the pillow. Ari took the opportunity to kiss the column of Dale's neck. "Morning."

"Good morning." She flopped onto her back and brought her hands up, letting her fingers trail over the strip of leather around Ari's neck. Ari smiled; she'd done the same thing every morning since putting it on. Dale's eyelids were still heavy, but her smile was lively as she traced the rough material. "Didn't you go for a run last night?"

"I decided against it. But I think the wolf disagreed with me. I'll probably have to go out tonight if I don't change for work."

Dale nodded and slid her hand down to Ari's hip. "Up. I want to shower."

Ari kissed her one more time and then rolled off. They pushed aside the blankets until Dale could get her feet free, and she tugged at her nightshirt as she walked to the bathroom. Ari took her phone off the charger on the nightstand and checked email, the news, and Twitter.

By the time Dale emerged from the shower, pink-skinned and wrapped in a fluffy blue towel, Ari was awake enough to appreciate the sight of her at the bathroom sink. The way she pressed her hips against the counter and leaned forward to get an inch closer to the mirror, her left knee bent so that the heel of her foot was off the tile, humming quietly to herself... Ari put aside her phone and climbed out of bed.

Ari undressed and stepped into the shower that Dale had left running so the water would still be hot enough to scald when Ari got into it. Ari undressed and tossed her pajamas into the hamper before she stepped into the stall. "I had a dream about you."

"Oh? Was I naked?"

"Pretty much."

"Sweet. Anything in the news?"

Ari ducked her head under the shower spray. "Nothing interesting. Still no word on Missing Melody."

She heard Dale cluck her tongue in dismay. It was the sixteenth day since her disappearance, and the sad truth was that the city had moved on. Even inundated with the girl's picture on every street corner and her face plastered on every news broadcast - local and national - after two weeks people reluctantly accepted the fact she probably wouldn't be coming back. The Saturday before, when it was clear the public's interest was waning, the girl's mother Brenda Scott made a final impassioned plea to whoever took her daughter. Rewards had gone unclaimed, and the information flood slowed to a trickle. The ubiquitous posters of Missing Melody began to disappear. Torn away by winds or rain, covered over by another flyer, or just simply taken down as new items were displayed in their place.

When Ari got out of the shower, Dale was in the bedroom and half-dressed. She brushed her hand over the small of Dale's back as she passed. "I'm going to run home and get a better change of clothes. Want to meet me somewhere for breakfast?"

"Sure. Adelaide's?"

Ari nodded. Their apartments were less than a mile apart, which made the idea of bringing clothes over easier and more confusing. If there was a concerted effort to move house, it would make the decision monumental. But as it was she could bring her things over to Dale's a little at a time and they could be cohabitating without actually making the decision.

"I'll see you there in thirty." She kissed Dale, tasting the mint of her toothpaste before pulling away. "Mm. See you then."

"Wear something blue."

Ari paused in the bedroom door. "What? Why?"

Dale shrugged as she put on a blouse. "I like you in blue."

Ari smiled and nodded. "Blue it is." She bent two fingers in a small goodbye wave and put on her jacket as she left the apartment.

Ten days earlier she had gathered everything she and Dale had discovered about Jenna Morris' disappearance and took it to Detective Lorne. He was, perhaps rightfully, angered and offended by the fact they had kept the information from the police. Withholding the kidnapping investigation was bad enough, but the fact a man was dead meant their silence bordered on criminal. Ari pointed out that Brandon Kent's death was what prompted her to come forward, and he informed her that was the only thing keeping her out of jail.

He initially promised to keep them up to date with whatever he found about the mystery shooter without providing a single scrap of news since. Whether that was his method of revenge or if the case had simply stagnated, Ari wasn't sure. She decided to give Lorne the benefit of the doubt and wait a few more days before she called to see if he had found anything.

A week earlier a thank-you card had arrived in the mail. Inside was a handwritten message from Jenna. "Thank you for saving me from the Bad Men. Love Jenna Pearl Morris (7)." The card was currently propped up against Ari's computer monitor until she found a more permanent way to display it. According to the note Madeline included with the card, Jenna was back in school and already putting the whole thing behind her. There were nightmares, of course, and Madeline had spent more than a few nights in a sleeping bag next to Jenna's bed, but Brandon and Mystery Man had treated her with relative kindness. "The road to recovery, I think, will be a short and relatively smooth ride thanks to you, Miss Willow. Thank you from the bottom of my heart."

The case was one of Ari's proudest moments, and one she hoped she would continue to look back upon fondly. She couldn't fully relax while Brandon Kent's killer was still at large. He was the one who had orchestrated Jenna's kidnapping for whatever reason, and until he was caught Ari couldn't completely appreciate the gratitude being heaped upon her.

At home she considered her schedule for the day as she examined her closet. She was scheduled to deliver two subpoenas for the law firm that had them on retainer after lunch, and she was going to spend the morning hours digging into Brandon Kent's life a little more. No matter how finished everyone else said it was, no matter how hard Lorne claimed the police were working on it, she couldn't just leave it be. Whoever had been pulling Brandon's strings used his gambling debts as leverage. They knew he would be the perfect fall guy. But how? And what was the goal in kidnapping Jenna Morris, of all the kids in the world?

With the process-serving case in her mind, she chose a pale-blue blouse with a navy tie and suit pants. Lawyers liked it when she dressed professionally for their assignments. She pulled her hair back into a semi-elaborate knot and stepped into the bathroom to apply her makeup. Her dream of cavorting with a *canidae* version of Dale flickered across the front of her mind briefly as she stared at herself in the mirror, but she dismissed it. She fingered the leather of her collar, then tugged the collar of her shirt up so that it was mostly concealed. So far only a few people had commented on her new accessory as most who noticed it decided they didn't need an explanation.

She decided she liked the collar. Dale assured her several times that she didn't have to wear it all day every day, but Ari had grown comfortable enough that she barely even noticed it. It was loose enough to stay in place even when she transformed, the risk of choking as her neck morphed remaining low enough that it wasn't worth worrying about. And in situations where she had to look professional, it was easy enough to cover or to make it look like a random accessory. All in all, it was a tiny price to pay for a constant symbol of their relationship.

She adjusted the knot of her tie and went to meet Dale for their breakfast.

Milo had houseguests. She could hear them moving around downstairs, preparing one of their proper English breakfasts, but she couldn't be bothered to go down and join them. She pulled the blankets up and rolled to face the wall. She wanted to pull the plug on the whole thing, but she knew the stakes were much too high for that. She hated what she was trying to do with Ari and Dale. In the short time they'd known each other their friendship had become something solid. Now her handlers were downstairs to make sure she finished the job.

She finally got out of bed but she didn't go downstairs. She felt like a child as she sulked in her nightgown, turning on the TV - quietly so it wouldn't be overheard and cause her to be summoned - and went to the window. It was covered with a thin sheen of frost but she could still see down onto the white-dusted lawn and the icy slicks that appeared her and there on the road. Winter had officially arrived and she was still spinning her wheels.

Someone knocked on the door and Milo clenched her teeth, closing her eyes as she rested her forehead against the cold glass. "I'll be down in a minute."

Footsteps retreated but she knew her return to privacy wouldn't last long. She put a jacket on over her nightgown and pulled on a pair of leggings, deciding that was as much dressing as she felt up to. She went down barefoot and found Ben serving up a fry-up with a side of bubble and squeak. Her stomach growled despite her irritation; she hadn't been eating well since she saw the collar Ariadne had started sporting. No *canidae* wore a collar lightly;

it carried a much deeper meaning than the Goth appropriators that had made them semi-fashionable.

She took a seat at the counter and looked toward the dining room for her other babysitter. "Where's Gwen?"

"She had business to attend." He passed her a plate and a cup of milk. "We spent a lot of time talking last night, she and I. We've decided we've given you more than enough time to complete your assignment. It's taking far too long. We're taking over."

"No."

Ben lowered his hands to his side but didn't look at her. "Millicent..."

"Fuck it, my name's *Milo*." She stood up and said, "I'm the one who was chosen for this, and if Dale doesn't come willingly, then I'm out, too."

Now he looked at her. "Don't be hasty, Mill... Milo. The consequences~"

"Fuck the consequences. She doesn't know anything about what's going on. We're using this poor woman like she's a pawn. She has a right to be told, to choose. Maybe she'll choose to come of her own free will. Maybe she won't. But I'll not force this decision on her, and I won't manipulate her into destroying the life she's building. You agreed to do this my way, Ben. If you want to go back on that promise, then I'll walk right now. You and Gwen can find another candidate. Good luck with that."

Ben was silent for a long time, gently twisting the knobs on the stove to make sure they were off. Finally he turned to face her fully.

"By the end of the year, Milo. You'll have this done by the end of the year or we will be forced to accelerate matters. Remember that we're not working on a timetable of our own devising; we are operating at the whims of our enemy, and they're growing closer every day. Lives will be lost if~"

Milo cut him off with a swipe of her hand and a grunt. "God, you're so fucking melodramatic. I get it. One way or another, I'll make it happen." She picked up her plate and the milk. "I'm going to eat in my room. If Gwen gets back, try and stick to the ground floor. I think I've already had my fill of the both of you today."

"The end of the year, Millicent."

She grimaced as she carried her food upstairs, idly wondering when the next flight to London left SeaTac.

Dale convinced Ari to spend her morning more productively

and, once she realized it wasn't a euphemism, they swung by the office to pick up their gym bags. They both had memberships at the Wellness Center, which Dale had set up in the hopes that it might ease Ari's transition between human and wolf. They only went infrequently, but Ari was eager to have something in her morning other than Brandon Kent's financial records.

The gym was practically deserted when they arrived, only a few intense-looking women on Stairmasters in the corner. Even in Lycra they seemed to be wearing power suits. One seemed to be dictating a letter into a small handheld device while another was in some kind of Zen trance. Ari assumed that her workout was the only time the woman let herself completely relax and felt sorry for them as she followed Dale to an area where they could stretch.

Dale was in tight shorts and a yellow tank top over a sports bra, her hair tied back in a ponytail that bounced with every step. She glanced back and caught Ari staring at her and smiled.

"Hey. Focus."

"Sorry. All those times we came here and I fought against ogling you. Now that I have permission, it's hard not to."

Dale turned around and walked backward with her arms crossed over her breasts. "I never gave you permission to ogle. You have to earn that."

"Right. My apologies."

Dale shook a finger at her and sat down. Ari sat in front of her and they stretched their legs out in a wide V pattern. Dale placed her ankles on top of Ari's. Ari leaned to the right and hooked her fingers around her sneaker, while Dale leaned to her right. Ari held the pose for a moment and then they switched to the left. Ari felt the burn in her thighs and lower back, felt the loosening of the muscles as she pushed herself just a little lower, held it just a little longer, and then released the hold with a sigh.

"Feeling good?" Dale asked.

"Feeling limber."

"Good to know." Ari laughed as they sat up, cupping Dale's face and kissing her softly. She dropped her hands and gripped Dale's arms just under the elbow. She pulled, leaning backward until her ponytail touched the mat. Dale matched Ari's grip and then pulled her up and forward. Ari smiled at Dale, who kept her lips pressed tight together in an attempt to stay professional.

They finished stretching and did a light circuit of the machines. Ari stayed on the treadmill an extra ten minutes remembering how hard she'd been breathing on the day of the ransom drop. Afterward she and Dale adjourned to the sauna and showered just as the lunch crowd began filtering in.

When Ari took her phone out of her locker, she saw that she'd missed four calls, all of them from Detective Lorne. He'd left a voicemail on one of them so she listened to it as she finished dressing.

"Willow. Detective Lorne. I think I've finally figured out where Brandon Kent was racking up his debts. I might need your help getting in there, if you're willing. I'm at Police Headquarters."

Ari finished dressing quickly. As sad as it was that Missing Melody was slowly being forgotten, maybe it meant the police had more time for "minor" investigations like finding out who had killed a degenerate gambler-turned-kidnapper in a park in broad daylight. Suddenly the idea of spending a little time investigating Brandon Kent didn't seem so dull to her.

CHAPTER FOURTEEN

THE HOMICIDE floor looked suspiciously like a furniture storeroom display. Neat rows of desks formed a grid around support beams, and a row of windows along the near wall created enough natural sunlight that the overheads were turned off. Lorne's desk was near the back of the room, near a glass cube occupied by someone who preserved their privacy with a row of dark blue pleated blinds. Ari's face was still stinging from the cold, and she paused at the doorway to blow into her hands as she looked around for Lorne.

The receiving officer had obviously called ahead to let him know Ari was on her way up as he was standing and watching the door when she appeared. He was an attractive man of indeterminate age, Ari's guess hovering around either side of forty. Today he was dressed for the weather with a thick sweater over his dress shirt. His salt-and-pepper hair could stand to be cut and introduced to a comb, but he made it look charmingly rakish. He always managed to look tired, even early in the day.

He motioned her over, speaking as soon as she was within non-shouting earshot. "Do you know anything about the Wandering Wolf?"

"It's an Encyclopedia Brown story, right? Bugs Meany stole Sally's dog."

Lorne held up a printout. "It's a bar a few blocks from Brandon Kent's house. According to one of his friends, that's where he used to go to play cards. I'd go down there and see if anyone would talk to me, but I think we both know how that would turn out."

"Aw, don't get down on yourself, Detective. They just don't know you like I do."

"Funny." He noticed her tie. "What are you all dressed up for? Where's the greasy jumpsuit and baggy sweaters I've come to expect from you?"

"They're at the dry cleaners. This is my laundry day hand-me-downs."

"Well, when you get them back, how about you head down to the bar and see if you can find out anything about the games. Who runs them, if there are any regulars, how much exactly our kidnapper owed. That sort of thing."

"Is the department picking up the tab?"

"I thought Madeline Morris hired you."

Ari nodded. "She did. To get her daughter back. This is just bonus, making sure she doesn't get taken again. I only do so much for free, Detective."

"Good to know." He paused and scratched his chin. "All right. I'll talk it over with my captain and see about getting you a check."

"Then I'll see about heading down there tonight. Wandering Wolf, huh?" She raised an eyebrow.

"Worried? Because in my experience, wolves usually mean trouble."

Ari shrugged. "When it comes to people, wolves are harmless until they're given a reason not to be. I'll let you know what I find out tomorrow."

"I appreciate it."

Lorne looked at the window. "Drive safely. Looks like a storm is coming in."

Ari nodded her thanks to him and left the building. She was outside before she realized that visiting the bar would interfere with her plans to go out for a run. She cursed under her breath. Sometimes being successful and busy was more trouble than it was worth.

Ari loosened her tie as she stepped into the office. "It's amazing how unreasonable people are when you tell them they have to go to court."

"Uh-oh." Dale moved her hands from the keyboard. "Did somebody throw something at you again?"

"No. But I risk slipping on icy sidewalks just to get called names? I had two papers to serve, and somehow I managed to get flipped off five times. If I was being sued, I think I'd want to know about it. Better than losing in absentia, right?" She went into her office and Dale followed. "I'm just doing them a favor. I'm giving them the knowledge they need in order to fight, and they act like I'm the one suing them."

Dale sat next to her on the couch and motioned for her to take her shoes off. Ari obeyed and twisted to lie against the arm of the couch, placing her feet in Dale's lap. Dale took the left one first, rubbing the arch with both thumbs.

"Poor baby."

"And even worse, I have to spend the night hanging out at some stupid bar where Brandon Kent gambled away all his cash in the hopes I can find a lead to Mystery Man. So I can't run tonight after all."

Dale's humor faded to real sympathy. "Aw, I'm sorry sweetie. You could go for a run now."

Ari considered it and shook her head. "Too many people even in the parks. The last thing I need is to spend a night locked up in the kennel."

"Well..." Dale pressed her lips together. "I know you've kind of been avoiding her since that kiss, but Milo has all that space behind her house. She'd probably let you run around for an hour or so just to get it out of your system."

"I don't know..."

Dale switched to Ari's right foot. "Come on, Ari. We've seen her, what, three times since that whole thing with her kissing you." She squeezed Ari's toes through her sock. "And I never told you that there was something... else that day I helped her find her stashes."

Ari had let the indirect comment from Milo drop, but now the memory came rushing back to her. "Oh? Praytell."

"It was nothing. I was trying to get up this embankment, and I slipped. She was right behind me and caught me, and she kind of... held on for a minute. It was a very awkward moment. And I think if it had happened before you and I got together, I might have let it turn into something more." She glanced at Ari. "Don't be angry, okay?"

"I'm not." She pushed herself up on her elbows and frowned. "That was the day before she invited me out to run, and she tried to kiss me. You're saying you felt like it was a romantic moment? Like she was coming onto you?"

Dale shrugged. "Well. A little. There was a definite sense that she would have let it happen if I'd gone for it." She squeezed Ari's foot. "Don't be mad at her, Ari."

"No, I'm not. You're a beautiful woman and she'd just spent the day with you. I'd be shocked if she didn't get a little swoon-ish around you. I'm just remembering when she was coming onto *me* her logic was that wolves should be with wolves. And then right before the ransom drop, she mentioned that you and she had a moment..."

Dale pulled her head back in surprise. "She mentioned it?" She thought for a moment and dropped her gaze to Ari's throat. "Is that why you bought the collar?"

"No." Ari shrugged and sighed. "Partially. But it was the way she brought it up." She sat up and dropped her feet to the floor. "Why would she come on to both of us on the same day?"

Dale pushed her hair behind her ears. "Maybe she wants a threesome."

Ari shook her head. "I think she wants to come between us."

"Sounds like a threesome to me." Ari looked at her and Dale shrugged. "Sorry. Trying to lighten the mood. Why would she want to break us up?"

"I don't know. But I'm going to find out." She bent down to retrieve her shoes and put them back on. "I'm going to use the pretense of needing a run and head over there. I'm going to bullshit her a little and see where it goes. Are you okay with that?"

Dale reached out and eased Ari's shirt collar down. She unfastened the leather collar and pulled it off. Ari reached up and brushed the skin where it had rested, feeling suddenly naked without it. Dale put it around her fingers and held it up.

"This will be waiting when you get back. Just don't carry the ruse too far, huh?"

"I promise." She leaned in and kissed the corner of Dale's mouth, whispering, "I love you," before she kissed her properly. Dale put her free hand on the back of Ari's neck and repeated it back to her when they pulled back. Ari kissed the tip of Dale's nose and said, "One way or another, I'll find out what's going on."

"One way or the other?"

"Either she'll tip her hand or I'll beat it out of her." She winked and stood up. She put her coat back on and, not wanting to sniffle through a confrontation, took her scarf as well. "Hopefully it won't take very long. I was planning to hit the bar around eight and depending on how long it takes for me to get into the poker game... you probably shouldn't wait up for me." She cupped Dale's cheek. "I'll miss you."

"I'll miss you, too." She kissed Ari's wrist. "And hey... no matter how late it is, if Milo kisses you, come over to my place. I don't want her to be the last person you kiss if the world ends tomorrow."

Ari wanted to smile, but she was too touched. She moved her hand up into Dale's hair and pulled her close. "I spent too much time not kissing you. I don't know what I was thinking." She kissed Dale as if she was trying to make up for lost time all at once, but she finally pulled back and touched her tongue to the corner of her mouth. "Okay. I should go."

"Yeah." She wrapped the scarf around Ari's neck and tucked it up over her nose. Ari winked and Dale blew her a kiss. Ari left, confident that whatever explanation Milo had, she was prepared to handle it.

The streets were all but abandoned on the drive to Milo's house. Ari hoped that it would lead to the bar being closed early on account of the weather. If she could skip out on her obligations to Detective Lorne, it meant she could put on some thick socks and snuggle under blankets with Dale with some hot cocoa. She idly touched her neck, surprised by how much she missed the negligible weight of the leather. Maybe it wasn't the physical weight she missed.

The rental car and another vehicle she hadn't seen before were parked in the driveway of Milo's house, forcing Ari to park at the curb. She was encouraged by the fact Milo had company, especially the woman whose presence had caused Milo to sneak Ari around the front of the house so she wouldn't be seen. As she walked up the front lawn she noticed the footsteps in the snow leading back and forth from the front porch. Apparently the house had seen a lot of activity in the past twelve hours.

She tugged down the scarf and made sure the top buttons of her shirt were undone to reveal the absence of the collar. She turned her face toward the cold wind and took a few deep breaths, holding them for a second and then exhaling a cloud of pale white fog. She was huffing now, her cheeks red, her eyes wet with tears that she tried to blink away as the door opened. She turned toward it, expecting Milo, but she was startled to find a light-skinned black man staring at her instead.

"Um. Hello."

"May I help you?"

She wiped the cuff of her coat under her eye. "Uh, i-is Milo here?"

"I shall see if she's available. Please, come inside to wait." He stepped aside so she could enter. "I'll just be a moment."

She watched him ascend the stairs, her face burning as her cheeks thawed out. One sniff had told her he was a *canidae* and a smoker, but that was all she could tell from him. She walked toward the dining room door, certain she could smell the perfume of the unknown female visitor but she couldn't see anybody. She rubbed her frozen palms together, wishing she'd brought gloves, and looked toward the second floor just as Milo appeared at the top of the stairs.

"Ariadne? What are you doing here?" She cast a panicked look left and then right. "Who let you in?"

"Some guy. He didn't introduce himself." She remembered she was supposed to be an emotional wreck so she rubbed at her eyes. "I didn't realize you had company. I can go."

"Don't be silly. They're interlopers and you're a guest. What's wrong? You're totally frozzed and you look as if you've had a terrible day." Her eyes drifted down to the hollow of Ari's throat, noting the lack of a collar. Ari realized she had noticed Milo noticing it ever since it had shown up, a simple glance that now seemed to speak volumes. "Is everything all right? C'mere. Let's talk about it."

Ari feigned reluctance as Milo guided her into the dining room. She brought her hands up as if she was ashamed by tears in them, and that gave her the leeway to watch Milo. She scanned the dining room to make sure it was empty and then quickly craned her neck to look into the kitchen. She pulled out a chair.

"Have a seat. I'll get you something warm to drink."

She went into the kitchen and left Ari alone. She twisted in the chair to look behind her. Where had the doorman gone?

"Just stay here and stay quiet, right?" It was hissed, barely loud enough for Ari to hear. A few seconds later Milo came back with two mugs. "One good thing about an unwanted American in the house, they make sure you have coffee for emotionally-needful guests. How'd'ya take it?"

"Ah, black. Black is fine."

Milo handed her a mug and sat next to her. "Now what's all this about? Where's your collar?"

Ari touched her throat. "Actually it was Dale's collar. She took it back. We broke up." Saying the words hurt more than she thought it would. Even knowing that Dale was back at the office and, in a few hours, would be waiting for her to come by for a goodnight kiss, saying it out loud caused a fresh wave of tears to glisten in her eyes. "Damn it..."

"Cor... you poor thing." She put her hand on Ari's shoulder and squeezed. "I can't believe... what happened? You two seemed so... right together."

Ari scoffed. "Right. You don't have to say that."

"But I believe it. Watching the two of you... I..." She seemed to get choked up and looked away. "You seemed so happy together."

"You don't believe it," Ari said softly. "I mean, why else would you have come on to both of us the same day? You saw it. You saw that we weren't happy. I don't know why it took us so long to agree with you."

She sniffled and hugged herself, feeling nauseated by this ruse. To fake it she had to believe it, and believing that she and Dale were breaking up was too much for her. Milo touched Ari's hair and then muttered something under her breath. She stood up suddenly and walked toward the wall, her head bowed and her hands on her hips.

"Don't do this, Ariadne."

"What do you mean?"

Milo turned. "I mean *fight* for her, god damn it. Forget about what I did. Go back to her like this, let her see how much it's killin' ya to be apart from her. Tell her you made a mistake or convince her that she made one. 'Cause I can't stand it. I can't stand seein' you like this and knowin' it's my fault."

"What the hell do you think you're doing?"

Ari turned toward the man's voice. He had slipped into the dining room from the foyer, hands behind his back in a casual manner that belied the fire in his gaze.

Milo was undaunted by the daggers he stared into her. "Forget it, granddad. Look at her! I'm not doing this to her."

Ari slowly stood up, dropping the act as she looked between Milo and the old man. "Milo, what's going on?"

The man glanced at Ari as if she was an annoying bug that had just landed on his dinner plate. Then he looked back at Milo.

"What's changed, Millicent?"

"I didn't expect to like her." Milo looked apologetically at Ari. "Why couldn't you have just been a bitch?"

"I am a bitch," Ari said softly. "At least three nights of the week, I am."

Milo laughed and tears rolled down her cheeks. "Well, fuck it. The rest of the time, you're a person I respect. I've gotten in the middle of relationships before. I've broken couples up. But I won't do it to you. You love Dale and she loves you, and I'm not going to be the one who gets in the middle of it."

"So you really were trying to break us up?"

A quick nod of the head and then, as if sensing it had to be said out loud. "I was. Yeah."

"Why in the hell would you do that, Milo?"

"That... is a very long story."

The woman had spoken from behind her, from the kitchen door, but Ari kept her eyes locked on Milo. Suddenly it was very hard for her to inhale, hard for her to breathe. She clenched her teeth and felt her face grow warm as the woman joined them in the dining room. The man who had answered the door looked at the new arrival and retreated a step, deferring to the woman's authority. Milo also tensed slightly, her eyes locked just over Ari's shoulder with an uneven mixture of fear and respect.

The sound of the woman's heels, a slow tapping, sounded like a giant clock ticking off the seconds. She seemed to accept Ari wasn't going to look at her, so she walked in a wide circle around the dining room table until she was standing next to Milo.

Her hair was still brown but streaked with gray. It had been pulled back and held with a clip that let it cascade down onto her shoulders. Ari's hands felt cold, as if they'd fallen asleep. She narrowed her eyes, trying to shut out her vision of the woman in the blood-red blouse, open at the collar to reveal an oval cameo. She wore a black skirt and black stockings, her heels making her almost a full head taller than Milo. She rested a hand on Milo's shoulder, causing her to flinch. She smiled.

"It's so lovely to see you again, Ariadne."

Ari's mouth was suddenly dry. "Wish I could say the same, Mom."

Chapter Fifteen

Ari was thirteen. From the outside she was indistinguishable from the other girls in her class. A little taller, more slender, but with the same rebellious attitude her peers affected. She lived in affluence, a large home in Seward Park with a view of Lake Washington from her attic bedroom. She had friends, tentative girlfriends with whom she had kissed or cuddled with but had never gone any farther. She liked baseball, she had experimented with cigarettes and beer but had not yet found anyone who'd offered her pot.

Her secrets were larger than her friends, however. Where other girls were educated about the changes their bodies were going through via giggle-inducing film strips in Health class, Ari was sat down in the privacy of her home and given a hushed speech. She was a *canidae*. Her education began a few nights afterward, when Ari woke in the middle of the night with cramps that she knew couldn't be natural.

Gwyneth had helped her through the first horrific transformation. She'd coaxed the trembling wolf out from underneath the bed where she was cowering and held her until she calmed down. When the initial panic was passed, Gwen demonstrated a transformation of her own to show Ari what it was supposed to be like. They left the house through a doggie door and ran through the wilds of Seward Park.

The next morning Ari woke unable to move. Her entire body was stiff, like someone had poured quick-set concrete into her bed while she slept. Gwyneth, certain it was just a result of a night of overexertion tried the tough love approach. She tried to force Ari out of her bed and accidentally broke her right arm.

The *canidae* doctor who examined her revealed that Ari's body was reluctant to the change. Going from one form to the other was more painful for her than it should have been and he had no idea why. He wanted to do tests, but Gwyneth asked to speak to him privately. When he returned he gave Ari a subscription for painkillers, set a date for her to get the plaster cast on her right arm removed, and flatly told her to call if she had any problems. Ari knew before they left the doctor's office that they would never go back to that doctor again.

"I don't want to do that anymore."

"You have to, Ariadne." Eyes on the road ahead, not on her daughter. "That cast isn't going to fall off by itself."

Ari shook her head and looked out the window. "I mean the wolf thing. I don't want to do that again."

Gwyneth was quiet for a long time. Finally she said, "Well, that's not your choice. It's who you are."

"It hurts." Ari hated the tears in her eyes, the tremble in her voice.

"Of course it hurts." She reached over and touched the back of Ari's head, but Ari shrunk away so she returned her hand to the steering wheel. "It was a bad first time. In time it will hurt less, I promise. Once your body realizes what it's supposed to do, it'll stop hurting as much."

Ari was implacable. "No."

Gwyneth just sighed and shook her head. The matter was dropped.

The cast came off six weeks later, the procedure performed by a different doctor than the one who put it on. The first night she was back at home Ari found herself pacing from room to room, pausing to look out the window at the moonlight bouncing off the lake. She locked herself in her bedroom, she did exercises, she even thought about going for a jog until the itch urging her to leave the house became too strong. She took a long shower and, when she emerged, her mother was waiting in the hallway outside the bathroom.

"Nothing's worked, has it? You still feel the draw."

She bumped past her mother and continued to her bedroom. Gwyneth grabbed Ari's arm and stopped her.

"If you're going to fight it every time, you will hurt just as badly every time. The wolf will take you, and it will dominate your body. A *canidae* shares its body with a wolf, but you're making it fight. And if you fight it, the human part of you will lose."

Ari yanked her arm out of her mother's grip and slammed the bedroom door behind her.

The next night she was too in pain to get off the couch. She sobbed, clutching her mother's hand until her fingers curled and her nails darkened. Gwyneth stayed with her until the transformation was complete and then carried her outside. The wolf took over, and Ari didn't remember anything for three days. When she finally came back to herself she was in the bathtub at home, her arms and legs covered with a crosshatching of scrapes and cuts. She lunged at the toilet and retched, throwing up again when she saw something small and furry land in the toilet bowl.

Her mother found her an hour later curled in the corner of the bathroom, trembling and sobbing. Gwyneth knelt beside her, stroked Ari's hair, and whispered, "Now then. Are you going to fight it any more?"

"No, ma'am."

"Good. Good girl."

After that Ari's true education began. Lessons in evading Animal Control, in how to slip through people's backyards, avoiding people who might hurt a stray dog just for fun. Gwyneth taught her the concept of stashes, bags of clothing and money hidden in various spots of the city in case she needed them. Ari learned to love the wolf, just as Gwyneth promised she would. She would look forward to Friday nights not because of hanging out with friends or late curfews but because the weekend was the only time she could be the wolf.

By the time she was fifteen, Ari and her mother were a dynamic pair. Hunting together, terrorizing small animals, exploring their environment. Ari had come to terms with who she was by that time, with her identity as a *canidae*. She became more mature, more serious, and she became her mother's partner in crime rather than her apprentice.

It was this newfound respect that prompted Gwyneth to finally tell Ari the truth. She was born with the gene to change but not the ability. The doctors examined newborn Ariadne and sadly revealed there was no chance she could transform. So Gwyneth took Ari to a specialist, a doctor with an untested and unproven method of naturally engineering a *canidae*. Historically *canidae* were either bitten as children or it was passed on genetically. With the gene already present, part of the work was done for him, but it was still a madly dangerous procedure.

At four months old, Ariadne Willow's blood was drained. The doctor replaced it with the blood of another *canidae*, using a wolf donor so that it would match the gene already present. She survived the procedure. Gwyneth didn't say how close she had come to dying, but she refrained from saying it in a way that Ari knew it had been dire.

The betrayal was too much for Ari. She left the house for the weekend, traveling across town in wolf form just to put as much distance as possible between her and her mother. She ran to Alki Park and walked the paths, watched the boats, and left her footprints up and down the beach until the sun went down. When the visitors left, the homeless returned to claim their pieces of land. One group took pity on Ari and shared what little they had with her. She ate two slices of bread for dinner and slept with her back against a wooden pylon.

In the middle of the night she woke to the sound of crashing waves on the surf. She watched it lap against the sand, hypnotized by the movement. Finally she got to her feet, took off her shoes, and walked down the sand until the water was touching her toes. She submerged herself to the knees, then the waist. It was freezing, but she kept walking until her shirt was soaked. A wave went over her head and she pushed forward against the surge of the Sound.

Her feet left the sandbar and the force of the water threw her back toward the beach. She landed hard, spluttering and sobbing as she stared up into the sky. She rolled onto her front and saw she was being watched by one of the homeless men who had shared his food and space with her. She felt ashamed of herself, broken from the trance of self-pity that had drawn her to the waves. She curled her fingers in the sand and pushed herself up. The man nodded to her as she ran past him, and she was certain he thought she was going home.

At that point home was still a possibility. Ari thought there might be a chance she would forgive her mother, and that she could get over the hurt and pain enough to move past it. But for that night, she had to be on her own.

First she missed a day of school, and then a week. She found a place to stay, a warm and safe place where she could forget what had been done to her. Two weeks after her arrival there she snuck off and transformed by herself for the first time. She took the long way back home and lurked in the shadows until her mother came outside. She stood on the porch for a long time and, although she never looked in Ari's direction, she knew she'd been spotted.

Ari waited until her mother went back inside before she turned her back on her home once and for all. She went back to her life on the streets, which led her to Eva and then to Glory and to Dale. And somehow as far as she had come, the path of her life led her back to another large house in a different affluent neighborhood, staring across the dining room table at the woman she'd long ago cut out of her life.

"What the hell are you doing here?"

Gwyneth smiled. "I paid for the house. Well, with Benjamin's help." She gestured at the man who had let Ari in when she arrived. "Millicent needed a place to stay while she was in town, so I agreed to finance it."

"You paid a woman to come here from England to break up me and Dale? Wow, that's... I've heard of parents disapproving of a relationship, but damn woman." She started for the door. "Whatever you have planned, forget it. I'm done being your paper doll."

Benjamin moved to block her exit. She glared at him but he maintained a look of apologetic ambivalence. "This is not the way we wanted things to happen."

Milo scoffed and pulled out a chair to sit down at the table. "Yeah. Tell her what the original plan was."

Gwyneth cleared her throat. "Ariadne, please have a seat. If you're going to be so bullheaded about this, then you deserve to know the truth." Benjamin's eyes widened at Gwyneth and she shrugged. "She's obviously not going to let it go. Our original plan won't work, and Millicent's plan is impossible now. We have to salvage this before wolf manoth."

"Before *what?*" Ari said.

Gwyneth gestured at the seat across from Milo. Ari hesitated, reluctant to follow any of her mother's orders. She walked around the table and sat next to Milo. Gwyneth sighed and closed her eyes before she took the seat she'd offered Ari for herself. Benjamin sat down next to her, and suddenly Ari felt like she was about to be fired by Donald Trump.

"Where should I begin?" Gwyneth asked.

"The beginning is good."

Gwyneth smiled. "The beginning? All right... eleven hundred years ago, *canidae* thrived in Great Britain..."

Ari rolled her eyes. "Oh, for crying out loud."

"That's the beginning." She continued. "We outnumbered humans and made it impossible for them to thrive and spread the way they wanted to. We were savages in those days, but show me a species that isn't a little wild for their first millennium or so. We killed their livestock. We desecrated their graves for the sport of it. Eventually the king had enough of it. Tributes were paid with wolf pelts, and criminals were spared the death penalty in exchange for an annual fine of wolf tongues.

"The king knighted a group of men to hunt and kill as many *canidae* as possible. They trapped us, destroyed the forests where we made our homes, slaughtered our children... eventually we got the message we were unwelcome so we left. We spread out to Europe, Asia, Africa... The king was satisfied and disbanded the knights. Some of them went peacefully to retirement, but others..." She looked down at her hands, flat on the table. "Sometimes when a soldier is trained to do something well, that becomes the only thing they can do. The knights became hunters, dedicated to hunting us down wherever we ran."

Ari nodded. "And yadda, yadda, yadda, now I have to break up with my girlfriend. Thanks, it all makes sense now."

Gwyneth pursed her lips. "If you're not going to pay attention then I'm not sure what the purpose of explaining is."

"Fine. Can you please just get to the point?"

"The two species were at war for centuries. Our side was hardly blameless. We retaliated. We were cast as monsters so we decided to earn the title. We slaughtered them. They massacred us. We desecrated their graves. They burned our children. Hundreds of years passed. We became creatures of myth, hiding in the woods and transforming in secret to avoid the blade.

"Events came to a head in the early nineteenth century during the Napoleonic Wars. A *canidae* named Simon Lehner wanted to become a god to our people. He set humans and *canidae* against each other hoping to cull the herd of any of us who didn't kneel before him. He was stopped when a hunter and a *canidae* realized what he was doing and joined forces to stop him. They fought together, bled for each other, and in the end they were victorious. But more importantly, but the time the last sword was sheathed, the hunter and the wolf had fallen in love with each other."

Ari stood up and turned to leave.

"Where are you going?"

"Johanna Brion and Agatha Westreich," Ari said. "My bedtime story. You told me this bedtime story when I was six, Gwyneth."

"Because I knew that one day it would be necessary. Johanna and Agatha were real, Ariadne. After years of bloodshed and fighting, they gathered their respective leaders and proposed a truce. They were handfasted to one another as a symbolic gesture, a joining of the two races. For the first time in eight hundred years, *canidae* could live in peace. Hunters put down their swords. We declared a truce, and it held for nearly one hundred and fifty years."

Benjamin said, "But the truce is fracturing. Our numbers have grown and, at the same time, the hunters have grown bored and they are coming for us again."

Ari looked at her mother. "I thought you said the hunters stopped hunting two hundred years ago."

Gwyneth nodded. "Yes, after eight centuries. By that point, hunting was a part of them as much as being a wolf is part of us. They passed down the legacy to their children, taught them how to fight and how to kill, but they were inert. They were a silent army with no enemy to fight passing along wisdom so it wouldn't die out. Just in case."

Benjamin said, "In the sixties, the hunters began attacking us with guerilla tactics. It took us a while to realize what was happening but eventually we understood the truce was falling apart. There has been no true declaration of war as of yet, but we fear it's imminent. Traditionally January is the start of a time known as wolf manoth, when hunters move in force to kill as many wolves as they can. We believe they're gearing up to start the war over again, and they're using the upcoming wolf manoth as an excuse to draw first blood. We've been monitoring their movements and we believe they are massing in America in order to begin the assault here, in the Pacific Northwest. Washington, Idaho and British Columbia have such large numbers of *canidae* that they can make a sizeable dent in our population."

Gwyneth said, "A group of us attended a summit on a neutral ground. We agreed to renew the peace between our races by recreating Johanna and Agatha's handfasting. The human delegates chose a *canidae* to represent our people. Millicent was relatively well-known due to her wealth, so she was chosen."

Ari looked at Milo, who was steadfastly staring at her hands.

"And the *canidae* delegates chose a human to represent the other side. Our decision was for the delegate to be Ms. Frye."

Ari looked accusingly at her mother. "And how exactly did they even know Dale existed, Mom?"

Gwyneth didn't avert her gaze. "Yes. I was a member of the summit, and I nominated Ms. Frye. She is a rare candidate, Ariadne. Thanks to you she not only knows about our people, she accepts us. She has fought alongside and bled for a *canidae* just as Johanna Brion did two centuries ago. I'm not sure you understand how rare it is for us to interrelate the way you are. Humans are afraid of us, and *canidae* have been taught how to distrust humans."

Ari's eyes were wet. "Go to hell."

Milo said, "Ari, you have to understand the stakes. If this treaty doesn't happen, then the hunters will come back in force and hundreds of *canidae* will be killed. Maybe they'll get all of us this time."

Gwyneth said, "Either this ceremony takes place or we go to war."

"You made me a wolf. I was born a human. So forgive me if I don't want to sacrifice the most important person in my life for your little treaty."

Gwyneth sighed and stood up. She took put her hands into her pockets and stepped around the table to where Ari was standing.

"Regardless of how you came into this world, Ari, you are one of us. The hunters have a new weapon they'll be using. It's called wolfsbane." She took her hand out of her pocket and Ari saw she was holding a clamshell case. "Would you like to see how it works?" She opened the top and blew a cloud of fine powder into Ari's face.

"Are you insane?" Benjamin shouted. Ari had both hands over her eyes but she heard Milo's chair hit the floor as she jumped to her feet.

"What the hell?" Ari leaned forward, rubbing at her eyes as the burning powder worked its way in. She lifted her head, saw her mother in front of her, and lunged. Benjamin managed to grab her arm and spin her around. He held her hand in his and extended the wrist so that her elbow was inverted, forcing her to the ground. Ari pistoned her other arm out and hit him in the solar plexus, giving her a moment to get free. She yanked her hand away, spun on her knees, and hurled herself at her mother.

Ari smelled blood, could almost taste it in her mouth as she slammed into Gwyneth. She grabbed her mother's neck and jumped, taking both feet off the ground and slamming them into the soft skin of Gwyneth's stomach. Gwyneth fell back onto the table and Ari perched on top of her. She felt her face twisting into a mask, her lower jaw extending out as her eyes turned black. She lifted her hand, fingers twisted into claws, and held the pose for a moment as she savored the fear she saw in her mother's eyes.

Milo pressed the Taser into the small of Ari's back and pulled the trigger. Ari howled in pain, giving Benjamin and Milo the opportunity to pull her off. They were none too gentle, hurling her to the floor. Milo flung herself across Ari's mid-section and held her to the ground as Benjamin pinned her arms.

Gwyneth was ashen, shaken by the attack, but she straightened her clothes and looked down at Ari.

"Millicent, did you bring the sedative?"

"On the table."

Gwyneth picked up the small black box and knelt. Ari felt her pants leg pushed up, the pinprick of a needle on the tight skin of her calf. Gwyneth stood again and looked down at Ari.

"Deny your true self as much as you want, Ariadne. But you've just proven that you are one of us no matter how much you protest. When this war comes, you will either be a soldier or a casualty. The time to choose is now."

She crouched down as the drugs began to do their work. Ari's rage, obviously induced but not wholly created by the wolfsbane, collided with the sedative and the two fronts created a storm in her mind. Her mother's voice sounded hollow as her body began to go limp.

"This is a war, Ariadne. And in a war, we are asked to make sacrifices. If you're not willing to give up Dale, then I am more than willing to give up the daughter who turned her back on me. Dale will mourn, but then she will do what she must in order to save lives. She learned to love one wolf... she can learn to love another."

Ari's vision swam. She saw Milo looming above her mother and the fight went out of her. The drugs won the battle and she passed out.

CHAPTER SIXTEEN

THE SCENE she woke up to was so dreamlike that she couldn't swear that she was actually awake or if it was some bizarre fevered hallucination. She was in an enormous four-poster bed and the windows were completely blanked out, as if the world had been erased. The room was so cold that Ari couldn't feel body under the blankets. Or maybe that was the drugs. Everything in the room seemed to be painted a monochrome blue-gray except for the woman sitting by her side. Dale. In a black shirt and a blue scarf, face bright pink and red hair pinned up at her temples by small silver barrettes, Dale was a splash of life and color in the dreary fog. Her eyes were wet and she was holding Ari's hand in hers.

Then, seemingly in the blink of an eye, Dale's shirt became white, and she was stretched at the foot of the bed. Then she was sitting up and gently running a wet washcloth over Ari's upper arm. She noticed Ari's eyes were open.

"Ari?"

She was sure she would fall asleep again. She waited for the quality of light to change, waited for Dale to disappear or jump across the room, but she just leaned closer and put her hand on Ari's cheek. The palm was unbelievably warm, and it was enough to wake Ari enough that she became convinced it was for real this time.

"Hi."

Dale smiled. "Hey there. How do you feel?"

"I don't know."

Dale touched the washcloth to Ari's forehead. "Yeah, she said that you might be a little out of sorts when you woke up."

"She?" Ari's eyes opened. "Mom?"

"She's gone. And Milo said her grandpa went back to England just before the storm hit. It's just me and Milo here."

Ari's expression changed, but it was a lateral shift. "Oh. You and Milo."

Dale nodded. "She explained everything to me when I got here. Apparently she kicked everyone else out before she called me. You've been fading in and out for almost three days. How much do you remember?"

"Everything that happened in the kitchen. They told you everything?"

"Yeah." Dale reached into her pocket and held up Ari's collar. She let it hang from her fingers for a moment, then leaned forward. "Lift your head a little?"

Ari did as she was told and Dale put the collar back on her. The effort of holding her head up for fifteen seconds was all Ari could manage, and Dale guided her head back down onto the pillow. Ari closed her eyes at the soft touch of Dale's fingers on the throat, and Dale leaned forward to kiss her dry lips.

Ari touched the collar. "That feels better."

Dale smiled. "She told me about the ceremony. It wouldn't work, Ari. The first time it worked because Johanna and Agatha were in love."

Ari shook her head, dismissing the conversation for the moment. "Can I have some water?"

"Oh, shit. Yes."

Dale reached for the nightstand and poured from a tall plastic pitcher. She tried to angle the glass so Ari could take a drink without sitting up, then gave up. She took a drink, then lowered her glistening lips to Ari's mouth. She stroked Ari's cheek as she pushed the water into her mouth, and Ari closed her eyes as she accepted the tepid offering. It could have been ambrosia as far as she was concerned. Dale pecked the corners of Ari's mouth and sat up again.

"If all it takes is a *canidae* marrying a human, then I'll just marry you."

"You'd do that?" Dale asked softly.

Ari shrugged. "I'm planning on doing it someday anyway. If the schedule has to be sped up to stop a genocide, then so be it. There are worse reasons to get married."

Dale smiled. "Well. As sweet as that hypothetical proposal is - and I would hypothetically accept - I already brought it up to Milo. Apparently it won't work."

"Why not? Because the humans chose her as the candidate instead of me?"

"I don't know. She said it was a personal reason."

Ari closed her eyes. "Detective Lorne must be going crazy. I said I'd check out that bar for him. I've been here for three days? Shit... I've got~"

"Ari, you're not going anywhere. Neither is..." She looked at the window and waved her hand. "Hell. No one in the city is going anywhere."

"What?"

"It's a blizzard, Ari. It was blowing in the night you came over here, and it was really starting to pick up when Milo brought me over. No one expected it, but it's stretched from Tacoma almost up to Vancouver. It's a mess. Roads and bridges are out and iced over, we lost power yesterday about... well, about a day ago. For the time being we're stranded. You're lucky you didn't miss much."

Ari grunted and shifted under the blankets. She supposed it could be worse; the storm could have come in before her mother left and stranded them all together. She found Dale's hand without opening her eyes and linked their fingers together.

The next time Ari woke, Milo was in her room. She was wearing a red and black turtleneck sweater and looked as if she hadn't slept in a week.

"I'm out."

Ari blinked at her.

"The agreement. I'm not going to go through with it. They'll have to compromise. They'll have to decide you and Dale are the right candidates and, even if they don't, I refuse to participate. Their original plan was just to take Dale. Leave you a note that said she had gotten tired of the danger and all the *canidae* shit, and they would tell her that you were dead." She chuckled and shook her head. "They're not the smartest pups in the litter, ya know?"

Ari managed a smile. After a moment of heavy silence, Ari

said, "You should have told us from the beginning."

"Yeah." She was standing by the window and hugged herself against the chill. "Like I said, I'd done this sort of thing before. Dive-bombed relationships just for the hell of it. Figured this was more of the same, but I wasn't prepared to like you so much. Both of you. Let me know if you need anything. I got a pretty full pantry you and Dale are welcome to take advantage of."

"What was the shit Gwyneth blew in my face? Wolfsbane?"

Milo winced. "You have to believe that I had no idea she was going to pull that. It was insanity, Ari. Her own daughter..."

Ari snorted. "You'd be amazed at what that woman has done to her daughter. Does it always hit that hard?"

"Yeah. Sometimes worse. Hunters came up with it by accident, discovered turns us feral without a transformation. Your mother is worried that they're going to release it in Seattle, let us go ape-shit, and then come in and sweep up the mess. That way it doesn't look like they're slaughtering innocent people, they're taking care of dangerous killers."

"You believe that?"

Milo shrugged. "Makes sense, right? You saw what it does first-hand. Imagine that on a grand scale, sweeping through Seattle and infecting every *canidae* it touches. We go crazy and the hunters save the day. It's bottled justification for murder. Hunters have done a lot worse."

"Like what?"

Milo pursed her lips and leaned against the wall. "Okay. A *canidae* woman was at college when a couple of other students realized what she was. The boys were sons of hunters, so they'd been taught that *canidae* are real. And now they had a real-live one to play with. So they spent a few nights tracking her movements, stalking her, just to see if they could do it. They were just boys playing until one night when they realized the wolf was all by herself in a big empty room. They may have gone hunting with their dads when they were young, but this wasn't an animal. This was just a pretty girl sitting in a library doing research for a paper. They couldn't kill her any easier than they could have killed a random shopkeeper.

"But she was a wolf. And they had been brought up with the legacy of being hunters. So the four of them surrounded her. Though she knew about the history, she never expected to be confronted by hunters. Far as she knew, the peace was still in place. They harassed her a little, teased her, but then it started to get mean. She tried to leave peacefully and they let her get as far as the courtyard before one of them knocked her down."

Ari wanted to tell her to stop the story, but she knew that it was the kind of tale that had to be finished once it was started. Milo's voice was detached, flat.

"They finished with her about an hour later. At one point they were almost seen so they carried her to one of their dorm rooms so they wouldn't be interrupted. When they finally got their fill of the fun and games, one of them drove her to a bus stop. Told her to consider herself lucky because most hunters would've just killed her. He made her say thank you 'fore he let her out of the car."

"Did the police ever catch them? Punish them?"

"Nah. No reason to make the report, right?"

"I'm sorry, Milo."

Milo shook her head. "It's not my story. It's your mother's. She found out she was pregnant a bit after that, and decided to keep the baby. Remember what she said about hunters getting it in their DNA over the past thousand years or so? Your father was a hunter, Ari, and your mother was a *canidae*. That's why you couldn't change when you were born. Your natures were fighting each other. Gwen just chose a winner. And that's why you're not a viable candidate for the ceremony. You're tainted with hunter DNA."

Ari's mind was swimming.

"I'm not saying don't hate her. God, what she did to you... I can't even imagine. I'm only saying maybe accept that she had a reason for what she did." She started toward the door. "I'm going downstairs. You want anything?"

"No."

"Want me to send Dale up?"

Ari nodded, and Milo slipped out of the room. Ari looked at the snow-blanked window and sank back against the pillows, trying to come to terms with the information she had just been given. She'd always known she wasn't the product of a loving relationship, but to find out the truth so bluntly was harsh. She thought about all the questions she'd asked growing up, begging for stories about her father. Gwyneth eventually demanded silence on the subject when Ari was ten, insisting that there are some things it's just better off not knowing. As much energy as she'd put into hating her mother over the years, she could feel her resolve slipping just a little now that she knew what she'd gone through.

The door cracked open and Dale stuck her head in. "Hey..."

Ari motioned her to the bed. Dale slipped out of her shoes, crawled onto the bed, and Ari cradled her close.

It had been a week since Ari's last transformation, and the wolf didn't care that she was recuperating from what amounted to a drug overdose. She was up and out of bed, wearing an outfit borrowed from Milo, and she could feel the animal clawing at the corners of her mind. She didn't know what it expected; even if she transformed there was no way she would let it outside. The drifts were almost up to the second story on the north-facing side, and the backyard was an unbroken sea of white.

On one of her meandering trips through the house she crossed paths with Milo in the sitting room. Milo smiled knowingly.

"Going a bit mad, huh?"

Ari nodded at the window. "I keep looking out the windows hoping that if the wolf sees the snow it'll realize running is a lost cause. It doesn't seem to have gotten the message yet."

"Yeah. They can be a bit stubborn." She hunched her shoulders and looked longingly at the door. Finally she tossed her head to get the hair out of her face and looked at Ari. "You know, we don't have to wait until the snow melts to go out. It's a big house. It's mine. Who cares about a few scratch marks on the floor? Better than freezing our tails off out in that mess."

Ari hesitated. She felt like she should refuse on principle, but the urge was even stronger now that there was a potential outlet.

"I don't know if it's such a good idea so soon after being sick."

"You'll be fine. Besides, I've been meaning to talk to you about some pain management techniques. I know a few good tricks we could use so you maybe wouldn't hurt so bad. C'mon."

"Where are we going?"

Milo walked backward so she could face Ari. "We're about to take off our clothes and do breathing exercises together. I think we both would feel a lot more comfortable if Dale was in the room acting as chaperon."

"I think she'd feel more comfortable with that, too."

They found Dale in the library, eager to put aside the book she'd been reading to supervise their deep-breathing session. Ari was in her undershirt and panties, and Milo was wearing baggy shorts and a tank top. Their legs were crossed in front of them and they were close enough that their knees were almost touching. Dale had turned out the lights but the sun was reflecting off the snow through the window so that the room was still shockingly bright.

"The massages are a great idea, but you've been focused on managing the pain once it's begun. It's great and it's brilliant. I'm not surprised it's helped you. But a big part is properly preparing yourself for the transformation. Ari, your body wasn't made for the change. It's not a painless experience for any of us, not really, but you're suffering much more than you need to be. It's the same thing that happens to the people who were bitten as kids when they grow up."

Dale said, "How did you learn about these methods?"

"I had a girlfriend from Sussex who was bitten when she was seven. She was big into trying new ways to manage her pain. Okay, Ariadne... deep breaths. Close your eyes and relax. No tension whatsoever. The world outside is blank and white and your mind should be the same. The wolf is in you. It's a part of you always even if you're on two legs. You feel her, you can hear her, just like she can hear you when you're on four legs. Your body wants to fight the change, but there's no reason to. The wolf has just as much right to the body as you do. Deep breaths."

Her voice had taken on a different cadence, and Ari found herself hanging on every syllable. She breathed in through her nose and released it through her lips. Her hands were resting lightly on her thighs, her feet tucked underneath her knees.

"Don't fight your wolf, Ari. You like how it feels when she takes over, especially times like now. When it's been so long and you're aching to let her take over."

"Yeah." It was barely spoken aloud, just a word carried on a quiet exhale. Her skin was tingling, as if anticipating the transformation.

"Okay. I'm going to keep my eyes closed out of courtesy, but it's time to undress. All right?"

"Yeah."

They undressed quickly and then sat on their knees facing each other. Ari took a deep breath and let her hands hang limp by her sides. Her fingers were twitching, their movements out of her control as something deep inside her began to swell and crest. Ari lifted her chin and parted her lips, and her right arm lifted as if pulled by a string.

"Dale..."

"I'm here."

"Don't look. I know you hate it when I change, so don't~"

Dale wrapped her fingers around Ari's outstretched hand, kissed the knuckles, and let it go. "I'm here for you, Ari. Completely and totally."

"I~" The words 'love you' transformed into a gasp, and then her mouth wasn't the proper shape to form words. She sagged backwards, dropping on her rear end and then rolling onto hands and knees as her body contorted. Her eyes snapped open and she saw Milo passing through the same transformation, her small breasts transformed into a convex breastplate covered with fine white fur.

Within seconds she and Milo were standing and facing each other in the middle of the room, giving their faces tentative sniffs before Ari moved over to Dale. She pressed her face against Dale's side, and Dale ruffled her fur with her fingernails curved into talons. Ari arched her back at the rough massage, making tiny sounds of pleasure before she pulled back. Milo was waiting by the door, so Dale smiled and petted Ari's head and nodded.

"Go on. Go play with your friend."

Ari licked Dale's palm, then turned and ran out of the room. Dale snickered and stood to follow them just to make sure they didn't run into any closed doors.

CHAPTER SEVENTEEN

THE WEATHER conspired to keep Seattle in permafrost for the length of the season. At noon the mercury climbed just enough to start thawing out the top layer of snow, but after dark it plummeted back down to re-freeze the melt until there was nothing but glass-smooth dunes as far as the eye could see. After a few flickering false starts, the power came back on at Milo's home long enough for them to watch a press conference where the mayor request power rationing. They didn't want to stress the generators by having everyone suddenly start switching on their computers and televisions and heaters, so they restricted their usage to cooking and raising the heat to bearable levels. Several major thoroughfares had been cleared to allow the city to stutter back to life, but again the mayor was requesting people stay off the streets except in the case of an emergency.

Ari and Milo were now making daily transformations, stretching their wolf muscles with races through the front hallway and up and down the stairs. At the moment Ari was in human form and dressed in a shirt and skirt she had borrowed from Milo. She was at the window, watching the water trickle off the roof so she could see when it turned from liquid to icicles.

In the parlor, Milo was playing the piano. Ari thought it was maybe something by Vienna Teng, but she couldn't identify the specific song. There was a break in the music and Ari heard footsteps behind her. Even without cheating with her advanced sense of smell, she knew who it was and smiled.

"Am I intruding on your brooding?"

Ari shook her head. "C'mere."

Dale crossed the room and slipped her arms around Ari's waist, hugging her from behind. She kissed the back of Dale's neck. "As hot as you look in it, you must be freezing in that skirt. Come sit on the couch with me."

Ari turned away from the sun-gleaming snow, squinting as her eyes adjusted to the relative dark of the room. Dale took Ari's hand to guide her to the couch, but Ari was more concerned with her partner's outfit. It was a giant red plaid shirt that hung to her knees and obscured her hands with billowing sleeves. A belt was cinched at the waist to make it a skirt, and she was wearing pants that were at least twice her usual size.

"What are you wearing?"

"Don't mock me."

"No, no." She stepped back and ran her eyes up and down Dale's ensemble with an appreciative head-tilt. "You are a lumberjack and that is *very* okay. Where did you get these, though? They're not Milo's, are they?"

"No, they're from a bag her grandpa left here when he left. Unlike the *canidae* in this house, I have things like breasts and hips so I can't borrow Milo's clothes like you can."

"I know you have breasts and hips. I'm a big fan of both. And I've enjoyed those skintight little T-shirts you've been wearing."

They sat on the couch and Dale tucked her feet up under her. Ari settled against her side, and Dale stretched her arm across Ari's shoulders to toy with her hair.

"What are you thinking about?"

"Everything that's happening. If this storm had hit while Jenna was still missing, or if Melody Scott is still out there somewhere. I mean, if she was just lost instead of abducted, there's no way she's still..." She let her voice trail off and Dale put her head on Ari's shoulder. Ari kissed Dale's forehead. "And I'm thinking about this whole mess with the *canidae*. I'm so sorry you got involved in it."

"You came with baggage. Who doesn't?" She sat up and they kissed. "You're worth a little global conspiracy." She settled closer to Ari. "Can I ask you something?"

"Sure."

"You and Milo both said that this whole thing is based on a bedtime story...?"

Ari shrugged. "Well, apparently it's a bedtime story that was based in reality. Do you want me to tell it to you?" Dale nodded against Ari's shoulder. She searched her memory for a time when Ari's mother was a mentor and guide instead of a manipulative monster. She remembered her bedroom, and her mother sitting on the edge of the bed and quietly speaking as Ari drifted off to sleep.

"This is an old story," Ari began. Without thinking she had slipped into the same cadence and tone her mother had always used. "A story of a hunter who disguised her gender so she could go to war. It's the story of a *canidae* who was so determined to protect her pack that she did the unthinkable and trusted the hunter. And it's the story of a dog that thought himself to be a messiah." She stroked Dale's hair and quietly told the story.

"Children were being killed throughout Prussia. It was a time before Grimm, a world where *canidae* were known threats. The soldier Johanna Brion, recently returned from a decisive loss with Napoleon's forces in Russia, returned to protect her people from the beasts in the woods. Agatha Westreich, whose pack was endangered by the families of young victims, was also determined to find the true culprit and bring him to justice.

"The wolf and the hunter clashed when they met. But they were as strong as they were wise, and they knew they could only find the truth together. So they put aside the hatred and mistrust of centuries and joined forces. They found a *canidae* named Simon Lehner whose followers killed children in order to incite the humans to war with the wolves. The wolves would then retaliate."

Dale frowned. "To what end? I mean, what does that accomplish?"

"Humans would kill wolves, and wolves would kill humans. By the time the dust settled, the only *canidae* left standing would be those loyal to Simon. He would become the leader of the species just by default. And then his army would grow and he'd sweep out across the continent."

"But Johanna and Agatha stopped him."

"They did." Ari stroked Dale's arm. "They learned to fight together, to trust each other, and then they fell in love. It was the first time anyone had ever heard of a human and a *canidae* becoming intimately involved."

Dale put her hand on Ari's stomach and chuckled. "I think I

have a new pair of personal heroes. I owe them a lot."

"So do I," Ari whispered. "They defeated Lehner and then traveled around stopping his word from spreading. Eventually they were able to create the truce by marrying each other."

"Mm."

Ari stroked the back of Dale's hand. "You know I'd marry you, right?"

Dale lifted her head and looked at Ari to see if she was joking, or maybe if she'd misspoken. "What?"

Ari shrugged. "Come on, Dale. We've been together for five years now."

"Yeah, but we both slept with a lot of people during the first four years of that."

"We took a while to get where we needed to be, sure. But now that we're here, I'm not giving up what we have. Not if we have some stupid fight, not if anyone tries to come between us, not even if breaking up with you would stop a war. I can't see a life without you, and I can't see a life with you where we're not partners in every sense of the word. When you take all of that into consideration, marriage seems microscopic in comparison. I'm going to marry you someday. This would just be moving up the time table."

Dale smiled. "But it wouldn't work. For the ceremony, I mean."

Ari shook her head and decided not to go into her parentage. "No. The summit chose Milo, so apparently it has to be her. And with my hunter's blood... neither side would ever let me represent them."

"Mm. Too bad. That would have been a nice compromise."

"Yeah." She bent down and lightly brushed their lips together. Dale tilted her head up, wet her lips, and Ari took advantage of the move to capture Dale's tongue. Dale whimpered and put her hand flat on Ari's chest, curling her fingers in the material before gently pushing her away and turning her face so that Ari's lips brushed across her cheek to her ear.

"Stop, stop..."

"Sorry."

"No, it's not bad." She cleared her throat and sat up a little straighter. She was flush, something she tried to hide by raking her fingers through her hair. She dropped her hand to the collar of her borrowed shirt and glanced toward the door to make sure they were still alone. "You and Milo aren't the only ones who are feeling an 'itch' that they need to scratch."

Ari mouthed, "oh," and glanced toward the door as well. They had been sleeping in the same room, but neither had really felt up to being romantic considering the way sound seemed to carry in the large, quiet house. Without the white noise to drown them out, every whisper seemed to echo. Ari pressed closer to Dale.

"I didn't know you were feeling amorous."

"Amorous?" She snorted dismissively. "I'm horny, Ari. I want to be with you. But with this damn snow..." She took a deep breath to steady herself, eyes locked on Ari's lips. "We just need a moratorium on the kisses that make me think naughty things."

"Or," Ari suggested in a low voice, "we could just be very quick and very quiet." She pushed herself forward and twisted, easing Dale's legs apart with her hips as she dropped to her knees in front of the couch.

Dale's eyes widened. "Ariadne... no... oh, wait..."

Ari undid the lower buttons of Dale's shirt and bowed down to kiss her navel. Dale pressed herself into the couch, trying to escape by passing through it as Ari teased with the tip of her tongue.

"Okay..." She ran her hands through Ari's hair and closed her eyes, sighing heavily with resignation. "Hurry, hurry..."

Ari smiled. "I can already tell it won't take too long." She wet her lips as she tugged down Dale's borrowed pants. The waist was wide enough that they came down easily, Dale working her hips from side to side and then lifting her feet. Ari kissed the inside of Dale's knee, making her hiss, and then eased her legs apart and began kissing her thighs. Dale whimpered and brought her hand up to her mouth, biting her index finger as she watched with half-lidded eyes. Her toes curled as Ari moved her hand higher.

"Did you borrow Benjamin's underwear, too?" Ari asked. The Y-fronts actually looked sexy, and she slipped her finger under the flap to tease Dale's hair. Dale dropped her leg heavily on Ari's shoulder and tried to pull her closer.

"I thought you said you were going to make this fast."

"I never make promises like that." But she relented. She pushed her finger and thumb apart, spreading the underwear to reveal pink flesh, and she lightly teased with the tip of her tongue.

Dale sucked in a breath through clenched teeth and arched her back. Ari pushed her hand up under Dale's shirt to her breast, squeezing it gently. Dale had been forced to go without a bra until the one she'd worn to the house was hand-washed, and Ari circled the nipple with the pad of her thumb until it was hard enough to pinch. Dale squirmed and murmured softly, dropped her hand to Ari's head, and opened her eyes to look down.

Instead she saw a shadow moving along the hallway outside the library. "Shit." Ari looked up, then flared her nostrils to indicate she had picked up a scent. Dale was frozen in place as Milo stepped into the room, saw what was happening, and froze. She looked at Ari, at Dale, and then took a step backward.

"No~" The word was just barely uttered, but as Dale had feared it was loud in the silence of the house. "Stay."

Ari and Milo both looked at her. Ari's head had lifted slightly, her lips still only wet from her own tongue instead of Dale's juices. Milo put a hand on the wall to pivot away, shaking her head in apology as she tried to shrink out of sight. Dale swallowed, dipped her chin once in confirmation, and then gently guided Ari's head back between her legs. Her hand was shaking and she was holding her breath, but after hesitating a moment to give Dale time to change her mind, Ari kissed her again.

Milo slumped against the doorframe, a blush rising in her cheeks and her hands resting limply on her hips. Dale brushed Ari's hair with her hands, focused on her, lifting her hips to meet Ari's tongue, moaning quietly and resting her head against the back of the couch to focus on her pleasure. She flattened one foot on Ari's back, bringing the other up to rest on her shoulder. Ari kept her hand on Dale's breast, the other holding her underwear out of the way, moaning as her tongue pushed deeper with every stroke.

When Dale opened her eyes again, Milo's jeans were undone. The fingers of one hand were under the waistband of black panties, and Dale wet her lips as she watched the muscles of her forearm move. She rolled her eyes back in her head and wriggled lower on the couch, angling her lower body up to meet Ari's mouth. Ari thrust her tongue deep and Dale cried out softly.

"Don't stop, Ari."

Ari dropped her hand from beneath the shirt and blindly sought Dale's hand. They linked fingers and squeezed. Dale bared her teeth, grunting as she fought to hold off her orgasm. She forced her eyes open and saw Milo's hand moving faster, her thumb hooked on her underwear, her mouth opened so that her ragged breathing was soft and inaudible.

"Puppy," Dale sighed, almost unaware she had spoken aloud until she felt the rumble of Ari's responding moan rolling across sensitive skin.

Dale pulled her lips back against her teeth, eyes squeezed shut, and tightened her grip on Ari's hand as she came. Ari stayed in position for a few seconds, then moved Dale's underwear back in place and patted the soft cotton of the crotch. Dale's entire body hitched at the light slaps on such a tender area, and she pulled Ari up to kiss her. Their tongues dueled and Dale sighed as she let Ari's weight settle on top of her and between her legs.

Ari finally broke the kiss and looked over her shoulder. Dale looked as well and saw Milo had vanished. They looked at each other again and kissed.

"How much did she stay for?"

"Most of it." Some of Ari's hair had fallen forward so Dale twisted it around her finger. "Are you mad I told her to stay?"

Ari shook her head. "No. She needed to see for herself... she can't get between us."

Dale sighed and dropped her hand to Ari's collar. "Never."

"How's that itch of yours doing?"

"Scratched. For now." She kissed Ari again and then looked past her at the door. She lowered her voice to a whisper. "And I don't think I'm going to be as nervous about Milo *hearing* us if you had an itch of your own."

Ari chuckled. "I'll keep that in mind." She kissed the tip of Dale's nose. "Love you."

"I love you, too, puppy." She licked her lips and looked down. "Don't take this the wrong way, but it's cold in here and I would really love to put my pants back on now."

"Oh... right."

She sat up and retrieved Dale's pants. As she put them on, Ari looked toward the hallway and wondered how far Milo had retreated. She smelled the air and could tell immediately that Dale wasn't the only one who'd gotten scratched. She smiled and went to keep Dale warm on the couch.

They didn't see Milo again until that night. The pantry was running bare, which meant that going out would constitute an emergency. And if they left for groceries, it only made sense that they would go back to one of their apartments until the weather allowed them to go back to work. Ari found Milo in the kitchen preparing a hodgepodge meal from what they had available. She coughed quietly into her fist to announce her presence before she approached.

"Need a hand?"

"Sure, if you've got one to spare."

Ari smiled. "At the moment I have two." She joined Milo at the center island and examined what they had to work with. "What is this?"

"Rice with various things chopped up in it. We don't have any meat so it's all veggie."

"Do you have any salad dressing?"

Milo tilted her head to the side and went to the fridge. She searched the door, clucking her tongue until she found a bottle. "Italian. And..." She clicked the top open and gave it a whiff before handing it to Ari. "Ah, it didn't go bad. What are you planning?"

"Well, it's not going to be much without chicken, but I think I can make a nice vegetarian soup. You have broth, right?"

"I got more broth than I know what to do with."

Ari motioned for her to bring it over as she chopped the vegetables. "I got an education in how to make a lot out of a little after I left home."

"Cool." Milo rested her elbow on the island, chin in her hand as she watched Ari. "This is probably as far as we can go with the ingredients on hand."

Ari nodded. "Yeah. I talked about it with Dale earlier. We should probably try to leave tomorrow. The neighborhood streets are still pretty icy but I heard it's clear sailing the closer you get to Downtown."

"Yeah. I just hope it's, ah, not... related to what happened earlier. In the library."

Ari looked up. "Not at all. Dale and I both knew you were there. If it was going to be a problem we would have told you to leave."

"I'm sure. I just wanted to be sure you weren't regretting what happened."

Ari let the knife hover over the broccoli clarets as she considered it. Finally she said, "Dale and I agreed that you needed to watch so you'd know you couldn't get between us. But I think you needed to see it because it was symbolic to who we are. Dale literally saved my life the day we met. She didn't create my business, but she made it workable and she made it a career that could support us both. I love her. I adore her. And you saw me on my knees to her because I really do worship her a little."

"Um."

Ari turned and saw Dale standing in the door. She chuckled and shrugged.

"So I guess Milo and I are all matched up on the 'walking in on intimate moments' tally board." She closed the distance between her and Ari and rested her head on Ari's shoulder. "I adore you, too."

Ari stroked Dale's arm. "Milo and I were just talking about the fact tomorrow we should venture out into the wilderness and get back to our lives."

"Good. I'm getting a little stir-crazy here."

"I saw," Milo muttered, making Dale burrow tighter against Ari. Milo smiled and winked before adding the chopped vegetables to the broth. "Anyway, we've only got a few days before Gwen comes back. She's not going to leave this alone."

"What about Ben?" Ari asked.

"He went back to England. Once you made it clear the ceremony won't be going forward, he wanted to make sure everyone back there was prepared for wolf manoth."

"How bad is it going to be?"

Milo thought for a moment and then just quietly said, "Bad. There hasn't been one for over two hundred years. The hunters have a lot of pent-up rage they want to take out on us."

Dale stepped back from Ari and took a position on the third side of the island. "I've been trying to come up with a way out of this mess, and I might have one. What if Milo and I just go through with the ceremony?"

Ari coughed and raised an eyebrow.

"I mean for appearances sake. It's just a ceremony to help seal the treaty, right? It wouldn't be an official handfasting."

Milo said, "So you'd marry me but you'd keep sleeping with Ari?"

"Yeah. We make it look good for the peanut gallery, and then everyone shakes hands and goes home. Wolf mammoth avoided."

"Manoth," Milo corrected.

Ari said, "Would that work? There's not some primae noctis thing where they force you to, you know, do the deed?"

"I have no idea what the procedure is. This was only done once in history, two hundred years ago. I doubt they would gather around to witness the actual consummation. I'm sure the ceremony is the important part."

Dale held her hands up. "Well, then fine. A ceremony is just playacting. If it's not, then I've been married to David Howell since the second grade."

Milo seemed willing to consider the plot, but she looked to Ari for the okay.

"Run it by them. If it'll work, it's worth it to stop a war."

Dale covered Ari's hand. "If you're uncomfortable with this at all, we'll come up with another way."

Ari reached up and touched her collar. "This is the only thing that matters. Everything else is just appearances."

Dale smiled, and Milo seemed utterly relieved as she joined them at the island. Ari didn't know if it was the best solution, but it was the only way she could see out of the mess. Now that she knew what Milo's endgame had been, any jealous or mistrust was alleviated. If Dale had to be sham-married to anyone, Milo was the only candidate Ari felt comfortable with. But just in case it wouldn't work, she was going to keep thinking of alternative courses of action.

CHAPTER EIGHTEEN

THE NEXT morning, Ari and Milo shoveled the driveway to free Ari and Dale's cars. The neighborhood roads still looked hazardous, although it was obvious a few brave souls had managed to turn some of the ice into slush. Ari's car had better brakes and more traction than Dale's, and Milo told them to just take it and pick up Dale's car when the roads were a little less arctic. They wished her well on her trek to the grocery store, then headed out. They took it slow, deciding on Dale's apartment as their destination before they even started the car. There was a grocery store within walking distance and, if that was picked clean, a nearby convenience store would provide the basic necessities.

The drive from Milo's house to Dale's apartment, normally completed in under ten minutes, took the better part of an hour. Fortunately everyone else desperate or foolhardy enough to be out that morning was being just as cautious. They were forced to reroute twice by snowplows, avoided streets where there were a lot of pedestrians. Ari hadn't been sliding much, but she wasn't going to take a chance when there were kids building a snowman on the curb.

Pulling into the garage of Dale's building was like being transported to a different planet. Wet tire tracks led down the ramp, and clumps of blackened snow trailed down to the bottom like clumps of dirty cotton. But it was warm, brightly-lit, and the sea of cars reminded Ari the city was actually inhabited. Dale's usual spot was occupied, so Ari drove farther until she found a different place.

"I feel like I just woke up from a really long dream," Dale said.

"Rip van Winkle." She put her arm around Dale's waist and led her to the elevator. "We'll see what the streets look like tomorrow. For now, as the boss, I'm saying... no work today."

Dale gave that idea the thumbs-up and slumped against Ari once they were in the elevator. "It just feels good to be home. With you."

The building was alive, compared to the silence of three people bouncing around in a mansion. They could hear music coming from the apartments they walked past, some doors standing open with signs that announced they had hot plates if anyone wanted to cook and another that advertised board games if anyone had kids they needed to entertain. There was a note taped to Dale's apartment door that announced the building was rationing their power until everything was back to normal, politely requesting that people shut off or unplug anything that wasn't absolutely necessary.

Dale unlocked the door and tested the lights on to make sure they worked.

"Dale?"

"Mm?"

"If the building didn't have power, don't you think the elevator would have been a little slower?"

Dale turned to her. "Shut up and undress."

Ari was shocked by the sudden change in tone. "Pardon?"

"You heard me, boss lady. You scratched my itch yesterday, but I didn't get to scratch yours. So take off your clothes before I take them off for you."

Ari backed into the living room while Dale advanced on her. "You know statistically, the odds of someone overhearing us now are much greater now than they were at Milo's house."

"Don't care. Pants off."

"You're a wild woman." Ari pushed off her shoes.

"You've got your wolf, I've got my libido." She put her hand on Ari's shoulder and pushed her down onto the couch, straddling her as she started unbuttoning Ari's shirt. "Let's find out which one howls louder."

They eventually made it to the bedroom where Dale finally

repaid Ari for what had happened at Milo's. Afterward they changed into clean pajamas - the first truly clean clothes they'd worn in a week - and napped until the mid-afternoon. Ari woke before Dale but remained still and silent so as not to disturb her, content to watch the weather out the window. A few flurries were drifting across the glass but Ari knew it was just the last whimper of the storm that had shut down the city for the past eight days. Soon the streets would be cleared and they would go back to their real lives. She made plans to call Detective Lorne to touch base, and the urge to call Madeline Morris to check up on her was strong enough that she decided she might as well give in to it.

She slipped out of bed to make the call without disturbing Dale. Jenna was fine, and they'd made it through the storm unscathed. They spoke briefly before Ari hung up and plugged the phone in to charge. She'd managed to keep it alive during the blackout, but now the little battery indicator seemed to eagerly suck power from the outlet. She put it on the arm of the couch so it could fill up and then tiptoed back to bed. Dale was still out, so Ari slipped back under her arm and stared at window.

Speaking to Madeline and hearing Jenna's chipper voice over the phone reawakened Ari's unanswered questions in regard to the case. It was driving her crazy that she didn't even have a clue who the mystery shooter was. The 'mean man' Jenna couldn't identify, the apparent mastermind behind her kidnapping. She wondered if it was possible he was also involved with the Melody Scott abduction. The Scotts were fairly well-off. Had they been unable to come up with a ransom or just unwilling? Was Jenna his attempt to get a quick payday?

Her mind wandered back to the story of Agatha and Johanna. Simon Lehner had kidnapped children to incite humans to raise arms against *canidae* in their midst. Could Melody and Jenna have been the first victims in a new wave? If the hunters were willing to use a drug like wolfsbane for their own twisted means, why not blame them for a series of abductions? Maybe Madeline had screwed up their plans by going to a private investigator instead of the police. But then why involve Brandon Kent? And if the exchange was a trap, why had the Mystery Man shot at Brandon instead of her?

Dale stirred and turned her head to rub her chin against Ari's shoulder. "Hi."

"Morning."

"What time is it?" Dale slumped back onto Ari's chest.

Ari looked at the clock. "A little after five."

Dale burrowed closer to her. "I want to sleep some more. Tell me a bedtime story. Not Agatha and Johanna. Tell me a better one."

"Okay, baby. Once there was a wolf who thought she was a girl. She didn't have a pack. She didn't really have friends or a family. And then one day, an angel with bright red hair swooped in and saved the wolf's life from some bad people." Dale giggled sleepily and spider-walked her fingers over Ari's stomach. "She took the wolf who thought she was a girl home and made her feel safe and warm and loved. And she showed the wolf what it was like to really be a girl. It took a long time, but eventually the wolf stopped thinking she was a girl and became one. A real one, with a heart and love to give. And she realized that in all of her life, the red-haired angel who saved her was the only person she had ever truly loved. And the wolf knew that she would do anything to protect the red-haired angel."

Ari looked down and saw that Dale was asleep. She lightly kissed Dale's forehead just above the eyebrow and Dale made a quiet noise of contentment without waking.

"You're the only person who has ever mattered to me, Dale," Ari whispered. "I'm not going to let anything happen to you."

She stroked two fingers up and down Dale's upper arm and closed her eyes. She finally joined Dale in sleep thinking about Madeline Morris, Jenna, Brandon Kent, Missing Melody, her mother, Benjamin Moss, and what could possibly tie together such a disparate group of people and if it had anything to do with a treaty from two centuries ago crashing down around them.

Dale lifted her head and blinked sleepily when Ari slipped away from her again. Ari shushed her, guided her back to the pillow, and kissed her cheek. She stroked Dale's arm until she fell back to sleep and padded barefoot out of the bedroom. The apartment was freezing, so cold that she knew she could have seen her breath if the lights had been on. She hugged herself against the chill and checked her phone's charge before she dialed Detective Lorne's number.

"Willow." He had answered on the fourth ring, which made Ari check the clock. She and Dale had slept away most of the day, but it was still only nine o'clock at night. "I'd ask where you'd been, but no one in Seattle is asking that question these days. How'd you fare in the storm?"

"All in one piece," Ari said.

A lamp clicked on behind her and she turned to see Dale pass through the light into the kitchen. Her hair was pushed up on one side and flipped over the top of her head, and her feet seemed to be turned sideways judging from the difficulty she had walking. Dale waved two fingers as she passed Ari and went to investigate their food stores. As she began investigating what was still good and what needed to be tossed, Ari focused on the call.

"Now that the city is lurching back to life, I thought I'd check in. If you still want me to check out Brandon Kent's money drain of choice, I could swing by tonight."

"I doubt they'll be open tonight. Most businesses are giving it until tomorrow so the streets can be cleared and the black ice can thaw a little more."

Ari watched Dale throw out a plastic bottle of mayo. "Tomorrow's fine. We were kind of cut off for a while. How did the city fare?"

"We're rebounding. The city burned in 1889, and now we've frozen. Fire and ice, right? In a hundred years they'll have to deal with a flood from rising water levels."

"Scary thought. Okay. I'll let you call you tomorrow when I'm heading over there." As she hung up, Dale opened a Tupperware container and offered it to her to double check. Ari gave it a sniff as she shut off her phone. "Wolf says it has three or four more days until it goes bad. We can have that for dinner tonight if you want to play it safe."

"Okay. You wanna heat it up while I finish with the fridge?"

"Sure." Ari stepped around the counter and placed the dish in the microwave.

"Was that Detective Lorne?"

"It was." She slipped past Dale and took a can of soda from the door of the fridge. Even without power, it would have stayed frosty and cold. She popped the tab and took a drink. "I confirmed that I don't have to go out tonight, so we can stay hunkered down in our bunker until tomorrow morning."

"Excellent." The microwave beeped. Dale checked the temperature, stirred the casserole, and nuked it for another thirty seconds. "After all the naps I've taken this week, and now being wide awake at my usual bedtime, my sleep schedule is going to be completely wonky for a few days. It'll be kind of nice to be part of your world."

Ari aimed a finger at her. "If you start singing songs from *Aladdin*, I'm out of here, blizzard or no blizzard."

Dale chuckled as she took the casserole out of the microwave. "Just promise me you won't venture too far from home until some of this snow melts. I worry about you on the best days, so I don't want to think about you freezing out there while you wait for me to come pick you up. How much do you want?"

Ari held her thumb and forefinger a few inches apart as she settled on one of the stools at the kitchen counter. Dale served up the food and got a soda from the fridge before sitting across from Ari. She crossed her legs and watched Ari for a moment before she spoke.

"We didn't talk about this when we were at Milo's because I thought you'd want privacy, but you never said how you felt about your mother being back."

Ari shrugged. "She's not back. She was always here, I just never acknowledged the fact. I happened to get forced into spending five minutes with her, but nothing's changed."

"You're sure? I think I'd have a few choice words for her if I was in your shoes."

"Oh, I have words, there's just no point in saying them out loud. And now that I know... what I know about how I came to be, I'm not really sure I can pull off the righteous indignation with the same authority. I have to rethink all the words I've wanted to say to her since I was a teenager. But if I decide I have to say them, I'll say them to you."

Dale smiled. "That's all I ask."

"Right now I want to get back to the case. Do you mind if I brainstorm a little with you?"

"Mm-hmm. Please."

"I was trying to connect Jenna and Missing Melody to the story about Johanna and Agatha. Back in the day, the bad wolves killed kids to make people take up arms against our kind. If the hunters are coming back, it makes sense that they might try that tactic again. Enough kids go missing, when the hunters come up with a scapegoat to blame, people won't hesitate. But no matter how I try to work it, Jenna doesn't fit. If her abduction was part of some *canidae* conspiracy scheme, why give her back? And why do it so easily?"

Dale raised an eyebrow. "Easily? You ran across Seattle, you got shot at, Brandon Kent is dead, and Madeline was terrified for days–"

"Granted. But given how it could have gone, that was easy as pie. Brandon cooperated from the very beginning. He let me call the shots."

"He was just taking orders. He was terrified because he was prepared to deal with a hysterical mother who would do anything to get her daughter back. You showed up and turned the tables on him. You were a better opponent and he caved."

Ari shook her head. "If it was that easy to throw their plans completely sideways, Mystery Man wouldn't have waited so long to kill Brandon. He would have just eliminated the middleman to talk with me himself." She took a bite of her dinner and chewed thoughtfully. "What about the ransom? Why not give a number?"

Dale gestured with her spoon. "It's like what you said. They were making Madeline decide how much Jenna was worth. To you and me, a million dollars is a fortune and to Milo she considers a hundred-dollar bill to be a nice tip. Money means different things to different people."

"So he's a philosopher kidnapper?" Dale shrugged. Ari looked toward the window. "And Brandon knew what Madeline was worth. Maybe not the exact dollar amount, but he had a good idea. He worked with her, he dated her, so he at least could guesstimate about how much she could afford." She stirred her meal. "So if it wasn't a scheme to get as much money as possible, then why let Madeline choose how much to give?"

Dale thought for a moment as she chewed her mouthful. Finally she shrugged. "Maybe they just wanted to get rid of Jenna. You know, like when a store is trying to get rid of something that won't move, they drop the price or let you negotiate a little."

"Kidnapper's remorse," Ari muttered, then pressed her lips together. "But they treated her kindly. They were being so nice to her that she doesn't even realize she was in danger. She thinks it was just an unusual couple of days. Even the gunfire didn't faze her because she thought we were playing."

Dale hummed and looked toward the window. The clouds were low enough that they formed a bulky ceiling over the city. Ari ate a few bites before Dale spoke again.

"Maybe Brandon wanted the cops involved."

"They said no police."

Dale rolled her eyes. "Everyone says that in every kidnapping movie, and who always gets involved? Cops or the FBI. They swoop in and take over the negotiations. Brandon didn't expect to be dealing with someone like you. What if the kidnapping went the way it did because of Missing Melody?"

"How so?"

"Brandon and Madeline broke up a year ago, but not because she hates him. It's because he's a gambler. She's worried he won't be a good provider for Jenna so she ends the relationship. She moves on, Brandon doesn't. He decides to show Madeline he can be a hero. He gets a partner who is smarter than him to make sure things go off without a hitch. They plan, they get everything ready, and they finally work up the nerve to actually grab Jenna. His plan is to be the one who brings her back. A knight in shining armor who has proven he can come through when it really matters. But Missing Melody ruins everything. Suddenly he's a kidnapper in a city where suddenly every cop is on high alert for a kidnapper. He panics and all he cares about is getting out of the situation as soon as possible. But he doesn't want to be arrested for kidnapping so he has to play the part for the exchange."

Ari considered it. "It fits. Mostly."

Dale looked crestfallen. "Where did I go wrong?"

"Jenna was taken *after* Missing Melody was already on the news."

"Shoot."

"Not to mention the part where Brandon hires someone to help him kidnap a little girl. How? With what money?"

"He gets half of the ransom."

Ari smiled. "He finds someone willing to commit a felony and be paid on the successful completion of the job? I don't spend much time with that sort of person but I very much expect they're the cash-upfront sort of businessmen."

Dale considered that and then brightened again. "Brandon *did* pay them. He clears out his bank account because he can just replace the cash when he's got the ransom."

"Kind of stupid..."

"This is a guy who spends every paycheck in a poker game. He's a gambler, Ari. That's exactly the sort of risk he would take."

Ari had to give her that. "Okay, but in that scenario Brandon's murder makes absolutely no sense. The girl was gone, the money was gone. Any sane kidnapper or accomplice is going to want to regroup. What would make you just pull out a gun and shoot your partner? Especially if said partner was the one who set the whole thing up?"

Dale pursed her lips and looked into her bowl.

"New theory." Dale looked up and Ari used her fork to punctuate her thoughts. "Mystery Man is the boss. He hired Brandon to kidnap Jenna and, if things went wrong, Brandon would be the one to take the fall. But who would want to kidnap her, if Brandon was just a patsy?"

"Madeline's ex-husband? Gerry or whatever? Has Detective Lorne checked up on him?"

Ari shrugged. "I presume so, but he hasn't told me anything. Madeline didn't seem to think he was a very viable threat, but she did say he was capable of killing her. She said he considered her a trophy. Maybe he was okay with her escaping but Jenna was his child. What if he decided she was stolen property and tried to get her back?"

Dale narrowed her eyes. "No. Because then why even have a ransom? Why not just take her and run back to wherever it was?"

"You're right."

They were quiet for a moment, focused on their food, but then Dale smiled. "That was a really shoddy theory, Ari. Did you offer it up because you felt bad about knocking mine down?"

Ari shook her head. "Nope. It was a valid theory."

"Uh-huh. A valid theory that you'd already discounted."

"We'll never know."

Dale took a drink of her soda and drummed her fingers on the side of the can. "I don't think either disappearance is connected to what your mother told you. If the hunters wanted to strike up fear of werewolves, the girls would be showing up mutilated. Jenna wouldn't have been given ice cream and left alone to watch TV for three days before they gave her back."

"Hopefully I'll find a few more pieces of the puzzle tomorrow at the bar."

Dale nodded and they finished the rest of their meal in contemplative silence. Outside the window, snow and ice continued quietly melting even though the sun had set hours before. Seattle was beginning to thaw out and come back to life. Ari watched the trickling water streak past the window and got back into a detective's mindset.

It was time to get back to work.

Chapter Nineteen

THE OFFICE felt like a tomb, ancient and abandoned, with the front entrance buried under snow instead of sand. Dale kept her coat and mittens on as the thermostat grudgingly brought the heat back up. She held her bare hand up to her window and the one in Ari's office to check for any air leakage, but both seemed fine. She checked their messages, not expecting much. She was sure that the storm had trapped all potential clients who might have called, but there were still a few messages waiting.

Ari came in fifteen minutes later with coffee for her, cocoa for Dale, and a small bag of doughnuts. She exhaled sharply and held her bounty with one hand as she unwound her scarf with the other. "The line was insane. Look out, Starbucks, Seattle is out of hibernation and we're hungry."

Dale rubbed her hands together. "What did you get?"

"I managed to get a chocolate." She paused to increase the drama and then smiled. "And I had to be quick, but I also got one of the last grape jelly doughnuts."

Dale put her hands on either side of Ari's face and rubbed their noses together. "My hero. Thank you."

"Ariadne Willow. Little girls rescued, cheaters photographed, and jelly doughnuts found despite wintry apocalypse scenarios."

Dale snickered and took her breakfast to her desk. "Looks like a few storm-related crimes might require investigation of a private variety. People who went missing during the storm and break-ins that happened while people weren't able to get home. That sort of thing."

"Anything I could take care of before I meet up with Detective Lorne this afternoon?"

Dale held out a memo pad. "I listed them in order of time-sensitivity."

"Good girl. Earned your jelly doughnut."

"I aim to please, Miss Willow."

Ari winked at her and went into her office. Dale booted up the computer which, despite the cold and its abandonment, came eagerly to life for her. She patted the top of the monitor and tried to get back into the groove of real life. Ari left half an hour later to check up on the first item on the list, promising to call if she could get free for lunch. Dale wished her well and opened a search window.

An hour later she had a fair amount of information gathered on Mr. Gerald Kimbro of Spokane, Washington, former husband of Madeline Morris and biological father of Jenna. He was the shift supervisor at a delivery company, recently married to the dispatcher from his company. Gerald and his new wife Emily both had Facebook profiles that Dale used to dig a little deeper. In each photo Gerald had his arm around his new wife's shoulders in a manner that reminded Dale of someone showing off a new car.

His posts further supported Dale's theory that she was less wife and more possession. Entries contained language like "my wife got a raise" and "the little lady recently completed a 5k for charity, mighty proud." Her accomplishments were laid out as if they were his, implying that her success was somehow due to his presence or intervention. His pet names for her - the little lady, my girl - all seemed to diminish her in one way or another.

Ari came back an hour and a half after she left. Her face was bright red, one hand clutching the collar of her coat closed. When she took it off and hung it on the rack, Dale saw that she was wearing a different shirt than the one she'd left in. She was also wearing sneakers instead of her boots, and both gloves were missing. She was shivering when she walked up to Dale's desk and deposited a check on the keyboard.

Dale looked at it, impressed at the amount, and then looked up at Ari. "Big morning?"

"I don't want to talk about it."

"Was this the person who called about the missing pet?"

Ari nodded, making a noise as she shivered again. "Missing *monkey*. Missing illegal monkey. Missing illegal mean monkey. Monkey in a tree." She blew into her fists. "I sniffed him out. Climbed up. Tree branches can get really icy."

Dale made a sympathetic face and stood up. "Come into the office." Ari followed her. Dale took a thick wool blanket from the wardrobe and wrapped it around Ari's shoulders before guiding her down to the couch. She took one of Ari's hands and held it in front of her lips, blowing softly on them before she took two of them into her mouth. Ari sighed with relief and slipped her other hand under Dale's shirt. Dale yelped as ice in the shape of Ari's hand pressed against her stomach, but she didn't let Ari pull it away.

"Mmm. You're warm."

"Thank you. I did some digging on Gerald Kimbro." She explained what she had found on the internet. By the time she finished, some of the color had returned to Ari's cheeks.

"Well... it supports Madeline's description of him. But it also confirms my theory that he didn't do it. Yeah, Jenna and Madeline were his property but they're gone. He lost them. He doesn't have to get them back because he's replaced them."

Dale nodded. "That's what I was thinking." She bit her bottom lip. "I was reading his posts and judging him for the way he treated his wife. And I realized that someone might think I'm being dismissive when I call you puppy. Maybe I should stop."

"No! Please, no." She moved her hand to the back of Dale's neck, her hands warm enough that Dale didn't cringe at the touch. "I would take down anyone else who tried to call me that, but you? I don't... it's..." She furrowed her brow as she searched for the right words. She finally gave up and met Dale's gaze. "I love being your puppy."

Dale smiled and ducked her chin, and Ari kissed the spot next to her eye. Dale stroked Ari's hands. "So I guess Gerald checks out. Back to checking out Brandon?"

"That's what it looks like. I just hope the bar isn't a dead end. And heated. I hope the bar is heated."

"Aw. C'mere, you big baby..." Dale climbed on top of Ari and pulled her close to share their body heat.

The Wandering Wolf was in a row of bars, taverns, and

warehouses that faced the harbor on the south banks of Lake Union. At the moment the flotilla of boats were stuck in their slips, ice formations in a frozen pond. Detective Lorne had offered to join her in the questioning but she passed. She would get farther without a cop at her hip, and if things got bad enough that she needed police protection... Well. She didn't intend to let it get that far.

The door finally swung open after almost ten minutes of knocking. Shivering on the front step, Ari glared at the black-suited goon standing in front of her. He was tall and broad-shouldered, well-earned muscle rather than show-off muscle accumulated at some pricey gym. He looked at her like she was crazy, one thick eyebrow raised in irritation.

"Dark windows and sign didn't tip you off? We're closed. Get lost."

"Come on. All these cars parked out here, the smoke coming from the back? You guys have something going. Let me come in and warm up a little."

He ran his eyes up and down her body and smiled. "Lady, I don't think you'd like how these guys would want to warm you up. Why don't you go find a hotel somewhere, all right?"

"Nicky." He glanced back but then returned his gaze to Ari. "Don't be a putz. It's freezing out there. Let the girl in for a minute."

Nicky sighed and hung his head before he straightened up and held the door open for her. She smiled as she stepped past him into the bar.

The only occupied table was near the empty bandstand. Nicky led her over as the men examined the new arrival. They were all older than Nicky, who was older than Ari, and seemed to be in the range of early forties to late sixties. The elder of the group took a cigar from his mouth and rested it on the edge of his plate before he turned to face her. He smiled, but there was nothing friendly about his expression.

"This is not a very good place for a young lady like yourself to be. Especially all alone."

A white dog came out of the back room, its footsteps sounding as loud as if someone was knocking on the floorboards. It stopped in place when it spotted Ari, lowering its head before continuing forward at a slower pace.

The man at the table grinned. "That's Bismarck. He's a Bully Kutta. You know anything about them?"

"Not really. Mastiff, right?"

"Yep. Pakistani mastiff. Hugely loyal dogs." He whistled. "All you'd have to do is give me a dirty look and Bismarck there would make you regret it. I don't think you fully thought through the act of coming here. I think maybe now you're rethinking your decision. I am a generous man, and I will let you turn around and walk out of here."

Ari tilted her head to the side and feigned confusion, never taking her eyes off Bismarck. He returned her stare without blinking. "But I have questions."

"They will have to go unanswered. Such is life."

"I think you'll answer them." She stepped forward and Bismarck leaned toward her.

"What's your name, young lady?"

"Ariadne Willow."

"My name is Huey Onatero. Does that name mean anything to you?"

Ari shook her head. "I don't really associate with your kind."

There was a brief silence before the other men at the table laughed. Huey, to his credit, smiled. "You have balls, Miss Willow. I will tell you that."

Ari shook her head. "Nope, last time I checked my balls were in my girlfriend's nightstand. And why is that a compliment, anyway? One good kick and you're out of play. Telling someone they have balls is saying they have a very vulnerable weak spot. I want to talk to you about Brandon Kent."

"I want you to leave. One of us will get what we want. Do you remember that I told you Bismarck is very, very loyal to me?" The dog's ears twitched at the sound of his name, but his eyes didn't leave Ari. "Nicky is a good soldier. I trust him to take care of my irritations. But he is only human. He'll hesitate and he'll think about his wife or his kids before he does real damage. He'll think about cops. Or he'll think about how pretty you are.

"Bismarck doesn't have that failing. If I tell him to make you bleed, he'll make you bleed. And because you are still on my property after I've asked you several times to leave, I'll be entirely lawful in doing so. Now I will ask you one more time to leave or I will be forced to give you a demonstration of just how loyal a Bully can be."

Ari squared her shoulders and pointed at Bismarck. "Wait a minute. Are you talking about this dog?"

"Do you see another?"

"I just assumed you were talking about a mean dog. One that I should be afraid of who was hiding in the back room or something. Not this sweetheart." She walked toward him.

Nicky seemed to be sincerely concerned for her when he said, "Miss, I really wouldn't do that if I were you."

Ari kept her eyes locked on Bismarck's. He was trembling with unspent energy, obviously waiting for the kill order. Ari stopped two feet in front of him and looked down, lowering her eyes without lowering her head. She flashed her teeth at him, wrinkled her nose, and gave a growl so low that the men at the table couldn't have heard it. He may have been a mastiff, but she was a wolf. He may have been an attack dog, but he was Tame while she was Wild. She towered over him. Her eyes were flat and cold, and there was no doubt which of them was Alpha.

Bismarck whimpered and dropped. He kept his belly just above the ground and inched forward, presenting the top of his head to Ari. She crouched and scratched him between the ears, and he turned his head to lick the inside of her wrist.

"What in..." Huey stood up and stared at the dog. "What did you do to my dog?"

"Not a thing." Ari bent down and kissed the top of the dog's head. "Go on back to your bed, sweetie-pie. Take a nap."

Bismarck got to his feet and trotted back the way he had come. Ari stood, wiped off her hands, and faced the men.

"Want to see if I can charm your men, or can we have a discussion about Brandon Kent?"

Huey was still staring at her as if she'd pulled a fast one on him. Treats in her pockets, lunchmeat smeared on her wrists, anything to explain why his security system had failed so spectacularly.

"I don't talk about my patrons. That's just good business. I'm sure you understand."

"I would, but he's dead. He got killed while he was picking up the ransom for the little girl he kidnapped. You wouldn't know anything about that, would you?"

Huey raised an eyebrow and shrugged noncommittally. "What goes on outside of this establishment, I have no control over. I can only manage my bar, not the world. And I'm sure you're surprised that the clientele who would frequent such an establishment are not exactly the most upstanding citizens."

"You're right. But if a client has a big enough debt, it could be used against them. It could be leverage to make them do all sorts of sordid things. If that was true, then you might be held accountable in some way. Unless, of course, you were to help clear the air. What do you say, Mr. Onatero? Feel like earning some karma points?"

"I suppose," he said carefully, "it would depend on what you want to know."

"Did Brandon Kent frequent this bar?"

Huey nodded. "Yes."

"And how much did he owe you?"

"At the time of his unfortunate demise? Nothing."

Ari looked at Nicky, who shrugged. "Paid in full."

"Nice timing. How long before he died was his debt paid off?"

Huey glanced at one of the men at the table. The man took out his phone, poked at the screen, and then turned it around so Huey could read it.

"One week prior, Brandon paid his full sixteen thousand dollar debt to us and re-entered our good graces. He paid in cash. And before you continue, we do not ask questions about where the money comes from. I prefer not to know. It's simpler that way."

Ari said, "You might want to rethink that policy. I'm pretty sure it was payment to get Brandon to kidnap a little girl."

Huey shook his head and melodramatically put one gnarled hand on his chest. "Horrible things happen in this world, Ariadne Willow. If I were to concern myself with each and every one of them, my sensitive heart would shatter a thousand times over. Now please, unless you wish to know which teams Brandon was foolishly loyal to, or if you want to know just how terrible he was at cards, I will kindly ask you to leave."

"Thank you for your time, gents. That wasn't so bad, was it?" She winked at them and walked back to where Nicky was waiting to escort her out.

"One minute, hold on." Ari turned to Huey. "What did you do to my dog?"

"I didn't do anything to him. He might be feeling a little emasculated right now but other than that..." She shrugged. "He should be fine the next time some unwanted pest shows up. Have a nice thaw, gentlemen."

Nicky escorted her out to the sidewalk and let the door swing shut behind him. He shoved his hands into his pockets and stopped her from crossing to where her car was parked.

"Hey. Brandon really kidnap a little girl?"

"Yeah. His ex-girlfriend's daughter."

Nicky looked at the icy lake, squinting against the sun reflecting off the flat surface. "The day after that girl went missing... Missing Melody, you know? Some guy was in here talking about it. I mean, everyone was talking about it. But this guy... he seemed really determined, you know? Wouldn't let anyone change the subject. He asked Mr. Onatero about anyone with kids. Daughters, specifically. They were just shooting the breeze, but Huey got a little creeped out eventually and sent the guy away. But it was right after that when Brandon came up with his payday. And if he had access to a kid, like you say, then maybe..." He hunched his shoulders. "I'm just letting you know about the guy I saw in here. I don't know his name, I can't even remember what he looked like. I just remember him 'cause he gave me and Huey the creeps. But if it helps you find out who kidnapped the girl, you know. People who do that to kids..." He shook his head.

"Thank you. I think it'll be a help. You say that he was looking for little girls after Missing Melody disappeared?"

"Yeah. At first I thought he was some kind of bounty hunter looking for the girl himself, trying to get that reward."

"I'll keep it in mind. Thanks, Nicky."

He held up a hand again, half-smiling. "You gotta tell me... what did you do to Bismarck? That dog still takes swipes at *me* when I feed 'im and I've worked for Huey for ten years."

Ari smiled and shrugged. "Sometimes you just have to have the louder bark."

"You didn't even make a noise."

"Doesn't matter. Bismarck heard it loud and clear. Thanks for your help, Nicky."

She walked back to her car and got behind the wheel, looking out at the lake. Someone went into a bar trying to find someone with gambling debts. He wasn't looking for someone connected specifically to Jenna, which meant any kid would have done.

The question was no longer who would want to kidnap Jenna Morris. The question was now who would go to all the trouble to kidnap a random child just to give it back in the easiest way possible? And what was the point of arranging a kidnapping where the victim's identity didn't matter?

Ari finally decided she wasn't going to find the answer sitting outside the Wandering Wolf and drove away.

CHAPTER TWENTY

BITCHES INVESTIGATIONS shared a building with a mysteriously quiet antique shop called Den of Antiquities. Dale had never seen anyone pass through the doors - customer or employee - but she knocked anyway just to see if she would get a response. After waiting a reasonable amount of time for someone to reach the front door, she gave up and ventured out to the neighboring building to a small record shop. She asked the man behind the counter if he had a shovel she could borrow so she could clear the walk outside their office, and he refused but promised to shovel it for her himself. After a bit of back and forth, Dale agreed to let him clear the sidewalk in exchange for buying him a cup of hot coffee when he was finished.

She carefully made her way back across the icy pavement. She noticed the wet footprints just inside the door so she wasn't surprised to find a walk-in client waiting in the office. The woman stood and turned to face the door when she came back in, and Dale offered an apologetic smile and waved.

"Sorry about that. I just had to step out for a second. Hi, I'm Dale Frye."

The woman was gorgeous, with waves of black hair that had hints of going lighter brown at the roots. Her smile dimpled her cheeks and chin, and just before it crinkled her bright blue eyes

Dale thought they looked oddly familiar. She wore a black silk blouse open at the collar to reveal a sapphire pendant on a gold chain at her collar, and her skirt looked like it cost more than everything Dale was wearing combined. The woman was tall, most likely even without the dangerous shoes she was perched upon, and she made Dale feel puny in front of her.

"Hello, Miss Frye. Would it be all right if I refrained from introducing myself for the time being? It's nothing personal..."

Dale cut her off with a wave of her hand as she walked around her desk. "It's fine. A lot of our clients request anonymity. You can give me whatever name you like, or you can refrain from giving a name until Ms. Willow is back. I understand the need for privacy. You can wait for her if you'd like. She shouldn't be too long."

"Thank you very much." The woman smoothed a hand over the back of her skirt as she sat, crossing her legs and lacing her fingers in front of one knee. "Ms. Willow is, um, out on an investigation, I presume?"

"She is." Dale gestured at the window as she took a seat. "We lost a week due to the storm so she's trying to make up for it by jumping right back on the horse, as it were."

The client nodded. "Yes. We all lost time during the storm. Sometimes it's not so easy to get it back."

"I'm sure. Ari will do her best to help you."

She smiled. "You have a lot of faith in her, don't you?"

"Of course. She's an amazing detective. In fact, the case she's on right now is one that was officially closed. She's not getting paid to follow up on it, but she has to make sure everything is tied up to her satisfaction before she can let it go."

"Mm." The woman nodded slightly and scanned the office as if she was appraising it. "A worthy aspect in an investigator. How long have you worked with her?"

"Five years. Feels like longer." She smiled. "In the best sense, I mean. I can't imagine not doing this, or not having Ari in my life."

The woman's expression softened slightly and she made a quiet sound in her throat as she examined the floor beyond the pointed toe of her shoe. "You obviously care a lot about her. Could you tell me - if it's not overstepping - how far exactly she would go in order to close a case? You mentioned she's working on something now without getting paid. How long will she pursue it if she doesn't get an answer?"

Dale considered the question, wondering how much she could

reveal. "This is kind of a special case. A little girl was endangered, and even though she's safe now, the police didn't catch the man who endangered her. So Ari is going to stick with it until the man is apprehended or else until she's positive the girl is safe."

"I see." She checked her watch, glanced toward the door, and uncrossed her legs. "Ms. Frye, thank you for your hospitality, but I'm afraid I have an appointment I can't miss. Can I come back later this afternoon to speak with Ms. Willow?"

"Of course. I'll make sure she's free. Say four o'clock?"

The woman nodded as she stood. "That would be ideal." She shook Dale's hand over the desk and smiled before she left the offices. Dale watched her go, admiring the line of the woman's body before she marked the appointment on Ari's calendar. Gorgeous woman, stately and elegant, refined. Since the Gavin case blew up all over the papers, they had been getting more and more calls from the elite parts of town. Dale had always had a thing for rich, done-up women so she was enjoying the procession of finely perfumed and beautifully jeweled clients that had passed through the door.

Alone again, she started polishing up the report on the Jenna Morris case with the speculation they had done at the apartment. All their theories had been shot down, but some bit of logic they had used might lead to the truth in an unexpected way when they had more clues to work with. Part of her mind was occupied with thoughts of her attraction to rich women to the point where she was imagining Ari as an heiress and wondering if anywhere nearby rented French maid costumes.

Ari came in just as Dale was finishing up the report. "Hey, puppy. I'm glad you're here. I have something I want to run by you." She looked up and saw Ari was standing just inside the door and slowly scanning the room as if she'd misplaced something. "What's wrong?"

"Was someone here?" She slowly took off her scarf and unbuttoned her jacket as she continued to look around suspiciously.

"Yeah. She wanted to talk to you about a case, but she had another appointment."

Ari shut the door. "Did she touch anything?"

Dale stood up. "I don't know. What's wrong?"

"I need... your hand, you shake hands with the clients." She gestured for Dale's right hand. Dale furrowed her brow but offered it. Ari took Dale's hand in both of hers and brought it to her face, breathing deeply.

"Ari, what's wrong?"

She exhaled and opened her eyes. "That wasn't a client, Dale. That was my mother."

Dale's eyes widened and she pulled her hand away, suddenly wanting to run into the en suite to wash the scent off.

"What did she say she wanted?"

"Sh-she didn't. I thought she was just... I respected her privacy." She tried to remember exactly what they had discussed. "We talked about you. How long I've worked with you, what kind of detective you were, that sort of thing." She realized something else. "Oh, God. She was in here alone. I went next door to borrow a shovel for the sidewalk, and she was already here when I got back. Could she have planted something?"

"Like what?"

Dale shrugged helplessly. "I don't know. A bug? A camera?"

Ari smiled and cupped the back of Dale's head. She pulled her forward and kissed her forehead. "That's not her way. Relax." She dropped her hands to Dale's shoulders and squeezed. "She just asked about me?"

"Yeah. I thought she was a potential client so I may have gushed a little. But otherwise I just told the truth. She said she was going to come back at four. Do you think she'll actually keep the appointment?"

"I think we have to act as if she will." She looked at her watch. "Okay. We have a couple of hours until we have to worry about that. Come on into my office, and bring your notepad. I found out some interesting stuff at the bar."

Dale picked up a pad off paper off the desk and followed Ari into the main office. She caught Ari scenting the air to see if her mother had snuck into the inner office, but she didn't seem to find any evidence of her intrusion. She sat on the couch and, when Dale was settled next to her, Ari recounted what she had learned from Nicky at the bar.

When she was finished she sighed and shook her head. "I thought it would clear things up, but I'm even more confused now than when I started. Why would someone go to all the trouble to kidnap a random little girl? If the Mystery Man wanted to get at Jenna, he would have gone straight to Brandon Kent. But instead he goes to Huey Onatero and asks him about anyone with access to kids. Beyond the creepiness factor, that doesn't tell us anything. Why would you do that and immediately give the girl back unharmed?"

"Maybe you're compounding your errors."

Ari looked at her. "What does that mean?"

"You're trying to figure out the logic of the scenario. But whoever the Mystery Man is kidnapped a little girl. Took her away from her mother for reasons unknown. Since you can't fathom doing that, you can't extrapolate to a scenario where you would give her back. You and Mystery Man are standing on separate islands. His crazy island has a bridge that leads him to the mainland, and you can't figure out how he got over there from your little sane archipelago."

"Okay. So how do I get to his island?"

"You can't. But you can change the situation so that it works for your island." She put down her pad and turned to face Ari. "You can't imagine taking a little girl, so change it from a kidnapped little girl. Let's say you stole, I don't know, the last slice of pecan pie from the fridge."

Ari blinked in surprise. "I can't believe you're bringing that up."

"It's a hypothetical." She tapped Ari's thigh with her fingers. "Okay, so instead of trying to figure out the logic of a kidnapper, imagine you're hungry and you go to the fridge~"

Ari interrupted, "And I see the pie you told me earlier you weren't planning to eat."

"Hush. I'm doing your job for you. We don't need to worry about the logic of why you took it right now. That will come later, and it's more important to figure out the second part. After you've gone to the effort of taking the pie, what would make you give it back? No arguments, no negotiations, no fight. You just randomly decide to give it back to me."

"This is a tortured comparison, Dale. It has no bearing on why Mystery Man took Jenna or why he gave her back."

"Just play along, Ari."

She sighed and closed her eyes. "Because I felt bad about taking the pie away from you. Which I would then extrapolate to the kidnapper feeling remorse for what he had done. But I didn't feel remorse about the pie until you caught me, and... what are we saying, that the kidnapper didn't realize he was doing something wrong until the moment he had Jenna?"

"Maybe he was worried about eventually getting caught."

Ari shook her head. "He planned too much to just suddenly change his mind once he had the girl. He had to know that he was risking prison the moment he took her. People who plan kidnappings this thoroughly don't suddenly realize it's a felony and then repent."

"Okay. Back to the pie..."

Ari groaned in frustration and stood up. "Enough with the pie, Dale! It's not an appropriate metaphor. The reasons for giving back pie are incongruous with giving back the little girl you kidnapped. You give back pie because it doesn't taste good, or because it's not the right kind, or it..." She trailed off, frozen in place. Outside they could hear the rhythmic scrape of the shovel as their neighbor cleared away the slush, snow and ice.

"What?"

"It's not the right kind."

Dale tilted her head to the side. "I'm not following you."

"Let's say you're a kidnapper, but you don't have a specific victim in mind. You want to kidnap someone because... hell, who cares about the why. It's on your bucket list. You find a guy with access to a kid, you pay him upfront to commit this felony. He stakes out the victim, sweeps her up, takes her to your evil lair, and you realize she's black."

"Why does that matter?"

"I don't know. I'm not that far across the bridge yet. But that's gotta be it. Huey and Nicky both said that Mystery Man came in looking for anybody. He wound up with Brandon Kent, who was Asian but might have passed as white if the lighting was bad enough. Maybe Asian would even have worked for whatever Mystery Man wanted. The point is, whatever he had in mind, black wouldn't work."

"So... what, he's a racist on top of everything else?"

Ari began to pace. "I don't know. But the ransom amount didn't matter, the identity of the girl didn't matter, so what's the only thing he could have been disappointed by?"

"He wanted someone like Missing Melody?"

"Sure." She flinched and shook her head. "No. It's not like an iPhone or something. You don't see someone with a kidnapped girl and think, 'Ooh, I gotta get me one of those.' It's not a competition or a status thing. And besides, people don't imitate a crime three days after it happens or while it's still being investigated. Why would two different people kidnap two different girls in the same week?"

"Are we sure it was two different people?"

Ari looked at her. "You think someone kidnapped them both

but decided they didn't want Jenna?"

Dale dismissed her own comment with a wave of her hand. "I'm thinking about the story again, sorry. Johanna and Agatha, the wolves leaving dead bodies of children lying around to rile up the villagers."

"Wait," Ari whispered. "Wait, wait." She pressed her thumb between her eyes, a pose Dale knew meant that she was thinking hard. "This isn't *canidae* and hunters, but what if it's something similar? Missing Melody was kidnapped three days before Jenna got taken. But Brandon Kent staked out the house for at least a couple of days before there was an opening to take her. So maybe we can presume that he was paid to take her around the same time Melody was taken. They weren't taken at the same time, but maybe they were supposed to be."

Dale looked down at her notes. "Is there anything to connect the Scott and Morris families?"

"No, but that's the point. They're strangers. Melody Scott is like one of those Precious Moments figurines. Whoever took her knew that there would be an exhaustive hunt. They knew there would be posters and news updates. They knew Melody's picture would be all over the city until she was found." Her eyes snapped open. "So the kidnapper planned to make sure she was found. Oh, God. Melody wasn't taken to be ransomed. Whoever took her wants to keep her."

Dale stood up. "Jenna was supposed to be a decoy."

Ari put a hand on her stomach, nauseated. "They were going to kill her. The plan was to grab a second girl, kill her, dump her somewhere, and let people assume she was Melody Scott."

"That would never work," Dale said softly. "There's DNA and dental records. The body would have to be identified by someone, a family member. And if the plan was to pass someone off as Melody, then the Mystery Man would have asked more questions about her. Height, age, hair color. He would want to make sure there was a resemblance."

"It depends on how much damage they were planning to do. If there were no teeth, no dental records. And DNA results take time in the real world. The truth wouldn't matter for the first few weeks. A little girl goes missing, and then all of a sudden a body turns up? If it's even close to right, the media isn't going to wait for DNA results before they declare a tragic end to the story. By the time the truth comes out, whoever took Melody is far enough away that they can't get caught. But if the body they find is black, the jig is instantly up."

"Oh, God, Ari, I don't... I don't like this line of thinking."

"Neither do I, but it explains everything. The timing, the set-up, the relatively easy ransom exchange. The second kidnapping was supposed to be a decoy to cover up the first. But Jenna didn't fit, so they gave her back as easily as they could without raising suspicion. Then Brandon was killed because he'd screwed everything up. Mystery Man didn't care about me, Jenna, or the ransom. The exchange was a trap, but it was for Brandon."

"Ari, it's been weeks since Melody was taken and Jenna was given back. If you're right, then whoever took Melody is long gone."

"No. They wouldn't take a chance while she's still in the news. There are still updates on KING5 every Saturday. The story went national. Everyone in this part of the country knows what Melody Scott looks like, so he has to bide his time. This is it, Dale. This explains everything. But if I'm right, then we've got bigger problems."

"I'm scared to ask."

Ari nodded toward the window. "A blizzard like this, it would be very easy to make a kidnapping look like a kid just wandered away from home and got lost. Now would be the perfect time for our guy to go hunting for a second decoy. He could be out there right now looking for another little girl to kidnap."

Chapter Twenty-One

ARI SHRUGGED back into her jacket and took her scarf off the hook. "We have to talk to Detective Lorne and see if anyone's reported a missing girl since the storm passed. Mystery Man wouldn't make the same mistake twice. He'll be looking for a girl that matches Melody as closely as possible. She just has to look right and the story will fade away long enough for him to get away with her."

Dale said, "What do you need me to do?"

Ari put her hand on her forehead and thought for a moment. "Come with me to the police. If we're both telling the same story, it might seem less crazy. Marginally."

"Okay." Dale shut off her computer.

As she was getting into her coat, someone knocked on the door and came inside without waiting for a reply. Ari tensed, smelling the intruder before she turned around. Dale took a step back, putting Ari between her and the new arrival as a way of firmly declaring which side she was on. Gwyneth noticed Dale's reaction and smiled.

"I see my daughter has told you who I really am. I apologize for lying to you earlier, Ms. Frye, but I just had to get a look at you. I was curious to see the woman who holds the fate of our species in the palm of her hand."

"Don't." Ari's voice was almost a growl. "Do not play on her guilt like that or so help me, I'll make you regret it."

Gwyneth eyed Ari and then looked back at Dale. "I also apologize for allowing your misconception to continue, but to be completely fair, I never lied."

"You said you wanted to hire us."

"No, actually, I didn't. I simply let you draw your own conclusions as to my presence. Dale Frye. Hm. Such an entitled little girl. Milo told me about your sham marriage idea. It won't work. This isn't a game, and it isn't posturing between two bored people. This is war. They want to kill us all. They want to eradicate us from the planet, and they will succeed unless you do the right thing."

"This thing has been falling apart for decades," Ari said. "As long as I've been alive. Well... since about nine months before I was born, right?"

Gwyneth's eyes flashed with anger mixed with enough shame that Ari almost felt bad for making the jab. "I suppose telling Milo was a way to get the information to you... I'm glad you know the truth after all this time, even if it doesn't change the way you feel about me."

"Even if I break up with Dale and she married Milo, how long will that peace last? They want to kill us all, they'll do it eventually. You say it's not a game, but that's exactly what it is. A game to buy time. To pass off the problem to the next generation. If the hunters want a war, let's give them one. We don't have time for this right now. Dale, come on." She walked past Gwyneth and Dale followed her into the hall.

Gwyneth pursued. "Ari, we don't have the luxury of playing to your hurt feelings. People are going to die unless we perform this ceremony."

Ari stopped at the door and spun around. She brushed past Dale and aimed a finger at her mother's face. "You destroyed my life once. The life I was supposed to have as a normal human, as a regular *person*. You took that away from me. But I made the best of it. I found a way to become the person I was meant to be despite you. And now you want to destroy it by taking away the only person I've ever loved? Get out of my life, Gwyneth. Leave me alone, and leave Dale alone, or else when the hunters show up I might show them straight to your house."

Gwyneth grabbed Ari's arm and squeezed. "Ariadne, listen to me. *Canidae* are going to die in genocidal numbers. If you turn against our people, you'll regret it."

"I'm not turning against *canidae*. And I'm not turning against you. I did that a long time ago. Now let me go."

Dale stepped forward. She put her hand on Gwyneth's hand, leaving it there until she relaxed her fingers. Dale stepped between Ari and her mother and looked up into Gwyneth's eyes. Now she knew why they had seemed familiar; they were Ari's eyes.

"Do you see what your daughter is wearing around her neck?"

"The collar?"

"My collar, Ms. Willow."

Gwyneth looked at Ari. "You let the human mark her territory. Quaint."

"It doesn't make her my property. It shows that I'm hers. I belong to her. Heart and soul. I couldn't marry Milo even if I wanted to. So do as Ariadne asked and leave us alone."

"You may change your mind when the bloodshed begins, but by that point it will be too late. Their blood will be on your hands, Ari, and on yours, Ms. Frye." Gwyneth stepped around them and opened the door. Air so cold it felt like a physical being shoved past her, lifting the belt of her coat to whip like tendrils. Her hair whipped across her face as she turned toward them again. "Ms. Frye... the hunters hate *canidae*, but do you have any idea how they feel about the humans who choose to consort with our kind? Ariadne, if you haven't changed your mind by the beginning of wolf manoth then you should take my advice. Take your pet and run. And never stop running."

She stepped out into the freezing gale, leaving Ari and Dale alone in the corridor. Dale pressed against Ari's side and slipped a hand into her coat to touch her stomach.

"Are you okay?"

"Yeah. Come on. Time's wasting."

To his credit, Detective Lorne listened to their entire theory before he cracked a smile. "You can't be serious. Half our missing kids' resources are still tied up with Missing Melody, and now you're telling me another girl somewhere in Seattle is at risk of being kidnapped. And this is unrelated to the girl your agency rescued a few weeks ago. And all of these kidnappings are the work of one person?"

"I realize how it sounds," Ari said. "If his plan had worked, no one would have connected the dots until it was too late. The police would have mostly ignored Jenna's disappearance--"

"I contend that hypothesis, by the way," Lorne interrupted.

Ari ignored him. "...but Madeline Morris hired us instead. And the fact that Jenna didn't suit his purposes meant he had to get rid of her and quick. He couldn't just drop her back at school and pretend nothing had happened. Once Brandon took her, they had to play the part of kidnappers for real. That's why they made it so easy for us. They let Madeline choose the amount of the ransom. They agreed to everything I asked, down to the ice cream I told them to buy for Jenna. And when Jenna was safe, the ringmaster killed the only person who could connect him to the whole boondoggle."

Dale said, "He had to lie low. Two kidnappings is a coincidence but three is a pattern. Especially if he grabbed a girl who looked exactly like Melody Scott. People would find it suspicious. People would wait for a DNA test on the body before they jumped to conclusions. But now..." She gestured at the window. "It doesn't have to be a kidnapping. It can just be a little girl who went missing in the biggest blizzard to hit Seattle since 1950. How many people have been reported missing since the city started thawing out?"

Lorne glanced toward his computer, which was currently showing a screensaver. Ari knew he was mentally reading that morning's statistics.

"Did any of them match the profile?" Ari asked. "She would have to be five to nine years old, blonde, slender..."

Lorne leaned forward and began to type. "Why go to all this trouble?"

"As long as Melody is missing, no one will stop looking for her. He'll never get out of the city. She'll be spotted on a security camera or some hotel desk clerk will see her and call it in. The only possible chance he has of getting away is if the public thinks the story is over and lets their guards down. The only way they move on is if there's an ending."

He scanned the screen and rubbed his bottom lip with his thumb. "Eight children have been reported missing. Five boys, a red-headed girl, a twelve-year-old girl... and one blonde girl from Beacon Hill who matches Melody Scott's age and description."

Ari's mouth was dry. "When did she go missing?"

"The report was filed this morning at noon. Her mother said that she left the girl at home alone when she went out for groceries.

It was too cold, too dangerous, the market would be too crowded, et cetera. When she got back four hours later... given the circumstances, that isn't exactly surprising... the girl was gone. She thinks the girl was most likely exploring or playing in the snow and got lost or trapped. We have K-9 officers searching the neighborhood, but they haven't turned up anything so far."

"They won't," Ari said. "Everyone is going to waste time looking for her in snow drifts while she's somewhere else. This is the person who took Jenna Morris. It's the person who is still holding Melody Scott somewhere. I need to know who that might be."

"How would I know?"

"The person who is taking these girls, who took Melody, has to know her. He has to know he'll be suspected in the abductions. That's why he needs to misdirect the police. Whoever it is, he's close to the family. You have to have looked at someone as a person of interest."

"Not me," he said. "I'm not on the Melody Scott case."

"Then find someone who is. If he already has the girl, then the case is going to end very badly, and very soon."

Detective Lorne finally agreed to take Ari and Dale's theory upstairs to the Missing Melody task force. Before he left he gave Ari the information on the girl who matched Melody's description and gave them permission to talk with the mother. He forbade them from saying anything about the connection to Melody Scott, and Ari was willing to agree in exchange for the opportunity to leave immediately. She feared being forced to wait for a police escort and giving the bastard even more time to get away.

The girl who had gone missing was Lucy Chabot, a second-grader at Beacon Hill Grammar School. The roads of her neighborhood were slick with snowmelt that was still liquid, the surfaces swept clear. The black-and-brown piles of snow stood tall along the gutter like slowly-diminishing ramparts. Ari drove past the Chabot house once, cursing at herself when she realized her mistake and flipped around to go back.

Dale followed her up the driveway. "How much are we going to tell her?"

"As little as we can get away with," Ari said. "We don't want to crush her hopes, but we also can't tell her that the guy has no reason to keep Lucy alive very long. Her sole purpose is as a dead body. He's already wasted weeks, so I can't imagine he'll waste much more time. Here's hoping he puts it off as long as possible. Killing a defenseless girl is a lot different from just kidnapping one."

The door was answered on the first knock. Ari felt guilty, well aware the mother was probably on pins and needles waiting for word on her daughter's disappearance. Her eyes were pink, her nose bright red, and she was holding a wad of Kleenex in one hand. She looked between them and her eyebrows lifted hopefully.

"Yes? Can I h-help you?"

"Ms. Chabot? I'm Ariadne Willow, this is Dale Frye. I'm a private investigator and I was hired to look into the abduction of a little girl named Jenna Morris. We think the same person who took her is responsible for taking Lucy. We'd like to try helping you get her back."

The relief that flooded her face was almost immediately replaced with grief. "I can't afford to hire you. I'm sorry~"

"The police are footing the bill, ma'am. Right now all we're interested in is getting your little girl home safe and sound as quickly as possible."

She stepped back and held the door open wider. "Then please. Come in out of the cold, detectives."

Chapter Twenty-Two

LISA CHABOT seemed eager to distract herself from thoughts of her daughter's disappearance by acting as hostess. When she insisted on making them cocoa, Dale offered to help her and they disappeared into the kitchen leaving Ari alone in the living room. Toys and various winter clothes were piled on a chair next to the hallway. She picked up one of the hats and turned it inside out, bringing it to her face and breathing deeply. The girl's scent was strong enough that she didn't need to be in wolf form in order to memorize it.

When Dale and Lisa returned with the refreshments, Ari was in front of the fireplace looking at the framed school photos of Lucy. Lisa used both hands to push her hair out of her face after placing a plate of cookies on the coffee table. She offered a tight smile as Ari and Dale sat on the sofa.

"You said you were hired to find a different little girl. Was... w-was she...?"

"She's home, safe and sound," Ari said.

Lisa closed her eyes for a moment and then dipped her chin. She was petite with mousy brown hair, a small woman swimming inside warm clothing. Judging from the photos over the mantle, Lucy had gotten her looks from her father. When Lisa had composed herself, she looked at Ari with tears in her eyes.

"I'll be happy to help you any way I can."

Ari said, "Where is Lucy's father?"

"Out, looking." She sniffled and glanced toward the front door. "He came home from work to organize the neighborhood... he's sure she's in a snow drift somewhere, just waiting for someone to find her." She furrowed her brow to fight another wave of tears. "You really think Lucy was abducted? Who would do something like that?"

"We're not sure. But two little girls have disappeared since Melody Scott. The fact your daughter bears a resemblance to her supports a theory I'm working on."

"What theory?"

Ari glanced at Dale. "I'd rather not say right now. It's still a work in progress. It would be very helpful if you could tell us anything about the day leading up to Lucy's disappearance. You said that your husband thinks Lucy is just stuck somewhere. Do you have reason to believe differently?"

"Lucy wouldn't have left the house while I was out. She knows better than to wander off. And I know any mother would say that, that there's a chance she snuck out all the time and I only found out this time because she didn't come home before I did, but she's so responsible. She prefers healthy breakfasts to the point where she scolds me if I buy a box of Pop Tarts. The only little kid I know who is offended by candy." She smiled and looked down at her hands. "So the idea of her playing outside without permission is so far beyond the realm of possibility that even though it's terrifying to think someone took her, it's the only thing I can think of that makes sense."

Ari nodded. "Had your daughter left the house since the storm passed?"

"Of course. She went to her friend Michelle's house to build snowmen yesterday. I went with her. I'm friends with Michelle's mother, so we had coffee in the house while the girls played."

"Where does Michelle live?"

Lisa pointed vaguely north. "Just a few streets away from here. We walked."

"Did you notice anyone who seemed out of place in the neighborhood? A car parked on the corner watching kids, or maybe someone who you just got a bad feeling about?"

Lisa closed her eyes, her fist resting against her mouth as she tried to remember. "There really wasn't anyone else out. The streets were still treacherous; that's why we walked. Everyone we saw was in their own front yard or on one of the side streets playing on the ice."

Ari thought. Mystery Man had left it up to chance before and ended up with Jenna. He wouldn't risk the same mistake again, so he either had to search on his own or just know where he could find a girl who looked right.

"Does your family have any connection to the Scott family? Kids in the same class, or maybe mutual acquaintances?"

"Brenda and Timothy Scott? No. I'd never even heard of them before their daughter went missing." Her eyes seemed to shrink as she tried to hold back her tears, and she pressed her thumb against her lips as she turned to look toward the door. "I remember thinking how terrible it must be for them. And now I know exactly how it feels."

Ari took a card from her pocket. "If you think of anything else, could you call us?"

Lisa took the card with trembling fingers. "You said two others girls had gone missing. The one you were looking for is home, but Melody is still gone." She sniffled. "So it's fifty-fifty whether or not I'll get the same happy ending."

Dale spoke for the first time since returning from the kitchen. "The girl who made it home safely had one thing Melody didn't. Jenna had Ari looking for her."

Lisa smiled at that. "Then I'll let you get to work."

They thanked her for the cookies and stood to leave as the front door swung open. The man from the family pictures came in. "Leese? I need to thaw out for a minute, but I'm going to go back out as soon as..." He stopped in the doorway and examined the unexpected guests in front of him. With his coat, mittens, scarf, and hat, the only skin visible was his cold-burned face. He had the face of a scholar athlete with the added weight of someone whose sports days were behind him. Ari had a brief moment of recognition that faded before she could grab onto it.

He looked hopefully at his wife. "Is there news?"

"Paul. This is Ariadne Willow and Dale Frye. They're private investigators. They think that Lucy's disappearance might be connected to the Missing Melody thing."

He tugged off his cap and his hair nearly went with it, standing up in messing blonde spikes. "You think the same person who kidnapped Melody took Lucy?"

"It's a theory I'm working on, yes sir."

Paul seemed skeptical, and Ari was prepared to defend the theory without explaining it when he spoke again. "Because of the school pictures?"

Ari felt a tingle in her palms. "Pictures?"

Lisa suddenly gasped. "Oh, my God. I completely forgot about that."

Ari looked between the two of them. "So you do know the Scott family?"

"No," Lisa said. "Not really. Last year, Lucy got school pictures done. All the schools in the area used the same studio. Apparently some photos got misfiled and we received the pictures of another girl." She looked at Paul. "That was Melody Scott? Why didn't you say anything?"

"You were already panicked about how much the girl on the news looked like our daughter. I thought if I reminded you that someone else made the mistake it would only worry you more." To Ari, he said, "Do you think it happened again? Someone meant to take Lucy instead of Melody in the first place?"

Ari said, "It's complicated. What studio made the mistake?"

Lisa didn't even try to remember, turning to immediately dart across the room to the bookshelf. She took down a photo album, laid it open on the table, and flipped through until she found the picture. She took it out and looked at the mark on the back.

"Gaspode and Son. They have a phone number here."

Dale took the picture, copied the number down, then handed it back. She also got their cell phone numbers so they could call if they had any further questions or news to report.

Ari smiled in what she hoped was a reassuring manner. "We'll look into that angle. Thank you for your help." She looked at Paul, knowing his search had been futile. "Did you find anything?"

"No. Not a damn thing." He tugged off his gloves. "Lucy isn't the kind to run off without telling us where she's going. But I just have to keep looking. If I'm not out there~"

"I understand," Ari said. "But I think you'll do a lot more good here with your wife. Dale and I can take over the search for a few hours." She didn't add that if Lucy wasn't recovered by nightfall she probably wouldn't be found alive. She thanked the Chabots and let Lisa escort them out. They followed the sharp imprints of Paul's boots down the yard to where the car was waiting for them at the curb.

"What do you think?" Dale asked when they were back on the

road.

"I think Mystery Man got desperate. The snow storm was a perfect opportunity to make a kid disappear, but he had to act fast. He didn't have the luxury to scour the city, so he went after someone vaguely connected to the family. He remembered a little girl who looked so similar to Melody that a photography studio mixed up the prints."

Dale said, "That was a year ago. Do you honestly think whoever this is remembered the family's name, let alone where they lived?"

"I'm positive he didn't. He took one risk by taking a girl from a family with with even a minor connection to the Scotts. I'm hoping he took another risk to find out how to find them."

Gaspode and Sons' studio was within walking distance of their own offices. The small reception area was dark, but the door behind the counter revealed the lights were on elsewhere in the store. Ari knocked on the glass until someone appeared in the doorway. He was young enough that he almost had to be the "Son" in the business name, with piles of shaggy black hair and a weak attempt at a beard. He made slashing motions in front of his throat, shrugged an apology, and then used both hands to try shooing her away.

Ari held up two fingers and mouthed "two minutes."

He sighed and stepped around the counter. He raised his voice to be heard through the glass. "We're closed! No one wants to come pick up their photos in this mess anyway. Come back Monday. We'll be open Monday."

Ari raised her voice as well. "The little girl I'm trying to find will be dead on Monday."

He stared at her for a moment, then flipped the lock. He pulled open the door a crack, wedging his foot against it so that it couldn't be pushed opened wider.

"What the hell are you talking about?"

"I just need two minutes of your time. A little girl was kidnapped this morning, and I think you may be able to help me find her."

He shrugged, still looking perplexed. "I've been here all morning, in the studio, trying to finish developing pictures people dropped off before the blizzard. None of my employees can make it in, so I'm all alone. You think I'd take the time to go kidnap some random girl...?"

"I don't think you did it. But I'm thinking you might have

gotten a phone call this morning. Someone who asked you about a school photo mix-up that happened last year."

He stared at her. "How'd you know about that?"

"So someone *did* call you?"

"Yeah. Said he'd found another picture and wanted to know where he could drop it off. I gave it to him. How does that lead to a kidnapping?"

Ari ignored the question. "The person who called, did he leave a name or a number? Any way you could get in contact with him?"

"No. Why would he?"

"Damn it." She stepped back and looked up and down the street. "What time did he call?"

"Right after I got here, so around nine." He hunched his shoulders against the snow. "Listen, you don't think this guy really kidnapped anyone, do you?"

"I do. Anything you can tell me about him would be helpful."

He thought it over and then stepped back from the door. "I got his number. It came up on the machine and I don't think I've erased it yet. You can come look if you want."

"Yes. Thank you." Ari followed him in, waiting on the customer side of the counter as he went around to check the Caller ID. She took out her phone and put the number in as he recited it. "Thank you," she said again. "This is a big help."

The irritation and arrogance was gone from his face by then. "Look, if I did something to put a kid in danger, I'll do whatever I can to help. I just thought it was part of this stupid mix-up that happened last year. We had a ton of pictures, some of them got mixed together, and we had to do a quick shuffle. Those two girls looked so alike, I just..." He sighed and shook his head. "If you need anything else, let me know, okay?"

Ari looked down at the number on her phone. Her plan was originally to take it back to the office and have Dale to a reverse look-up on it, but maybe there was an easier way to find out who had called.

"Actually there is something you could do." She motioned for the phone and he placed it on the counter for her. She dialed the number and listened to the buzzing in her ear as it rang. Her heart raced and she prayed that whoever the Mystery Man was, he would be stupid enough to–

"Hello."

It was flat, a man disturbed at his work, and it was all Ari could do not to shout in victory. *Gotcha, you son of a bitch.* She wanted to demand his name, but she doubted a real clerk would ask the person she had just called to identify themselves. When she spoke, she gave her voice a lighter, more air-headed accent. She inflicted up at the end of each sentence to turn everything into a question.

"Hello, this is Sondra down at Gaspode and Son Studio? You called us earlier about some photographs that had gotten mixed up?"

"How'd you get this number?"

"Well, sir, it's right here? On the Caller ID? We're getting in touch because your call made us think there may have been a further mix-up in the orders? Gosh, we're awful sorry about this, but we have a big pile of pictures here with two different girls. If you wouldn't mind coming down here and helping us sort them out, we'd be awful grateful."

There was a pause as he considered. She knew that he was imagining a big pile of Melody Scott pictures mixed together with Lucy Chabot, damning evidence that the two girls were connected. When the DNA tests came out, the pictures would provide a connection that he couldn't afford. The fact that they had his number on Caller ID, and a clerk who remembered speaking to him that morning, meant that he couldn't possibly ignore it if he still hoped to get away clean.

"I'll come down. I'm..." He sighed heavily. "I'll be down there in about an hour. I haven't, ah, I haven't yet dropped off that picture I called about earlier. Why don't I just sort of the pictures at your studio, and then I'll take the ones that aren't my daughter to the proper family? No sense in both of us getting out in this mess."

"Well, that's very kind of you, sir. We'll be expecting you in about an hour? All right. Thank you. Bye-bye."

The young Gaspode raised his eyebrows when she hung up. "So I guess you'll be the one behind the counter when he shows up?"

"No. My partner will be here inside." She drummed her fingers on the counter and then looked at his bright blue shirt. "She'll need to borrow one of those uniform shirts."

CHAPTER TWENTY-THREE

IN ADDITION to the staff shirt Dale got from Kenneth Gaspode, Dale put on her black-rimmed eyeglasses and let her hair hang down on either side of her face. The plan was for her to pretend that she was doing work, but she thought it would be a better cover if she was actually occupied with something when the Mystery Man appeared. She also thought it was only fair to help Kenneth out, since he was helping them. He found the negatives for Melody Scott and Lucy Chabot in their records and ran off a half dozen of each, which Dale left in an envelope under the counter as she busied herself organizing the prints that were ready to be picked up when the store opened on Monday.

An hour and twenty minutes after Ari made the call, a black truck pulled up at the curb. Dale noticed it from the corner of her eye and whispered, "Show time." Kenneth looked, saw what she meant, and disappeared into the back room in keeping with Ari's plan. Dale tried to keep up the ruse of being busy, but she tracked the man from the corner of her eye as he approached the door, unable to deny curiosity at the man who had kidnapped three girls in the past few months.

The man who had kidnapped Melody Scott, Jenna Morris, and Lucy Chabot was completely average. In height and weight, he matched maybe five hundred other people in the general vicinity.

He was balding in a way that left a peninsula of brown hair in the center of his forehead, a fact he tried to hide by growing it long and letting it fall to either side. His brown coat ended at mid-thigh, revealing pressed trousers over brown loafers.

He was completely unassuming, unthreatening. If Dale had seen him on the street she would have offered him a smile and kept walking without ever thinking ill of him. She was a little disappointed, having expected a monster. This was the bogeyman? The shooter who had killed Brandon Kent just because he was a loose end? It was almost enough to make her angry. If this guy could be a kidnapper and a murderer, then anyone could.

She stepped around the counter to let him in, forcing a smile. "Sorry to make you come all the way down here. You try to do a good deed and you end up being put to work."

"Don't worry about it." He glanced around and then looked at his watch. Dale wondered who was watching over Melody and Lucy. Surely he didn't leave them alone.

"I have the pictures right here behind the counter. Whichever of these little girls is your daughter, sir, she is just a lovely little girl. They're both so beautiful."

He nodded absent-mindedly and rested a hand on the counter as Dale retrieved the envelope. She took the photos out and then, acting as if it was an afterthought, reached for a book of receipts. "Oh. You'll have to sign this."

"Sign?"

"Yes, sir. In case there's an issue we can have a record that they were picked up by someone whose name is on the account." She smiled sweetly.

He looked at the pen as if it was a knife, then picked it up and quickly signed. Dale put it aside as if it was the least interesting object in the world and put the photos on the counter. The girls were extremely similar, but only someone in a hurry would have made the mistake of mixing them up. The man quickly picked out the three photos of Melody Scott.

"These are mine."

"Excellent. And Kenneth said you offered to drop the other pictures off at the address he gave you earlier?"

He seemed surprised but then nodded. "Oh. Right, yes. Of course."

Dale separated the photos into different envelopes and handed them back across the counter to him.

"There you go, sir. Again, very sorry for the inconvenience."

He nodded dismissively, thanked her quickly, and carried both envelopes out the door. As soon as he was gone Dale picked up the receipt book and looked to see what name he had signed.

Luke Becker.

She smiled as Kenneth came back out. "Was it him?"

"Oh, yeah," Dale said. She tore off the receipt and sent Ari a text with the name. She hurried around the corner to see which way the truck went, hoping she would see Ari in pursuit. When she stepped out her eye was drawn down the block to where Ari had been waiting to follow whoever showed up. Dale stopped walking when she saw Ari's car was still parked, idle and dark at the corner.

Ari wasn't in the car.

She'd been expecting a car.

When the truck pulled up in front of Gaspode and Son, Ari knew that she had seconds to decide whether or not she was going to change the plan. She had been anxious about trying to follow someone through the still-barren streets of Seattle, certain he would see her and get spooked. The truck was a golden opportunity to follow him without being seen, but she would have to hurry. She opened the door a crack and cold air seeped in as she quickly began to undress.

She banged her knees on the steering wheel, certain that Mystery Man would come out and drive away before she could get ready. Her jeans pooled around her legs and she kicked them out of the way. She thought about the relaxation method Milo had taught her, but it was impossible to calm down enough for it to work.

She dropped out of the car on all fours, transforming quickly as she sagged her shoulder against the door to close it. The pavement was freezing under her bare hands but they quickly formed pads and covered with fur after only a few steps. Her spine stretched and elongated and her legs, one moment too long and the next just the right height, propelled her across the street. She crouched and leapt, landing in the back of Mystery Man's truck with a heavy thump that she prayed hadn't been heard inside the shop.

The bed of the truck was filled with tools protected from the elements by a thick burlap tarp. Ari got her nose under the edge of it and squirmed underneath, crawling forward until she reached the back of the cab. She braced her forepaws on the floor and curled her spine against the side of the truck, her head down so that it wouldn't make a tell-tale bulge in the material.

A minute passed, maybe two, before she heard the bell over the studio's door. Footsteps crunched in snow and then the truck's door opened. Ari had a flashback to hitching a ride to a dog-fighting ring in the trunk of a car, wishing she had some way to signal Dale that she wasn't in danger. The truck engine came to life with a growl and Ari stumbled slightly as Mystery Man began his trip home.

She lost track of their direction almost immediately, but she had the vague feeling they were going south. The truck was forced to go slowly and make frequent stops, sometimes idling for nearly five minutes before it began crawling ahead again. She sank down onto her belly and crawled back to the edge of the tarp, sticking her head out just enough to sniff the air. She smelled sea and salt to the right which supported her directional theory. Seagulls cried overhead, swooping back and forth across the prematurely dark afternoon sky. The birds were scattered by a small plane flying low to avoid the cloud cover, its engine chugging along as it angled in for a landing.

They had been on the road for nearly thirty minutes. Ari allowed for the bad conditions and cautious driving and assumed the plane meant they were somewhere near Boeing Field.

The truck stopped and Ari held her breath as Mystery Man got out. The engine was still running so she knew they weren't at their final destination. She heard his footsteps crunching through snow and risked lifting her head up enough to see above the sidewalls of the truck bed. The man had his back to her, standing atop a tall mound of snow pushed out of the way by plows. He was carrying two envelopes which Ari knew contained the pictures of Melody Scott and Lucy Chabot.

He disappeared over the hump of the mound, so Ari ducked back into her hiding place. Whether he planned to rip them up and dump them into the sewer, if there was a furnace somewhere he could incinerate them, or if he was just going to shove them into a dumpster on a construction site, Ari knew those pictures would never been seen again.

He was gone for nearly half an hour, the engine rattling noisily under the hood. Ari had a horrible vision of being stranded and out of gas while the temperature continued to plummet and wondered about just how smart her plan had actually been.

She was shivering by the time she heard his approach through the snow. The chassis sagged under his weight and he began driving again.

Their progress slowed even further as they entered a neighborhood. She could feel the truck's traction suffering as they pushed through deeper snow that hadn't been plowed, sliding a manageable amount on slick surfaces as he carefully took the corners. He finally pulled up onto a slight incline, she felt the set of the brake, and he shut off the engine.

She remained very still as she listened to his footsteps recede. He walked for a long time before she heard a door open and close, so she was expecting something rural when she finally squirmed free and lifted her head to take a look around. She sniffed the air and looked in all four directions before she narrowed down the location to somewhere between Interstate-5 and Beacon Avenue, on a large plot of land closed off by a wooden fence and embraced on two sides by thick woods. A light came on in the front room and Ari jumped out of the truck to the tightly-packed snow that covered the twin ruts of the driveway.

The pads of her paws were numb from the cold, and she tried to ignore the snow as it was caught in clumps until she had twin pairs of snowy white boots clinging to her feet. She reached the building and lifted her head until she picked up Lucy Chabot's scent. It was very faint, but she hoped and prayed that only meant she had been inside since Mystery Man abducted her. She skirted past the windows, ducking down even though they were too high for her to be seen, lifting her head toward the frame and sniffing quickly to determine if anyone was in the rooms she was passing before she moved on.

At the back of the house was a small greenhouse, a half-arch of glass that seemed to hang off the dark brown brick of the main structure. The lights were on inside and Ari could see empty shelves along the walls and rows of empty tables filling the space. She paced along the edge of perimeter looking for weak spots, but nothing presented itself. At the door she could see that it was unlatched, so she finally surrendered to the inevitable. She closed her eyes and transformed back into her human body.

It was like plunging into a frozen lake, her skin immediately contracting into goosebumps and her arms clinching over her naked chest. The snow that had been clinging to her fur cascaded down off her body and she quickly threw the latch and ducked into the relatively warm greenhouse. The door clicked quietly shut behind her and Ari sagged against the freezing glass to catch her breath. The pain was numbed by cold, her fingers curled into hooks in front of her breasts as her brain worked out the conflicting signals of pain, hypothermia, and relief from the cold. Finally, naked save for Dale's collar, she moved quickly forward in the hopes a laundry room would present itself.

The home's original back door stood open to the greenhouse, and she paused to smell the air. She didn't smell any deodorant or body odor, but she still gave the hallway a visual check before she stepped out. Mystery Man was in the kitchen; she heard him opening cans and the splash of liquid into a cup. She moved to the left, away from the kitchen, and peered into a dark room that, fates be praised, was a laundry room.

Less than a minute later she was dressed in a black T-shirt and a pair of boxer shorts, both fresh from the dryer. She had to tuck the shirt into the shorts to keep them from falling, but they would suffice for the moment. She also took a pair of socks, putting one on and saving the others for her front paws if she had to go back out into the elements on four legs. The thick cotton not only warmed her toes, it made her movement across tile floors even more silent.

Just beyond the laundry room was a wooden door with a heavy padlock on it. She pressed her ear to the wood and heard cartoon music on the other side. She searched for a key or something to break the lock with. She couldn't get this close and then leave empty-handed. The drink he was preparing in the kitchen was probably liquid courage to do the dirty job ahead of him. Lucy Chabot was going to die in the next few minutes unless Ari got her out of the house.

She looked toward the kitchen, came up with a dumb plan, and pushed away from the door with a mental promise that she would return.

Mystery Man had his back to her when she entered the kitchen. She pushed her hand into her hair, feigned a yawn, and blinked sleepily.

"Hey, sexy. There you are."

He jumped as if she'd announced herself by firing a gun into the air, spinning around so fast he nearly lost his footing. He grabbed at the counter, eyes wide behind his glasses as he stared at the impossible person standing behind him.

"Wha... y-you... who are you?"

He was torn between anger, fear, and confusion. If she'd been a man or less attractive, she was certain one of the defensive qualities would have kicked in. But she was a pretty woman wearing his underwear. All he cared about was how she had gotten into his house; he would deal with the why later. Ari decided to play on his alcohol and anxiety and smiled.

"Aw. Don't be like that. I know last night was rushed, but don't tell me you forgot my name." She swayed her hips as she walked toward him. "'Course, we were a little preoccupied at the time, so I can't be too offended. I'm Tule. And you? Was the name you gave me last night your real name, sexy?"

"I-I don't... I don't know who you are. Last night? Last night I was *here*. I've been here f-for... wh-who are you looking for?"

"Dale Frye," Ari said. "This is his place."

"I don't know who that is. This is my house."

She raised her eyebrows. "You're Dale?"

"I'm Luke! Luke Becker. This is my house, and I don't know... Are you wearing my clothes?"

She winced and sucked in a breath through her teeth. "I am. Gee. Don't you hate it when people take things that don't belong to them?" She stepped around the counter and he backed away from her. The bottle of Captain Morgan was on the counter with only enough for one more glass clinging to the bottom. "Hey. Where are the keys to the TV room?"

His eyes moved to the right. "Uh."

"I want to watch TV, sexy. And I thought I'd free those girls you had kidnapped in there."

His anxiety and confusion evaporated in an instant. His awkwardness became anger, and he stood up a little straighter. She saw realization dawning in his eyes.

"Wait a second. You're the woman who was at the baseball field."

"Yep." She grabbed the Captain Morgan by the neck and swung it upward. Becker deflected the blow, knocking her arm back as he brought his half-full glass around and tossed it at her. Ari ducked and it shattered on the back of her head, sending a torrent of warm liquid down over her.

Becker rushed her, using his arms like braces to keep her from moving to either side. She hit the fridge hard enough to knock the wind out of her, coughing as Becker backed up and punched her in the side of the head. Ari's vision exploded in sparks as she dropped to her knees in front of him. He grabbed a handful of her hair and bent down, his breath hot on the side of her face as he spoke.

"This is over. It's *finally* over. And I won."

Ari punched him between the legs.

She put all of her strength behind it, delivering the blow with enough force that Becker toppled backward. The scent of alcohol floated around her like a pungent cloud, blocking any other smells so effectively that she felt as if she'd been muzzled. Becker opened a drawer and pulled a knife, swinging blindly as he lunged at her. Ari ducked toward the stove and grabbed one of the coiled burners. She pulled it off and used it as a shield. When he thrust the knife at her, Ari caught it on the curved metal and twisted to get it out of his hand.

Becker stumbled off-balance trying to keep hold of his weapon and Ari punched him in the face. His glasses broke and he fell, landing unceremoniously on his ass. He looked up at her, dazed, and Ari tossed the burner onto the stove. It landed with a clatter and Ari moved closer.

"It is over. You lost."

She took a dishtowel off the counter, lifted his arms, and bound his wrists to the door of the fridge. It wasn't going to hold him long, but she hoped it would be enough of a trap for her to do what needed to be done.

Ari snagged the padlock key off the hook next to the kitchen door and hurried back to the TV room. She got the lock undone and pushed the door open, taking the lock with her so Becker couldn't just lock her in with the girls if he got free. The room was sparsely furnished, with a couch along one wall and an armchair in the other. The TV was in the corner, set at an angle so it could be seen from most points in the room.

Lucy Chabot was sitting on the floor with her back to the couch, her knees drawn up and her arms resting across them. Her head was tilted to the side, her cheek fat where it rested against her arm. Melody Scott was laying on the couch like she had been drugged, obviously bored and frightened by her long ordeal. Lucy turned toward the door when it opened, but Melody only shifted her eyes away from the TV with disinterest. When they saw her, however, they both perked up.

"You're not him," Melody said. Her voice started flat, but just three brief syllables Ari heard the beginnings of hope stirring.

"Nope. I am definitely not him." She scanned the small room and saw two coats - one burgundy and the other blue - tangled in a pile in the corner. "Get your coats, ladies. I'm taking you both back to your parents."

Chapter Twenty-four

Melody moved with renewed vigor, tugging on her jacket before helping Lucy into hers. Ari heard Becker banging and clattering in the kitchen as he tried to free himself. She didn't want to rush them, didn't want them any more scared than they already were, but if they didn't leave soon Becker would be back into play. She kept her voice as calm as she could.

"Okay, girls. You got everything?"

"Yes."

"Okay. My name is Ari. I'm going to call the police and they'll come take you home."

Lucy said, "You're not supposed to call the police except in an emergency."

Ari smiled, remembering Jenna's reluctance to use her mother's phone. "It's okay, honey. I have permission."

She ushered the girls out ahead of her, trying to remember if she had seen a phone in the kitchen. They had just crossed the threshold of the TV room when something crashed and clattered to the tile floor and she heard Becker falling to the ground with a shout of victory. She put her hands on the girls' shoulders and stopped them from continuing on.

"Okay... new plan. Come on, this way."

She turned the girls toward the greenhouse and urged them to move faster. They hurried past the laundry room and Ari slammed the door behind her once they were inside the empty glass cube. There was a dial on the wall to operate the lights, and Ari twisted it until the light was intense enough to turn the glass walls into mirrors. She knew that Becker should have been able to get to the greenhouse from the kitchen, and only one thing would have delayed him.

He was arming himself.

The greenhouse door didn't lock from the inside, so she guided the girls to the exterior door. They went outside into the cold, the girls huddling together as Ari looked for something to block the door with. There was nothing that would stop a man of Becker's size, so she gave up looking and began to examine their escape options.

The truck was at the top of the driveway. They would be out in the open for far too long, and Ari didn't feel like tempting the man who shot Brandon Kent from across a baseball field. Their only real option was the woods. She was still wearing the underwear and T-shirt, her feet no longer cozy in the snow-soaked socks, but she wasn't about to strip naked in front of two kids no matter what the danger was.

"Girls, I want you to close your eyes. There's going to be a dog here when you open them again, and it's going to be wearing this collar." She touched her throat. "I want you to grab hold of the collar and get on the dog's back. You won't hurt it, okay? Just hold on tight and cover your faces."

Lucy nodded and, a few seconds later Melody did as well. They put their arms around each other and covered their faces. Ari quickly shoved down her boxers and pulled the T-shirt over her head, transforming as she dropped to her knees. She remembered her socks too late, her feet twisting and shaping inside the cotton.

The door to the greenhouse opened and Ari turned to face the exit. With the light reflecting off the interior walls, she could see Becker but he couldn't see her. He was carrying a rifle in one hand, reaching out with his other hand to open the door. He was moving fast since, in his mind, Ari and the girls had started running as soon as they were outside. Ari crouched on her forepaws and timed it.

Becker pushed the door open and continued forward. Ari lunged and slammed her weight into the door, knocking it back into his face. Becker recoiled and tripped over his feet, falling flat on his back and lying dazed. Ari spun and barked at the girls.

Melody jumped, looked at Ari with wide eyes, and then looked at the discarded clothes. She scooped them up, tucked them into the front of her coat, and hooked her fingers on Ari's collar. She hunkered down as Lucy did the same, then rose with an extra hundred pounds weighing down on her. She was big as the wolf, but carrying two riders was pushing her strength to the limit. Her breath wreathed her head in thick clouds of fog as she steadied her feet under her passengers. Lucy was practically hanging off Ari's side, and Melody had her leg hooked over Ari's hips.

Ari was nearly to the woods when Becker slammed through the door again. She heard him cock the rifle and braced for impact, but he didn't fire. His neighbors might be far away, but a gunshot would carry. Ari slipped between two trees and let the shadows obscure her. She heard Becker shout a curse and knew he was giving chase.

The woods weren't really woods at all, more of an undeveloped strip of land between neighborhoods. Ari shoved through the scrub and found spacious stretches between trees. Snow had accumulated in waist-high drifts around the trees, nearly drowning Ari as she tried to shove through with the girls. The trail she was blazing through the snow would make it impossible to evade Becker, so Ari stopped after a few minutes to think of a new plan. She ducked down and lowered her head, grateful when Melody took the hint and let go of her. She tugged the clothes out of her jacket and held them out, and Ari took them in her teeth. Melody seemed to understand what Ari was and turned Lucy's head away.

Well aware of Becker's pursuit, Ari forced her way through the transformation faster than she should have. She tugged the shirt over her head and stepped into the underwear.

"Girls..." Melody turned to face her and Ari pointed. "Go straight through the trees. When you get to the street, go to the first place they have lights on and ask them for help." She saw Becker coming toward them. "Stay together. Just find someplace with people and ask them to call the police. Go, go..."

Melody took Lucy's hand, looked back toward the man lumbering through the snow toward them. Becker's face was beet red, his hair falling limp around his face as he high-stepped through the drifts. His glasses were fogged up, blinding him while at the same time making him look like a cartoon villain. When the girls were gone, Ari ran at Becker. He saw her coming through the condensation on his glasses and swung the rifle up.

"You stupid~"

Ari jumped and slammed into him before he could finish his thought. The gun swung up and hit him in the chest. Ari grabbed the barrel and twisted, throwing her weight to the left and pulling him down with her. She landed hard on her side with him on top of her, her vision filled with his strained expression, the spittle on his lips and the crazed eyes behind glasses that had been knocked askew. The snow partially cushioned their fall but Ari didn't give him a chance to recover. She gripped the gun like she was on a bench press and shoved up, slamming it into his jaw. The blow dazed him enough that she was able to take it from his weakened grip. She tossed it aside and Becker reared back to deliver a punch with all his weight behind it. The blow kinked her neck back, and her teeth caught on the inside of her bottom lip. She brought her hands up inside the brace of his arms, sweeping outward and taking away his support.

When Becker collapsed on top of her, Ari bent her knees and fitted her feet in the hollow of his hips. She shoved backward and he was knocked back. She scrambled away from him, kicking up plumes of snow as he lunged for his rifle. She doubted she would be able to match him physically, but she was going to do everything in her power to keep him occupied until the girls could get somewhere safe.

She turned to face him, crouched low in a fighting stance made ridiculous by her trembling knees and the pallor of her exposed skin. Blood trickled down her chin as she motioned him to come at her. Becker kept the gun low, trying to catch his breath as he scanned the clearing around them.

"Who the hell are you?"

"Ariadne Willow. Nice to meet you. Put down the gun, asshole."

He looked down at it, then swung it up as if he had just remembered what it could be used for.

"Why would I do that?"

"Because if you shoot me, police are going to descend on this neighborhood like the wrath of God."

He shrugged. "I can still get the girls. I can still salvage this."

"Yeah? You go to all this trouble to get away clean and you're going to risk having a police report like that lying around? Neighbors report a gunshot, dead body of a private investigator lying in the woods a hundred yards from your property... you think you'll be able to get Melody away from here with something like that hanging over your head?"

Becker bared his teeth and then angrily tossed the gun away. "Fine. I can kill you quietly."

Ari curled her fingers in a 'come on' taunt, rolling her shoulders as Becker moved toward her. He was still outside of arms' length when a large gray stone rebounded off the back of his skull. His head was thrown forward with enough force to knock off his glasses and Ari saw his eyes were wide with surprise. He spun slowly to see Melody standing at the edge of the clearing. Her face was bright pink above her burgundy jacket, tears glistening on her cheeks as she reared back to toss another rock.

"Leave her alone, Uncle Luke! Leave her alone!" Her voice was little more than a shriek as she let the second rock fly. Becker's arms came up to protect his face and the rock bounced off his forearm just beneath his elbow. Ari rushed him from behind and jumped, bringing her left arm up and bending it so that the fist was braced against her neck. When she came down she slammed the elbow into the back of Becker's neck just below the base of his skull.

Becker went down on his knees and Ari's weight pushed him the rest of the way to the ground. She slipped her arm around his neck and grabbed her wrist with the other hand. She pulled and Becker choked and flailed, blood matting the back of his head where Melody's first rock had hit him. Ari bared her teeth as she tightened the noose of her elbow until his body went limp. She kept up the hold until she was certain he wasn't faking, then she let him go and pushed herself up on all fours.

When she lifted her head she saw that Melody was still frozen in place, her shoulders shaking with the force of her sobs.

"Sweetheart, go get~"

Lucy appeared through the scrub, leading a uniformed security guard by the hand. He looked confused by what was happening, but the confusion vanished in an instant. He let go of Lucy's hand to draw his Taser, aiming it at Ari. She showed him her palms and slowly sat up on her knees. Before she could offer assurances that she was on his side, Melody broke her paralysis and ran across the clearing. She threw her arms around Ari and the impact nearly knocked her over. Ari met the guard's eye.

"Can I put my hands down to hug her?"

"Uh. Sure."

Ari hugged Melody as the guard moved to check on Becker. Ari's adrenaline faded and the pain of every transformation, the fight she'd just had, the exhaustion of running with two seven-year-olds hanging off her collar hit her in a wave. She held on tight to Melody and closed her eyes, grateful for the chance to relax. Behind her, she heard the guard calling for backup.

"We didn't stay together," Melody said against Ari's neck.

Ari chuckled. "You did the right thing, honey."

"When can I go home?"

"Soon. Really, really soon. I think you've been gone long enough."

The police flanked both sides of the wooded area, one team focused on Luke Becker's house while the other acted as the command center near the site where he was arrested and the girls were recovered. Ari was questioned by the first officers on the scene, and again by the first detectives. When she was finally cleared of any wrongdoing, she was given a pair of coveralls and boots from the crime scene unit.

The detective in charge was a woman named Amy Hensler. Ari approached her and suggested maybe the girls could wait somewhere warm until their parents arrived, and the detective agreed. Ari escorted them across the street to a strip mall that was glowing in the gloom with soft and inviting light. The first shop in the row was a frozen yogurt shop.

Lucy tugged on the cuff of Ari's sleeve. "Can we have ice cream?"

"It's ten degrees out here." Ari looked down and saw the hope in the girl's eyes and crumbled. "Ice cream, huh? Why not. You want ice cream, Melody?"

"Yes, please."

Ari smiled and led them into the shop. The girl behind the counter had obviously been watching the drama across the street. She tried to act disinterested, but she had the same wide-eyed awe of someone who was playing it cool when they crossed paths with a celebrity.

"Hi," Ari said. "I don't have my wallet~"

"It's fine. On the house. Looks like you three had a hard enough night." She looked down at the girl clutching Ari's right hand. "Are you Missing Melody?"

Melody pressed against Ari's side, trying to disappear into her shadow. "I'm Melody Louise Scott."

The clerk smiled brightly, almost giddy at the realization that the long citywide nightmare would have a happy ending after all. "Well, a lot of people are going to be very glad you're okay. You can have whatever you want."

Melody was quiet for a moment, no longer the rock-hurling beast that had saved Ari's life. Finally she said, "Pink."

Ari smiled. "Do you want sprinkles?"

"Gummy bears."

Ari and the clerk both laughed. Ari put her hand on top of Melody's head. "I like the way you think, girl. One strawberry with gummy bears, please. And..."

Lucy said, "Can I have chocolate and vanilla?"

"And a swirl."

The clerk smiled. "Coming right up."

They took their ice cream to a booth. Melody and Lucy sat on one side and Ari sat on the other. She tried to disguise how badly it hurt her to move, but she'd been beaten up rather badly over the past few hours and the smooth plastic seat of the booth wasn't exactly helping. She rested her arms on the table and rested her chin on her crossed arms. The shop felt impossibly hot after running around through the snow for an hour. She broke out in sweat that evaporated as her body acclimated to the normal temperatures.

The girls were almost finished with their ice cream when the door opened and Dale came in. She spotted Ari and let out a breath she'd obviously been holding for a while. Ari slid aside so Dale could sit next to her.

"Are you okay?"

Ari nodded and took Dale's hand. Dale put her head down on Ari's shoulder, and Ari sagged against her as the girls ate their desserts. A few minutes later a uniformed officer came to retrieve them, and Ari reluctantly handed them over. After everything she'd gone through to save them she was reluctant to just let them go again. But the Chabot and Scott families had arrived and were understandably eager for a reunion.

The officer stopped at the door to look back at Ari. "I'm sure they want to meet you, too."

"Not right now, they don't." She smiled. "They have more important things to do right now."

Lucy slid out of the booth first and came around to hug Ari. "Thank you for saving us."

Ari returned the hug, fighting the emotional response. "My pleasure."

Melody paused at the edge of the booth. "There was another girl. Before. Jenna. She went away."

"She's at home. She's safe."

"Oh. Okay." She breathed an exaggerated sigh of relief, behavior so obviously copied from her parents that it made both women smile, and slid out of the booth. "Okay. Thank you, Diana."

Ari blinked in confusion and watched as the girls were escorted out. Dale twisted around to look at Ari once they were gone.

"Diana?"

"I have no clue."

Dale slid her hand into the small of Ari's back. "Are you okay? Sore?"

"I'll need an epic massage tonight."

"I think that can be arranged." She pecked the corner of Ari's mouth, and Ari turned her head to make it a full-fledged kiss. "It's the least I can do after everything you did today."

"Thanks."

Dale nodded toward the window and Ari turned to see Brenda Scott on her knees clutching her daughter and sobbing uncontrollably. A few feet behind her Paul and Lisa Chabot were cradling Lucy between them, both looking to shell-shocked and relieved to cry. Ari knew the tears would come later and closed her eyes as Dale kissed her neck just behind her ear.

"You're a hero, Ariadne. Nice work."

Eventually Ari's pain had lessened enough that she could stand. She draped an arm across Dale's shoulders and let her lead the way out of the ice cream shop.

Chapter Twenty-five

"Puppy... wake up." Dale stroked Ari's arm to wake her. After an hour-long full body massage, a leisurely hot bubble bath, and making out in bed, Ari was sufficiently exhausted but there was something she didn't want to miss. She sat up and rubbed the sleep from her eyes as she leaned against the headboard. Dale sat back as well, their shoulders touching as Dale turned up the volume on the late news.

A reporter was standing in front of Luke Becker's house, and Ari could see people in CSU jumpsuits moving in and out of the building like ants. The pretty brunette wore a bright blue parka with her station's insignia on the right breast, clutching the microphone up just below her bottom lip as she held her wind-whipped hair out of her face with the other hand.

"Have they said anything interesting?"

Dale nodded. "The kidnapper was Brenda Scott's brother. They think he'd been obsessed with her since they were kids, but he'd always held it in check. Then Melody comes along like a little carbon copy, and he has a second chance to have his little sister back."

"Ick," Ari muttered.

"Well... I mean, the way they talked about it, I don't think it was a sexual thing. It was more like his sister was a doll that got broken when she grew up and became a woman. Melody was a replacement for it. Kind of like how Jenna and Lucy were supposed to be replacements for Melody. The guy has something wrong with his head. Other people just aren't... people. They're things to him. And things can be replaced."

The reporter on TV was finishing her report. "...just why Becker took the other girls - Jenna Morris and Lucy Chabot - is unknown at this time, but investigators believe he planned to use them as part of his plan to escape with Melody."

The lead anchor, a sculpted plasticine talking head safe and warm back in the studio, said, "Savannah, there's a bit of an unusual twist as to how these girls were rescued, isn't there?"

Savannah smiled. "Yes, a bit of much-needed levity to the proceedings. If you ask Melody Scott who is responsible for her rescue, she has a very definitive answer for you."

The scene abruptly cut to Melody sitting in the back of a police car with her mother. "It was Diana. Jenna's friend."

They cut back to the field reporter. "Her mother enlightened us that Diana was Jenna Morris' invisible friend. When Jenna was rescued last week, she claimed she would send Diana back to save the other girls."

"Well," the head anchor chuckled, "it looks like she showed up just when she was needed."

"It certainly does."

Dale rubbed Ari's thigh through her sweatpants. "Invisible friend, huh?"

"I can live with that." She lifted Dale's hand, linking their fingers. "Some stuff came up the past few weeks that we haven't exactly had the time to deal with."

"The stuff with your mom and Milo?"

"Not specifically, but in that area. I'm worried Milo may have put the idea in your head that I belong with another wolf instead of a human."

Dale looked away. "Oh. Well, the thought had crossed my mind in a vague..." She pressed her lips together. "Don't you feel the urge sometimes? Somebody who can run with you and prowl, and you who can help you do werewolf yoga?"

"Those are the same benefits I'd get running with a pack. Support, understanding, comfort when I'm hurt... someone who will come running when I need them. I'm not going to break up with you in order to join a pack. You're my pack."

"Even without changing into a wolf?" Dale whispered, smiling as she leaned in for a kiss.

"A wolf wouldn't be able to handle you, baby." She brushed her lips across Dale's. "So don't worry about me running off with Milo or worrying that I'm missing something by being with you. I'd trade a dozen Milos for one of you."

Dale smiled and kissed Ari properly. "I know you're tired and hurt, but I really want to have sex with the woman who saved three little girls before she gets too famous to give me the time of day."

Ari smiled and glanced at the clock as she slid down until she was lying flat on the mattress. "It's 10:15." She hooked her hand under Dale's arm and pulled her close. "Now give me my reward."

Ari was more than happy to let the media cling to the "Invisible Friend, Guardian Angel" story. The families and the police knew the truth, of course, and Detective Lorne ensured that Bitches Investigations received the Missing Melody reward money. Brenda Scott came by the offices to drop off the check personally so she could thank her for what she'd done. Ari awkwardly accepted the check and the gratitude, quickly turning the conversation back to Melody.

It had been a week since the ordeal ended, but Melody seemed to be adjusting well. She and Lucy had only been kept in the same room for a day, but they seemed to have taken the time to form an extremely strong bond. Melody wouldn't rest until she was shown living proof that Jenna had made it out okay, and a play date had been arranged.

The three victims of Luke Becker were reunited in Oxbow Park, where a shared imprisonment with Melody was enough to unite Jenna and Lucy. Ari was invited to attend and, at Dale's urging, she showed up. Melody saw her walking across the parking lot and ran to greet her, motioning for her to bend down so she could whisper in her ear.

"I know you're not really Diana."

Ari was surprised to hear that. "Oh?"

Melody nodded and whispered again. "She just had to use you as her hands."

Ari smiled. "She did. It's okay, though. I don't mind."

"Good." Melody kissed Ari's cheek and ran back to where her mother was waiting.

Jenna was so thrilled to see her friend that she cried, clinging to the little blond girl's burgundy coat. The words had poured out of her almost too fast to be heard, but Ari eventually learned that Becker had threatened to come back and grab her again if she ever told anybody about Melody. She was so relieved to have the secret out and to see her friend again that Madeline eventually stopped trying to keep her still for more than a few seconds. When she finally left the park, Jenna was teaching her new friends a secret handshake-slash-dance move, and Ari realized that the only thing Luke Becker had successfully done was creating a group of friends who would now be impossible to break up.

When she got back to the office, she knew almost immediately that they had a visitor. By the time she reached the office door she knew who it was.

Milo was standing up as Ari opened the door. She wore a white tank top under an unbuttoned white blouse with the sleeves rolled up past her elbows. Her hair was bundled into a thick ponytail and topped by an olive green military cap that shaded her eyes. She smirked. "There she is. I smelled you coming from a block away."

"I don't have to be a wolf to smell you. All that British crap you eat..."

"Girls," Dale chided. "Play nice."

Milo grinned. "Just wanted to drop by and say farewell."

Ari's smile faded. "You're leaving?"

"Yeah. Wolf manoth's only a few weeks away. When things get bad, I want to be with my mates in England."

"Right." Ari glanced at Dale and then down at her feet. "I wish the plan had worked out better."

Milo snorted and rolled her eyes. "No, you don't. Liar. But I understand. I wouldn't let her go either." She looked back at Dale and winked. "Truth is, you were right. Ceremony worked before, but it won't work again. Hunters don't want fixes, they don't want peace. They're sick of the peace and want to fight us. I say we give 'em what they want."

"How does my mother feel about that?"

"She helped set up the summit and arranged the treaty. She won't be happy about it fallin' apart, but there's nothing she can do about it. Ceremony or not, wolves would have started dying when wolf manoth started. At least this way we'll be prepared."

Ari nodded. "I'm glad you understand."

"Yeah." She stooped and picked up her rucksack, slinging the strap over one shoulder. She held out her hand. "I'm sorry for the way we met, but I'm not sorry I met you."

"Same here." Ari shook her hand. "Give them hell in England."

"Thanks. And while I'm gone, the stashes I planted are yours. Dale knows where they are. And speaking of the lovely lady who brought me all this way..." Milo turned to look at Dale. "Miss Frye. It was more than a pleasure getting to know you. Makes it easy to see why Ariadne is willing to go to the mat for you. I'd've not minded being married to you."

Dale blushed. "In another life, maybe."

"Yeah." She reached up and pinched the brim of her hat between her thumb and forefinger, pulled it off, and flipped it around. She leaned over the desk and placed the hat on top of Dale's head. "Something to remember me by. Looks better on you anyway."

Dale settled it better on her head and stood up. "Thank you, Milo."

Milo smoothed down her hair and nodded. "Well... you two take care of each other, all right?" Her voice cracked a little and she took a deep breath to steady herself. "All right. Got a plane to catch and all that. Hope to see you both again under better circumstances. So long."

Ari shook her hand again before holding the door for her.

Dale looked at her new hat in the reflection off the window, then looked at Ari. "She wasn't so bad after all, huh?"

"She was okay," Ari said with a smile. "And you got a hat out of it. Bonus."

Dale chuckled. "Do you agree with her? Does it look better on me?"

Ari scoffed and winked as she went into her office. "Sure. But what doesn't?"

Dale chuckled and took the hat off and sat it on one corner of her desk as she went back to typing.

EPILOGUE

SLOWLY BUT surely, evidence of the blizzard melted away and Seattle got back to business as usual. To Ari the end of the year loomed, the beginning of wolf manoth becoming a threatening glow on the horizon. She hadn't seen her mother since her unexpected arrival at the office and she wasn't going to go out of her way to have a conversation with her unless it was vitally necessary. In the meantime, she was quickly inundated with new cases. The police department agreed to sign them on as freelance consultants on a case-by-case basis due to their performance on the trial run. Word of mouth had spread and they were soon overwhelmed with requests for cases.

Ari was sitting in the client's chair in front of Dale's desk going through the memos, separating them into piles. One was for referrals, potential clients she would send to agencies she trusted. The middle was for cases she was willing to take herself, basically anything that didn't have to do with little kids. Just because Jenna and Lucy had gotten home safely, Ari wasn't going to press her luck. The third pile was cases she planned to hand over to the police so they could get full investigations.

Someone knocked and Ari twisted in her seat to see Detective Lorne as he came in. "Detective. What can we do for you?"

"I brought by the check for your help on the Lucy Chabot

case."

"Another check? How many times are we going to get paid for this case?"

He grinned. "Hey, the families are grateful and so is the Seattle Police Department. This could have been a mess of epic proportions."

Dale said, "You said 'help.' By that, do you mean the fact we solved it for you?" Ari smiled at Dale, her head down so that Lorne couldn't see the expression.

"Semantics." Lorne smiled. "And there's actually something I wanted to talk to you about, Willow, if you have a second."

"Sure." She put the rest of the memos down on Dale's desk. "I'll finish these later. Step into my office."

Lorne followed her in and shut the door. Ari leaned against the desk as he crossed to the map of Seattle hanging on her wall and perused the pins that indicated where her stashes were buried. He turned away from it after a few seconds.

"So, Ariadne Willow."

"Yes, Don't-remember-your-first-name Lorne?"

"There's something that's been bugging me since the first time we worked together. And I thought now that we've got a few more cases under our belts and maybe trusted each other a little bit more, you might give me an honest answer if I just asked the question." Ari shrugged and gestured for him to continue. "Last year when you went into Katherine Gavin's house, you wore a wire. She called you a werewolf."

He smiled and Ari returned the expression as best she could manage. She tried to keep her posture casual, arms crossed over her chest as she listened.

"Afterward you told me that you have to use unusual methods in your investigations, and that it's too difficult to explain but that they produce results. I was willing to go with it last year and after what just happened it's impossible to deny you're definitely doing something right. But now I just have to ask... I've been feeling something when I'm around you, and I have to know if it's completely off-base."

For a moment Ari thought he was asking her out on a date, but then she realized what he meant. "Wait. You've been feeling something around me? You mean like we're alike?"

His eyes widened slightly. "You feel it, too?"

She took a deep breath, subtly trying to smell if he was a wolf.

She didn't pick up anything, but he may have just been better at hiding it than Milo was. He certainly wore too much cologne but it shouldn't have been enough to obliterate his scent.

"Vaguely," she lied. "I can't believe this."

Lorne chuckled. "Wow. Explains a lot, I guess."

Ari smiled and relaxed. "It'll make it a lot easier on me whenever I show up at one of your crime scenes."

"Well, sure. Now that we know we're on the same side." He put his hands on his hips and chuckled. "You know, I've never met anyone who was like us. I mean, outside of my family."

"Really? I've run into a few here and there. I could introduce you."

"That would be great. But I don't want you to think I'm going to be a third wheel, invading your group of friends. Pretty soon there will be enough of us in town that it'll be a damn country club." He crossed the office to examine the map again on the wall.

Ari furrowed her brow. "What do you mean?"

"You know, for wolf manoth," he said without looking back at her. "Hunters are coming in from all over the world. We've had fucking wolves coming out of the woodwork up here for decades. It's about time we did a little exterminating."

Ari's breath was caught in her throat. He hadn't sensed the wolf part of her, he had felt the part of her that came from the rapist. She felt nauseated but forced herself to hide it as Lorne looked at her again.

"Did you hear the wolves were trying to renew the treaty?"

"I didn't. What stopped them?"

"Who the hell knows? Maybe they got distracted sniffing each other's butts. Real shame, too. That ceremony would have been hunter heaven. A dozen of the mutts with their guards down? It would be like sending engraved invitations to a slaughter."

Ari had visions of picking up her paperweight and smashing it into his skull. If she had caved, if she had let the ceremony occur, then the hunters would have killed everyone there. Her mouth was dry.

"So. When Katherine Gavin called me a werewolf, you didn't~"

"No! The ultimate insult to a hunter, and it just slipped by me. And when you talked about having 'alternative methods of investigations'... I never even dreamed you meant hunter skills." He laughed. "Some detective I am, huh?"

Ari forced a smile. "I guess we both deserve to feel a little humiliated."

"I finally put it together when you managed to track down all three of the missing girls in no time flat. I mean, instincts like that, gotta be a hunter."

She smiled vaguely. "Yeah. Well, as amazing as it is to know we have this in common, maybe we can catch up later. Dale and I have a lot of work~"

"Oh! Yes. Of course. I just couldn't hold back any more. I finally put the pieces together and I wanted to... you know. Let you know I knew."

"I appreciate it."

He glanced at the door. "Does she know...?"

"No. Dale is, uh, out of it."

He nodded and mimed zipping his lips as Ari led him out. Dale looked up and smiled. "Good to see you again, Detective."

"And you, Miss Frye." He looked at Ari and smiled. "I'll see you around, Ariadne."

She could only nod dumbly, watching the door long after it had closed behind him. Dale stood up after he was gone, watching Ari and then coming around her desk to touch Ari's elbow. "Sweetie? Is everything okay?"

"No. Lorne is a hunter."

"What?"

Ari nodded. "And he thinks I'm one, too."

Dale blinked slowly and then shook her head. "Wha... what does that mean?"

Ari inhaled deeply. "It means wolf manoth is going to be much more interesting than we thought."

ABOUT THE AUTHOR

Geonn Cannon is the author of over fifty novels, including the Riley Parra series which was adapted into an Emmy-nominated webseries by Tello Films. He's also written two tie-in novels for the television series Stargate SG-1. He was the first male author to win a Golden Crown Literary Society Award for his novel Gemini, and he won a second for Dogs of War. Information about his other works and an archive of free stories can be found online at geonncannon.com.

Dogs of War: An Underdogs Novel
Seattle is under siege.

An ancient ceremony known as "wolf manoth," in which human hunters kill as many *canidae* as possible, has been revived. The hunters have arrived in force, focusing on the Pacific Northwest due to its high wolf population. Ariadne Willow, alerted to the danger by her mother, goes undercover with a group of hunters in an effort to minimize the damage. Unfortunately the hunters have a new weapon, a drug that brings out the feral side of any *canidae* exposed to it. With her safety and sanity both at risk, Ari is forced to trust a friend turned enemy in order to stay alive.

Meanwhile, Dale is cut off from her friend and partner and faces the wrath of drugged *canidae* and hunters who are eager to make an example of a human who has been consorting with a wolf. Chased through the city and forced to take refuge wherever she can get it, Dale receives help from unexpected corners.

Separated by circumstance and under attack from threats both human and wolf, Ari and Dale must do everything in their power to keep the body count down while also staying alive long enough to find each other again.

Riley Parra: Season One

For years the forces of good and evil have waged war in the confines of No Man's Land, the wasteland on the edges of Detective Riley Parra's city. When what should have been a routine case opens Riley's eyes to the true fight going on behind the scenes, she finds herself drawn into the endless battle between angels and demons. Reluctantly taking up the mantle of good's champion, a mortal fighting on the side of the angels, Riley can only rely on the guidance of an angel in human form to help her survive the coming war. A war that will put her closest friends at risk and make Riley question her sanity before it's over. Becoming a champion wasn't Riley's idea, but she's not going to let her city fall without a fight.

Tilting at Windmills (Claire Lance, Book 1)

Claire Lance is on the run. For the past year, she has kept on the move, keeping her head down, keeping out of trouble. Until she reaches a tiny town in Texas and trouble finally corners her. Forced to take action to save another woman's life, she suddenly finds herself over her head. Blood on her hands, forced to go on the run with the woman she was protecting or end up in prison, Lance finds herself forced to revisit the life she thought she had left behind and reopen painful old wounds.